I0524720

KEEP BREATHING

A novel by

Adam Grace

Published by New Generation Publishing 2011

Cover design by Norman McLeod

www.newgenerationpublishing.info

By the same author

THE TINA PROJECT

Adam Grace is a former Fleet Street journalist. He has worked for local, regional and national newspapers culminating in 20 years with *The Daily Telegraph* – a Tory newspaper where, he says, most of its journalists were closet socialists.

A survivor of the 'hot metal' era, he accepts that electronic word-processing has revolutionised authorship but is appalled by the internet's dark side, which he believes will inevitably destroy civilisation if euthanasia doesn't do the job first.

Acknowledgements

Novelists tend to be less reliant on literary agents these days but I would have been lost without mine. The late David O'Leary represented several distinguished authors yet still found time to advise and encourage me during my work on *Keep Breathing*. He complimented me on a controversial page-turner free from the popular crutches of high body count, profanity, prurience and obsessive introspection. Not many modern agents would do that!

Sincere thanks also go to Phil Temple, of BBC Drama Production, Prof Edward Hulmes, of Harvard University, Alex Schadenberg, Robin Haig, Bob Salmon, Neil Gee and Norman McLeod. Above all, I'm deeply grateful to my wife Jean, a retired nurse, who has never failed to enlighten me on medical ethics and end-of-life issues whenever I have turned to her for help.

And finally…a heartfelt tribute is reserved for my grandson-in-law, Chris Newton, who as my long-suffering computer consultant, will be almost as relieved as I am to see this novel published.

ONE

'And now for something completely different...!'

Howard Mitchell's retirement card, propped up on the Bluthner baby grand in his lounge, featured a cartoon scene of a wild bacchanalian orgy. He smiled as he read the caption one more time and recalled his emotional leaving party in The Swan with Two Necks after his final shift at *The Announcer*. Everyone in the newsroom had signed the card – reporters, sub-editors, feature-writers, photographers, even the tea lady – wishing the paper's longest-serving journalist a happy retirement.

Where had it all gone, that "distinguished career" the editor had referred to in his speech to the assembled hacks? It had been a career that scaled the heights only to end with a heart murmur and a derisory company pension. He might have made news editor but his GP had other ideas. He diagnosed stress-induced angina – a legacy of investigative campaigns exposing 'untouchable' villains in high places.

The average expectation of life in Fleet Street was 54, the medic informed him. He'd bucked the trend by 10 years. If he wanted another 10, early retirement was a no-brainer. Occasional freelance work might be possible but regular nightshifts were out or he'd be likely to discover another meaning of the word 'deadline'. He was in urgent need of daily medication and a nitrolingual spray for the chest pain he'd mistaken for indigestion. He didn't surrender without a fight but was bullied into submission when his wife, Barbara, a nursing sister, joined forces with the GP. Faced with this formidable medical alliance resistance was useless. It was all of two months since his world had turned upside down and the shock still hadn't worn off.

Making ends meet on Barbara's salary and his *Announcer* pension until qualifying for his state handout at 67 was all the more daunting since what should have been a 'golden handshake' more closely resembled a kick in the teeth. His Lordship, the paper's autocratic owner, had 'reorganised' the company's pension fund years ago to help finance an ocean-going yacht. The exercise left senior journalists no longer eligible for the 'top hat' scheme they'd been promised. It was the point where Howard's lifelong Right-of-Centre proclivities took a sudden lurch to the Left.

People assumed that if you worked for a Centre-Right newspaper like *The Announcer* you were of a similar persuasion. Readers were often shocked to discover that, due to His Lordship's primitive approach to labour relations, most of his editorial staff were to the Left of Ken Livingstone. They were hacks but *principled* hacks – with an allegiance to a higher authority than an aristocratic capitalist cowboy.

In Howard's case, the allegiance went back to a conversation in his first job as a cub reporter on a country weekly. He and his young colleagues had been drinking with the chief reporter, Alistair, a quietly spoken Scot. (Every newspaper office has its Scotsman, though not always quietly spoken). Howard's degree course had taught him the basic rules of journalism: always spell people's names correctly; question everything, accept nothing at face value. Bringing into the open what some people want hidden would make you deeply unpopular. You would be likely to face harassment, threats and worse[1]. They were an unavoidable part of the job.

But there was one basic question the fresh-faced idealist straight out of university still needed to ask:

"Who do we serve?"

The trainee wordsmith had been pondering the issue throughout his finals and wanted the view of a real professional. "As journalists, do we serve the paper's proprietor, the advertisers or our readers?"

Alistair, a seasoned hack who'd worked for almost every publication in Fleet Street, conceded it was a good question. The answer, he said, was all of them and none of them. "We work for our dear proprietor, of course. He pays our wages. We also work for the advertisers – they *help* to pay our wages."

"So do the readers," Howard reminded him. "They buy the paper…they pay us to tell them the news."

"Quite right. But they also pay us to tell them the truth. Above all, you see, journalists are servants of the truth. Don't ever forget that, laddie."

Howard never did. He knew of staff at certain daily and Sunday tabloids who regularly took liberties with the truth. But for him and colleagues on other serious newspapers the NUJ code of conduct served as their

---

[1] During the past 20 years 2,000 journalists and media staff throughout the world were killed in the line of duty. Source: International Federation of Journalists.

bible. That was the difference between him and his employer. The only bible His Lordship recognised was his company's balance sheet.

This ethical dimension to their job could spark lively debate during *The Announcer* hacks' liquid supper breaks in The Swan with Two Necks but now Howard only had Barbara for an audience and she'd heard it all before. She made no secret of the fact that, after a hard day in theatre, she preferred the soaps on TV. Which did nothing to improve his growing feeling of inadequacy or lift the melancholy of the long empty evenings.

It was the same every night. As edition time approached, the adrenalin would kick in. He'd become restless and his wife would tell him to calm down. But without the challenge of a deadline, the smooth teamwork needed to meet it, the wit and the buzz of producing a 32-page national newspaper in five hours, the sense of anti-climax was physical. Throughout his career he'd complained about the pressure and now it was gone he missed it like hell.

He'd tried watching TV to take his mind off the withdrawal symptoms but it simply sent him to sleep. There was no way he could watch any of the soaps with their clichéd, computer-generated storylines set in the same locations as last century: pub, betting shop, caff, courtroom (characters were still 'lovable villains'), prison visiting area and church – for weddings and funerals that always went wrong. Viewers had waited over 50 years for a ceremony to run smoothly.

The alternatives were endless wildlife documentaries and food programmes, inane game shows, impenetrable American football, women's boxing and, even more unedifying, cage fighting between humans reduced to the level of wild animals. The 24-hour news channels occasionally recaptured a slight frisson of excitement but it could never be the same as the real thing. The only light relief – albeit unintentional – was provided by the weather forecasts, still the joke they'd always been.

On an evening in late March, which the Met Office had predicted would be cool and dry, Barbara had taken two hours to drive home from the hospital through a blizzard and snowbound traffic on untreated roads. The journey usually took 20 minutes. Now she lay flaked out on the sofa in their cosy lounge with its log fire and softly shaded lamps, seemingly oblivious to events unfolding in EastEnders – the indestructible soap still churning out its nightly dose of barely-relieved human misery.

Unaccountably, for someone who worked with human misery all day, it was his wife's favourite programme. Howard knew that the moment he switched off the banal and ill-tempered dialogue (he called it 'direlogue') she would wake up. So he tip-toed across the deep-pile beige carpet to the bookcase where Solzhenitsyn, Orwell and Steinbeck rubbed shoulders with John Grisham and Dick Francis, and took down his own form of escapism.

There were three large, leather-bound volumes in all – loose-leaf scrapbooks containing cuttings of every news report and feature article he had worked on for *The Announcer* since joining the paper as a young newshound. The cuttings in the earliest book were turning yellow but those in the latest were well preserved under cellophane interleaves inserted by Barbara and his children. This was the scrapbook he chose.

With his wife snoring gently on the sofa, her gin and T barely touched, he poured himself a large Scotch and dry ginger before settling in an armchair and revisiting his personal archive – stories that made headline news during his last ten years with the paper. Starting with 2008:

*Year of the 'R' and 'P' words. Recession followed rapidly by Panic afflicts all levels of society in the credit crunch. As the economy hits rock bottom the government starts to dig, bailing out profligate private banks with public money. Unemployment takes off despite frantic juggling with statistics to disguise it. **Fears that the Large Hadron Collider** beneath the Alps might cause Earth to disappear in a black hole fade when the machine malfunctions. The only black hole contains an* Announcer *sub-editor whose mistyped headline reads:*

LARGE HARDON FLOPS

Then in following years:

Barbecue summer never happens but meltdown of financial system does. Treasury conjures cash out of thin air through 'quantitative easing'. It sounds technical – as if they know what they're doing when, in fact, nobody has a clue.

MPs' Great Expenses Fiddle sweeps away any lingering respect for politicians when they're found with snouts deep in trough of taxpayers' money. Public follows the MPs' lead and crime rate soars. Government responds by cutting police numbers.

Rotten Parliament replaced by a hung version. Coalition of Tories and Lib-Dems cobbled up after bizarre power struggle. Emergency Budget raises VAT to 20 per cent, freezes public sector pay levels and taxpayers' handout to royal family.

United Nations blames global warming for droughts, *floods and famine throughout the world. Under Copenhagen and Cancun Accords, 80 countries promise swingeing cuts in carbon emissions to save planet from 'mutually assured destruction'.*

Home Office computer error frees hundreds of prisoners *prematurely. Many give themselves up, indignant at rude interruption of comfortable lifestyle behind bars. Commonwealth dissolved after member states revoke allegiance to the Crown.*

Hyperinflation takes off as Treasury try to inflate their way *out of trouble by printing still more devalued currency. VAT levied on food and children's clothing. Petrol rationed. Widespread power cuts. Winter fuel payments for elderly axed.*

Death toll from hypothermia among UK pensioners at *record level after harsh winter. Racketeer gas suppliers charged with corporate manslaughter but cleared on a technicality. Property market collapses. Manchester United relegated from Premier League. Plus headline of the decade:*

PROF DAWKINS CONVERTS TO RC CHURCH

Assisted Dying Act sanctions physician-assisted suicide for *the terminally ill. Minimum retirement age raised to 67 for men and women. State pension frozen at existing level. The National Institute for Health & Clinical Excellence (NICE) denies patients life-saving drugs available throughout Europe.*

United Nations forecasts 'unsustainable' world population *of 9 billion by 2040. Rationing of food and energy likely in wealthy countries unless they take urgent action to 'halt and reverse' population growth.*

Howard downed his Scotch and poured himself a top-up. Barbara was still out to the world on the sofa. The soap's drama queens had given way to queens of a different ilk in a homosexual dating game, the ultimate prize being a lavish civil partnership ceremony paid for by the promoters. He returned to his scrapbook and rolled back more years in a momentous era of British history:

Change of monarch. A king now sits on the throne. House of Lords truncated following a referendum which also calls for abolition of the monarchy. Newly-crowned monarch lets it be known: 'One has no plans for going anywhere except Ascot, Goodwood and Cannes.' Bus passes for OAPs abolished.

A new political party rises from the ashes. When internal divisions destroy the Con/Lib-Dem coalition, Lib-Dems rebrand as the New Phoenix Party, their icon of a startled starling a symbol of hope for a demoralised public. Led by Australian feminist Dame Jessica Sykes, they win outright power in their first general election.

In his last VIP interview before retiring, Howard is tipped off by the director-general of the International Development Agency to expect a UN directive on mandatory 'population contraction' for Britain and other overcrowded countries.

The last page of the scrapbook, focusing on the year 2018 and containing pictures of Howard's retirement party, brought the record of his *Announcer* career up to date. Any future clippings would result from occasional freelance work. Little did he suspect that the book would require several more pages.

He finished his Scotch and cast his mind back to his last major story as a staffer – the tip on population control from the IDA director-general. The guy was one of the few public figures whose head was screwed on the right way. "Something dramatic" had to happen, he'd predicted – as if there hadn't been enough drama already. When pressed for details 'off the record', all he would say was the marginalised older generation should prepare themselves for a new role: that of an endangered species. They still didn't understand the gravity of the crisis. Matters were likely to turn ugly – a euphemism usually reserved by such people for something unspeakable.

The new recruit to the ranks of an endangered species replaced the scrapbook on the occasional table next to his chair, leaned back and closed his eyes. Retirement looked like being a lot less boring than he'd expected.

TWO

How ugly? The answer arrived a few days later with a resolution passed by an emergency session of the United Nations Assembly. The resolution *demanded* that all member states take immediate action to preserve food stocks and eliminate waste to combat the devastating effects of global warming on food supplies. It further *demanded* that all developed nations implement effective strategies to reduce overall population by 10 per cent over the next 22 years. Methods of implementation would be delegated to individual governments according to internal demographic factors but failure to realise this irrevocable target would result in stringent economic sanctions.

The ensuing panic came as a godsend to New Phoenix's policy makers – not that many believed in God. As Lib-Dems they had long advocated humane population control to pre-empt mounting social chaos, but their visionary stance had been frustrated by reactionary pro-life supporters. Now the chaos they'd forecast had become a serious threat to mankind they had finally been vindicated. The UN's timely intervention provided the vital stimulus to invoke their enlightened reforms without further opposition. Gone was the need for the charade of public consultation documents and important-sounding but impotent committees. The way ahead was clear and exhilaratingly inviting.

The reformers calculated that the United Kingdom population of 70 million people would need to shrink to 63 million by 2040 – a reduction of 7 million spread over 22 years. Much of that might occur through 'natural wastage' and allowance had to be made for wars, pandemics and other hypothetical horrors, based on a statistical database covering the past 40 years. Distinguished mathematicians skilled in creative extrapolation and guesswork fed forecasting modules into their sacred mainframe computer like ritual sacrifices. After much deep thought the deity handed down its infallible pronouncement: to be sure of meeting the United Nations target, overall UK population needed to be reduced *every year* for 22 years by at least:

318,182 souls

or IUCs (individual units of consumption) as New Phoenix preferred to call them.

All that remained was to identify the appropriate candidates according to UK demographic factors. They fell into three groups: immigrants, the unborn and the undead. While reversing the influx of foreigners was a logical solution, New Phoenix had never allowed logic to stand in the way of ideology, especially when it attracted the dreaded PC label of 'racism'. As for the unborn, mass abortion had eliminated millions of future taxpayers already. To kill off more would be counter-productive.

A more realistic solution was a 'cull' of the undead and the legal sequestration of their oppressive pensions. A new parliamentary Bill would be needed, extending the powers of the Assisted Dying Act. It would now apply not only to the terminally ill but to everyone of pensionable age, ill or healthy, who could be persuaded to opt for physician-assisted suicide.

In time-honoured parliamentary tradition, they waited for a good day to bury bad news. It arrived courtesy of a major earthquake in Turkey. The soaring death toll kept the reformers' announcement off the front pages while TV and radio news bulletins relegated it to 'other major news stories'. The statement, issued by the newly-formed Department for Population Control, brutally down-graded the image of older people from the cuddly old codgers they'd been sentimentally portrayed for centuries to that of a growing social burden.

'Everyone agreed' society needed to change the way it viewed its old people. They contributed nothing to the economy but consumed more than any other age group. Their pension handouts were by far the largest drain on the welfare budget. The inconvenient truth was these IUCs were no longer affordable. Tough, unflinching action was long overdue in the interests of the nation and the planet.

A White Paper was drafted setting out a restructured state pension scheme to reflect the nation's changing economic and social priorities. Its key points were:

1. Basic state pension payable for 15 years only – from retirement at age 67 or, for those continuing to work, from date of retiring.
2. After 15 years a 'Maturity Contract' would take effect, offering the choice of assisted terminal sedation on the NHS or an opt-out clause. For those opting out, the state pension would be progressively reduced by five per cent a year to a fixed minimum of 50 per cent.

The Paper's authors congratulated themselves on an ingenious system of population control to meet the UN demand while at long last stemming the relentless haemorrhaging of resources by the ever-growing army of pensioners. The Maturity Contract was a genuine breakthrough – the first time voluntary euthanasia had been incorporated as an instrument of socio-economic policy. Although admittedly Draconian it was pragmatic and it was fair. But it was also highly controversial. They fully understood the media would give it a hard time. All great reformers had suffered at the hands of reactionary and religious bigots, they told themselves. If it were left to such people we'd still be living in caves.

Opponents would seize on the stressful Catch 22 choice between terminal sedation and opting out in return for a decreasing pension. It would be a tough decision but the old were generally tough people. They'd try to survive for a year or two, relying on savings, family or charity support, before inflation inevitably eroded their purchasing power like an invisible stealth tax. It wouldn't take long to reach crisis point. What then? That, New Phoenix claimed, was the subtle beauty of their reform. Sooner rather than later it would focus the minds of pensioners – many suffering chronic age-related pain – on what was really in their best interests: more years of increasing hardship or the 'other' option: comfortable, stress-free life closure.

The stark fact was that terminal sedation *would be doing them a favour*. It was modelled on the medically approved Liverpool Care Pathway, a gentle and completely painless end-of-life procedure reserved strictly for the terminally ill with only hours to live.

Originating from a Liverpool hospice in the early 2000s, the method relieved suffering by syringe driver to sedate continuously and deeply until death. It was compassionate and entirely civilised – none of your Gothic poison chalices associated with Swiss suicide clinics. And none of the exorbitant fees they charged either.

Anticipating negative moral arguments from misguided pro-life elements, New Phoenix gave their revolutionary plan a positive spin. They called it the Health of the Nation strategy. Suitably manipulated by their PR team, it could provide the beleaguered government with a last gasp lifeline – a pathway leading not to death but to economic rebirth.

In the midst of death there was life.

*   *   *

Even though he'd been tipped off about Britain's new 'endangered species' Howard was still shocked by the state's declaration of war against its senior citizens. His instinctive reaction was to check his own 15-year deal if the scheme became law. He would be 82 on reaching the 'contract' stage – supposing he lived that long, which was unlikely in his present health. By then, opting out would probably cost 10 per cent a year of the state handout. There was no way his company pension could make up the difference. It would be the same for Barbara? *And what about his mother?*

In her mid-eighties, her 15 years were already up. He'd need to make sure she opted out. Without his help she'd be swept aside in the stampede to register. The scheme had the potential for massive social chaos. It was wide open to abuse. Government computers had a track record littered with blunders: millions of income tax records lost without trace, nuclear secrets discovered online, prisoners released prematurely, personal medical details sent to wrong addresses. If this electronic fallibility – not to mention the human version – extended to the Maturity Contract God alone knew what might happen.

The contract was based on a deeply flawed principle of presumed consent: that pensioners accepted terminal sedation unless they opted out. But what if the computers lost their opt-out details? The terminally ill, Alzheimer's and other dementia patients without family or legal support and unable to fight their corner might end up being heavily sedated and wheeled off for 'termination' against their will. Many such cases had been reported in Holland and Belgium.

With his help, his mother would survive that nightmare scenario, but then they'd start clawing back her pathetic widow's pension. How would she manage? His mounting anxiety took on a sense of desperate urgency. What was needed when politicians spectacularly lost the plot was the power of the Press to step in and straighten them out. Sadly, the media's response had been overshadowed by the devastating earthquake in Turkey.

Although splashing on the catastrophe, the following day's *Announcer* did squeeze in a front page cross reference to the shock waves nearer home. It was headed: *Elderly face pensions 'contract' threat – Page Three*, with the full startling story on the inside page. But as the quake carnage mounted and a UN relief operation faltered, subsequent issues devoted less space to the Maturity Contract. The national outcry it had provoked soon died down – even on the Letters Page which, after

21

a few days, reverted to more familiar topics of swearing on TV, how to make marmalade and the nesting habits of swifts. The restructured state pension was still at the White Paper stage, subject to committee hearings and public consultation.

But Howard knew that White Papers could be fast-tracked, committees wound up and consultation procedures reduced to a sham PR exercise. He repeatedly telephoned ex-colleagues, urging them to keep the issue alive by way of in-depth news features. He'd always been prepared to listen to constructive criticism himself, especially from more experienced colleagues. No doubt the latest crop of executives would appreciate similar guidance.

How wrong could you be? The Maturity Contract was just another hare-brained idea that would be watered down or dropped altogether, they told him. There were more newsworthy stories of immediate importance. In addition to the earthquake, another war was brewing, this time in Sri Lanka where scientists believed they had located an offshore oilfield the size of Texas. A soap actress was dying of cancer. The Health and Safety Executive had banned Christmas crackers (people might fall backwards and hurt themselves). Some of the alarmingly youthful editorial executives had problems remembering him. Others had never heard of him (after only two months!). All were too busy to deal with a 'yesterday's man' panicking over the fate of geriatrics.

There was little point in pestering people already stressed out by 'multi-tasking' – a management euphemism for extra unpaid graft on their complex website and online newspaper. Ever the realist, he was forced to accept that, once retired, you were out of the loop very quickly and there was no way back. *The Announcer* would wake up to the danger sooner or later. They were journalists after all…servants of the truth. But would truth summon them to their duty sooner rather than later?

Oddly enough, it was *The Announcer's* cryptic crossword that supplied the answer. The puzzle was one of the paper's most popular features on account of its challenging complexity. It was an institution in its own right. But it had always been too time-consuming to tackle previously. Time was now something he had plenty of. To his surprise, he found the clues remarkably easy – and that was when the penny dropped. The paper was being 'dumbed down'.

It all made sense…the superficial treatment of news stories, obsessive royal family arse-licking, celebrity tittle-tattle, frivolous features, the arrival of a dire agony aunt and the departure of common sense from the editorials. In a desperate attempt to prop up circulation, *The Announcer,* that timeless embodiment of serious thought and sobriety, had abased itself to popular culture. In other words, it was going down market. Not even the crossword had been spared.

For a positive thinker like Howard, the disillusionment, after a lifetime's service to the newspaper, was hard to bear. Nothing like this would have happened in the old days. You needed to be a journalist at the top of your profession to work for it rather than a glorified computer operator fresh from university.

Sensing her husband's despair, Barbara did her best to counsel patience. She agreed that the proposed Maturity Contract was open to abuse. It would give doctors too much power and they had more than enough already. Some did like to play God, she knew from daily experience. But it *was* only a White Paper – a discussion document. Hopefully, everyone would see sense and quietly drop the idea as unacceptable in a civilised society. But if Howard's worst fears materialised, she knew that, retired or not, he would fight it. His time would come. It always did.

In the meantime, they should count their blessings. They still had their family and their detached South London home. Their eldest son, Christopher, was about to present them with their first grandchild. Howard would have time to devote to the child – a luxury, which, due to his job's unsocial hours, he'd rarely enjoyed while his own children were growing up. Patience had never been Howard's strong point. In a world dominated by deadlines a sense of urgency was essential. But the stark reality was he no longer belonged to that world. He finally accepted that he needed to let go.

Throughout his career he'd sought refuge from the job's traumas by playing snooker at the Press Club. It was his form of escapism and it kept him sane. Now he could relax regularly at his local Liberal Club where they had two excellent tables, although increasingly arthritic joints restricted him to a couple of frames per evening. Sometimes, his former *Announcer* colleague, Bernard Baxter, now also retired, would join him for a beer. They would chat about old times and laugh at the ineptitude of the younger generation. Howard had been invited to join the bowls team but politely declined. You had to draw the line somewhere. Bowls was an old man's game.

He didn't feel like an old man. The only time he felt no longer young was at 10-o-clock in the morning when

Barbara would waken him as part of his adjustment to normal life. After working night shifts for most of his life, rarely rising before the crack of noon, he regarded 10 am as an indecent hour. There was no way you could feel normal at that time. But he had reluctantly agreed that his wife would rouse him progressively earlier and she was not the sort of woman to be deflected from her duty.

"You're missing the best part of the day," she would chide him, flinging back the bedroom curtains in the brisk manner of a nurse who knew what was best for a difficult patient. Startled by the sudden flood of light, he'd turn over and try to go back to sleep. But Barbara was having none of it. She would lift the duvet and tickle the soles of his feet. Cruel but effective. Slowly, grumpily he would sit up, shielding his eyes from the light in a theatrical manner. Then she'd hand him his coffee, *The Announcer* and, if it was a postal delivery day, his mail, which usually comprised bills, cruise line brochures and other marketing material aimed at the newly-retired.

One bright winter's morning, with snow lining the bedroom's leaded lights, there was a letter that looked important. The envelope bore a government imprint – surely not another tax demand? Inside was a single sheet of embossed, fine quality notepaper and, as Howard read its message, apprehension gradually turned to incredulity. After reading it a second time, he began to shake with suppressed mirth, before subsiding into his crumpled pillows in a fit of uncontrollable laughter.

THREE

If, as they say, laughter is the best medicine, Howard might have skipped his daily medication without any ill effects that morning. When his wife heard the guffaws from downstairs, she hurried back to their bedroom in alarm. Groans she could handle but not hysterics. She found him sitting up in bed, waving the letter aloft and still chortling.

"Now I've seen everything," he exclaimed, handing her the single sheet of cartridge paper embossed with the Cabinet Office crest. "What do you think of that, darling? They want to give me the Order of the Non-Existent British Empire!"

Barbara put on her spectacles and took the letter. It informed her husband he'd been nominated to receive the OBE for services to journalism. She was rarely lost for words but the prospect of such a dazzling honour left her overwhelmed. "I can't believe it," she said at length.

"Neither can I. It's got to be an elaborate joke or else a mistake. There's no way the Powers that be would ever give me a medal – not after what I did to their dodgy business scams."

She knew what he meant. The Powers that be and Big Business were interchangeable. Years earlier, Howard's investigative campaigns had exposed corruption at very high levels including Parliament. 'Sleaze-busting' he and his colleagues had called it. Some of the crooks were public figures who'd tried to intimidate the journalists and gone to jail as a result[1].

"But that was years ago."

"Our ruling class have long memories…and they're the world's worst losers. It'll be a computer error, you'll see."

He was probably right, his wife thought, but she didn't want to believe it. A mental picture of the family posing outside Buckingham Palace, dressed to the nines, was beginning to form. "How could they make such a mistake? It's from the Cabinet Office, after all."

Howard eased himself out of bed and started to get dressed. "Government computers make mistakes every day. Remember the famous case of the 'lost' 25 million taxpayers…the tax refunds for people who'd never paid any tax… millions went down the drain." He paused for breath after pulling on his socks and shoes, and sat

---

1. The first decade of the 21st century gave rise to the term 'Rip-off Britain' as the nation succumbed to a pathological obsession with money. The example, as always, came from the top, with more than half MPs caught fiddling taxpayer-funded expenses. Many claimed for phantom second homes, some for double glazing, groceries, toilet rolls and porn videos. Others even claimed for their annual poppy wreaths. Spivs running major banks awarded themselves mega bonuses, driving the UK to the brink of bankruptcy. When the abuse was outlawed, they doubled their salaries. Blue chip companies paid 1 per cent corporation tax, millionaire footballers 2 per cent income tax. The mantra of the age was supposed to be 'education, education, education'. In reality it was all about money, money, money.

down again on the rumpled sheets. "Then the old Child Support Agency that managed to lose half a million non-paying fathers without trace. And the Home Office computer that released hundreds of prisoners by mistake…most of them still on the run, happily committing more rapes and murders."

"Yes, but computers are more sophisticated now."

"Maybe, but they still crash. Glitches and scams still happen. They're not secure…they can be hacked into. They don't work at all if there's a power outage and the battery's flat. Computers…" he made a throat-cutting gesture "…one big hassle!"

Barbara knew he had no faith in computers, which was why the latest model laptop presented by his former colleagues as a retirement gift stood unused on his desk. But she knew from data processing work in her ward office that they could be blamed unfairly. "Might there be another explanation?" she asked, sitting next to him on the bed.

Howard considered the possibility of a prank by ex-colleagues. It was the sort of thing Bernard Baxter might dream up. The Liverpudlian former sub-editor had always been a practical joker. He would have enjoyed the incongruity of Howard being awarded an ONEBE, as they both called it. But it didn't seem possible that, without his previous Press credentials, he could have penetrated the Cabinet Office.

One other theory was taking shape in his mind. The award could have been intended for Hugo Michaelson, *The Announcer's* Old Etonian editor. The initials were the same and the names similar. Someone in the Cabinet Office, perhaps a junior civil servant, could easily have mixed them up. Human error as well as computer error was not unheard of. The theory started to stack up. The editor was a shooting crony of His Lordship and a committed monarchist. If anyone deserved the Order of the Non-Existent British Empire, Hugo did.

He stood up and struggled arthritically into his well-worn jacket. "The only other explanation is that they've mixed me up with dear old Hugo." There was an acceptance slip in the envelope, to be signed and returned to the Ceremonial Secretariat. Howard extracted it and felt inside his jacket pocket. "Where's my pen? I'll tell them to give their meaningless medal to Hugo!"

Before he could find his pen, Barbara gently relieved him of the letter and reply slip. She sat him back down on the bed. "Hold on a minute, Howard. Let's think about this. Why not accept the offer? You really deserve it, you know."

"I don't want the wretched thing!"

"But I do, Howard. It's only right you should be honoured after all you achieved as a journalist... thousands of *Announcer* readers would agree with me."

"But this isn't an honour, it's just the opposite. Where *is* this British empire? It doesn't *exist*. It's history, along with the Roman and Ottoman versions. We don't even have a commonwealth any more. The medal no longer *means* anything."

"It has *symbolic* value. That means something to lots of people, including your former readers. They still remember all the lost causes you fought for... and won."

"I wouldn't bet on it."

She took his hand and squeezed it gently. "And it would mean a great deal to the children. They'd all be so proud of you."

Howard laughed. "Aren't they already?"

Barbara knew he didn't always see eye to eye with Christopher, their eldest son, whose wife was about to present them with their first grandchild. While Howard's turbulent career had turned him into an ardent socialist, it had propelled Chris in the opposite direction, favouring capitalism and even the monarchy – institutions his father detested. A visit to the Palace by his father would work wonders for their relationship.

"Of course, darling. But Chris would be impressed, don't you think?"

"That's it then? I accept this so-called honour for you and Chris?"

"Something like that." She kissed him tenderly, just like old times. Now in her early sixties, her fine fair hair was turning grey and the green eyes had lost some of their sparkle. But her smile was as beguiling as the night they met at a campus disco over 40 years ago. He remembered, word for word, the conversation they'd had that night about clones – Dolly, the sheep, being the main subject of debate at the time.

"Just imagine," she'd said, "everyone'll be exactly the same when the scientists finish with us."

He'd blurted out: "I wouldn't mind if they were all like you." He was smitten then and he was still smitten now. He took the letter from her and folded it. "You could be right," he conceded.

"It has been known."

"I'll think about it."

Barbara beamed. She was already planning what to wear for the investiture.

*   *   *

30

Glancing in the bedroom mirror as he dressed in his shabby everyday clothes and casual leather slip-ons, Howard tried to picture himself in a hired morning suit. The spectacle brought him swiftly back to reality. The only time he'd worn 'fancy dress' had been at Christopher's wedding and he'd looked a total berk, as the photographs often reminded him. Everyone had described his appearance as 'distinguished', attempting to justify the expense of hiring the outfit. He didn't do distinguished. To him it meant 'elitist'.

But he realised Barbara was thrilled at the prospect of an investiture and the accompanying VIP status it would bestow on him and the family. Christopher, for one, would no doubt bask in the reflected glory. His son had abandoned journalism as a career while at university and gone into business studies. He now worked as a high-powered advertising executive and was into words like 'prestigious'.

Howard regarded prestige as uncomfortably close to privilege. It meant pomposity and pretentiousness. He was too old for such things. The idea of cringing in front of a member of the ruling class to acquire prestige seemed a ludicrous contradiction. All it did was strip you of your self-respect. He was a journalist not a dog.

If he were to go through with the ordeal, he would wear his trusty brown jacket with leather patches on the elbows plus his red trade union tie. Perhaps not the cap he'd bought for a fiver at a charity shop in 1998 although it would be a difficult decision. It wasn't your ordinary cloth cap but a jaunty version in blue cavalry twill with a broad peak and a rather splendid maroon silk lining. He wore it everywhere. People called him eccentric. In an upside-down but concentric world, he could live with that.

FOUR

The road to Cheam was less busy than usual for a weekday. Since he'd retired, Howard frequently drove along it to visit his mother in her sheltered apartment. He'd noticed a steady decline in traffic but on this afternoon in late February it was almost deserted. A heavy stillness wrapped itself round the frost-bound scene. Not a breath of breeze stirred the monstrous wind turbines that lined both sides of the dual carriageway. They stood motionless, becalmed... impotent giants brooding in silent reproach at the folly of their creators, who had left Britain's landscape as ruined as its economy. The technocrats' vision at the turn of the century had been a 30 per cent reduction in carbon emissions. Now, in 2018, the result was a 1,000 per cent increase in power cuts.

At a roadside battery-charging station a long queue of electric-powered cars waited for their plug-in high voltage fix. They were likely to wait a long time. A large sign read: NO POWER. Back in the days when renewable energy seemed like a good idea, the silent, non-polluting vehicles had been the 'green' answer to global warming. Socially responsible drivers were exhorted to buy one and save the planet. That was before the Great Depression, when the price of energy on the international markets soared beyond the reach of a government already on its uppers.

All-electric cars, like computers, were built round a fatal flaw. For all their state-of-the-art innovation and high-tech wizardry they were useless without electricity to power them. The problem was that wind power, tide power and recycled fish-and-chip-shop-oil power were never going to meet the demand. As Howard sailed past the stranded motorists in his ancient petrol-engined Rover, he was thankful he hadn't bought one of their luxurious status symbols. Although petrol was rationed and consumption had to be watched carefully, at least he could be reasonably sure of reaching his destination. That was the real luxury these days.

It was growing dark when he turned into the car park outside the gaunt, featureless building his mother called home but there were no lights on anywhere. He let himself in at the main door with the key she'd given him. The lift was out of order so, carrying his usual bunch of flowers, he slowly climbed the dark, stone stairs to her first-floor apartment. When he reached her door with its enamel nameplate, Susan Mitchell, he rapped three times very loudly with the heavy knocker. It was their pre-arranged signal. She was profoundly deaf, needing hearing aids in both ears.

When she opened the door Howard saw a dimly lit flat behind her but his little old mother was almost lost from view inside a voluminous overcoat, thick scarf and woollen gloves. As always she greeted him with a hug and a wet kiss.

He took off his cap and, as always, asked: "How are you, Mum?"

"I'm just the same, Howard. How are you?"

"I'm just the same, too." They laughed at their shared catchphrase and he kissed her wrinkled but still delicately beautiful face.

She accepted the bouquet with girlish delight. "They're lovely Howard. I'll put them in some water." She led him into the tiny lounge, illuminated by several candles on saucers. The room felt like an ice-box. "As you can see, there's another power cut so you'd better keep your coat on. I can't make a pot of tea but I keep my Thermos topped up just in case. Would you like a cup?"

He said that would be fine. He pulled his sheepskin coat closely round him and tried to relax on the two-seater chintz sofa, watching her in the gloom of her mini-kitchen. Her movements were slow due to painful arthritis and osteoporosis. The natural light brown curls he'd tenderly touched as an infant when she'd stooped to tie his necktie and his shoelaces were now a silvery grey. Her hairdresser had suggested a tint or dye but there was no way his mother would ever succumb to such vanities.

Apart from the flickering candles, everything in the room was just the same too. There was the same battered sideboard in which he'd kept his toys. A handle was missing from a drawer. It had been missing for over 60 years. The same Victorian standard lamp with its green-fringed shade, inherited from his grandparents, grandly dominated a corner. The ornaments and brass trinkets his father (a sailor who died several years ago) had brought home from the Middle East were grouped on the electric fire surround. Family wedding photographs and portraits of Howard's children, Christopher, Sally and William stood on the old bureau and on a small table near the window, along with his father's naval binoculars. His mother still used them to watch birds and squirrels in surrounding trees.

She brought in a tray with plastic cups of tea from the Thermos flask, daintily cut potted beef sandwiches and slices of sponge cake. "It's the best I can do, I'm afraid. These power cuts are getting worse…you can't use the kettle, you can't use the cooker, you can't use the telly…and, worst of all, there's no heating. All the radiators go off – and the electric fire, of course. Hot water bottles are no good as there's hardly any hot water. The gentleman next door died last week…pneumonia…same age as me. Believe me, Howard, it's no fun being old and cold."

Howard sipped the warm tea. "You know you can always come and stay with us, Mum." He and Barbara had a wood-burning stove offering immunity from the prevailing national hardship. But he knew what his mother would say. They'd offered her a home many times. She was far too independent to accept.

They huddled together on the sofa in the soft candlelight. "It's just like the war, Howard. The power cuts and the blackouts. We had to use candles *then*. Nothing's changed!"

"That's progress, Mum."

"Only then, of course, we also had the Blitz." She had been an infant at the start of the Second World War and had vivid memories of the air raids. "Night after night they came over…the Germans. It was awful. Those terrible wailing sirens would wake you and you'd have to run out to the shelter in your night clothes…in the freezing cold. I can still see the searchlights and hear the anti-aircraft guns…and the planes going over…and feel the fear – that there were men in them trying to kill us."

35

She sniffed and her tired old eyes filled with tears. "On top of it all we had rationing. We couldn't get enough to eat...a bit like now really. Only now we can't *afford* to eat. They'll be rationing food next, you'll see...like the petrol. Then it'll be clothing coupons..."

Howard had heard it all before but never tired of listening to her. It wasn't just nostalgia, it was history. There were very few people left who remembered the war. The traumatic experience had left them strong and stoical. They were a different breed to the modern generation who expected counselling if they were thrown off a TV talent show.

"You were a tough lot in those days!"

She dabbed her eyes with a tiny handkerchief and gave him a sidelong grin. "You're right. Look at young people today...twisting and jerking about on the telly...they call it dancing. A gust of wind would blow them over!"

As if joining in the hilarity of the moment, the lights, electric fire and TV all came back on. Power was restored, at least for the time being. The sudden transformation made them both jump. "Praise be!" his mother exclaimed, rising stiffly to her feet. "Let there be light." She snuffed out all the candles and returned to her sponge cake.

"What's happening to the country, Howard? Nobody seems to know. Where did it all go wrong?"

It was a good question, he thought. You couldn't simply say it was all down to the calamity of 2008. That had been 10 years ago – time enough to recover if the country's leaders had been fit for purpose. People said that a nation got the leaders it deserved but what had everyone done to deserve New Phoenix?

He finished his tea, now stone cold. "I wish I knew, Mum, but I believe it goes back to the 1970s and 80s...you remember, when schools stopped teaching the Three Rs? That's when the rot set in. Children left school semi-literate. Exams had to be dumbed down to boost the 'pass' figures."

"Yes, I remember. Everyone passed!"

"That's right...including today's leaders. We've become a nation of dunces led by dimwits."

"They can't all be dimwits, surely."

Howard snorted. "Just read the papers, Mother. One farcical blunder after another. It's been going on for years."

"I do, Howard, and I watch the news on the telly. But I think there's another explanation. Something else happened before then...in the 1960s. They legalised abortion...terrible mistake. Until then, human life *meant* something. It means nothing now. They want to kill off us golden oldies. We're living too long!"

So she knew about the White Paper. He sighed and stood up. The electric logs had started to melt the Arctic atmosphere and he removed his coat. "Let me make that pot of tea, now we can use the kettle."

She offered only token resistance as he cleared away the tray and rinsed out the used crockery in the sink. When he returned with a fresh pot of tea and clean cups she had removed the top layer of her thermal insulation to reveal a woollen cardigan over a 1990s-style blue and yellow floral dress. "You shouldn't be doing this, Howard. You should let me do it." She added pointedly: "While I still can."

He got the message. "Look, Mother...I don't know what you've seen on the telly but it's only talk at this stage. It's just a White Paper. You know what politicians are – professional talkers. It might never happen …and even if it did…"

Perhaps it was her faulty hearing aids but she wasn't paying much attention. "They say I'll have to take a cut in my pension now my 15 years are up…either that or let them euthanize me!"

The retired wordsmith smiled at the neologism. His mother had just given the English language a powerful new verb. She'd finally removed her gloves and he took hold of her wizened, skeletal hands. They were still icy. "You're not listening, Mum. It's what they call a public consultation exercise. They'll chatter about it on TV then forget it. Even if it went ahead, it'd take years to become law." He hoped she didn't know about fast-tracking.

"How long, about? I was looking forward to my telegram from the Palace."

You had to laugh. The things old people valued! "Like I say, Mother, it won't happen. But if it ever did, you've still got Dad's private pension. I'd take care of the rest." He wasn't entirely sure how. Freelance work was poorly paid and hard to come by even for journalists who were young and fit.

"I could never let you do that. I'd rather let them put me to sleep than be a burden on you and your family."

"You'd never be a burden, Mother. It would be the least we could do after all you've done for us."

She twisted her handkerchief between her bony fingers and sighed. "There's always *someone* trying to kill us. First it was the Germans, then the Irish, then the Muslims and now our own government. What have we *done* to deserve it?"

It was a good question but he knew that trying to explain British foreign policy would upset her. Before he could offer something non-committal she asked another.

"What happened to the sanctity of life, Howard?"

He concentrated on reassurance. "Search me, Mum. But look on the bright side. You're doing well for your age. I mean, look at you, you're still in your prime!"

It seemed to work. When her wheezy laughter subsided, she told him: "My doctor's very worried about my blood pressure."

He laughed, a trifle wheezily himself. "You're not alone, Mum. So's mine!"

*　　　　*　　　　*

What *had* happened to the sanctity of life, Howard wondered, as he drove home through the grimy, litter-strewn streets of south London. Was it really a casualty of the 1960s, as sociologists would have you believe, when the pill, punk rock and legalised abortion opened a generation gap between young and old? And at what point had the gap widened into its present unbridgeable gulf?

The young had always been intolerant of their elders but the hostility they showed them now appalled him. On radio and TV they were allowed free rein to vent their abuse, smart-arse satirists routinely mocking the aged under the guise of comedy. But nobody was laughing once the politicians joined in, branding pensioners parasites, the enemy within and 'coffin-dodgers' hanging on long after their expiry date. By an imperceptible incremental process, the abuse had turned into full-blown, state-endorsed elderphobia – and there was another sinister new word for the English language.

Cynical opportunists to a man (and woman) the politicians had been quick to exploit the social trend. Their Maturity Contract not only screwed victims financially it also subjected them to subtle emotional pressure at an age when they were least able to resist. They would feel under an obligation to sign up for assisted suicide rather than become dependent on family support. His mother had said so in as many words. It was exactly the reaction New Phoenix's psychologists anticipated.

The last thing her generation wanted was to be a burden on their families. Replicated across the nation, the sentiment would ensure a willing walk along the death pathway. The word 'willing' answered accusations of a coercive element. No-one would be forced into it…at least not yet. But gradually the public would be conditioned to accept the Maturity Contract as a form of modern, planet-friendly social engineering. The opt-out clause would be watered down until it evaporated completely. It was just a matter of time before…

Howard swerved violently to avoid a drunken youth urinating in the centre of the road, egged on by a crowd of half-dressed teenagers drinking from cans and bottles. They were staggering along the street, eating their junk food and hurling their litter into the rat-infested gutters. We'd become a throwaway society in every sense, he reflected. Once the government's designs on the elderly were realised, life itself would be thrown away just as carelessly.

On reaching your expiry date you'd become so much human litter.

FIVE

True to form, Barbara had been right about Christopher. Soon after hearing the news of his father's OBE, their eldest son swept into the drive in his expensive, electric-turbo convertible with its personalised number plate. His mother had pointed out when she'd telephoned that Howard had still not decided whether to accept the honour but Christopher must have thought she was joking. As far as he was concerned, acceptance of such a prestigious award could only be a formality.

Howard was in the kitchen staring in disbelief at his latest telephone bill, which had somehow increased by over 90 per cent since the last quarter, when his son burst in brandishing a magnum of Moet.

"Hi, Dad," the dynamic advertising executive breezed, gripping his father's hand and shaking it vigorously. "Heard the news...couldn't have happened to a more deserving old fella."

Howard felt a spasm of pain in his arthritic fingers but grinned bravely. "Hi, Chris. You're very kind. But actually I'm not sure if it's the sort of thing..."

"You've got to be kidding, Dad. Of course it's the sort of thing. They should really have given you a knighthood after all you've done." He plonked the bottle on the pine table and turned to Barbara. "I'll open it if you like, Mum. Let's have some glasses."

They drank a toast: "To Howard Mitchell, OBE." Howard half raised his glass automatically but didn't take a drink. Then they drank another toast: "To Howard Mitchell, junior." That was something else, of course. The grandfather-to-be drained his glass in one. Barbara was ecstatic. She knew her daughter-in-law's unborn child was a boy and they'd discussed possible names. A short list had been compiled including Sebastian, Jeremy and Alexander. But Howard had never been mentioned. She hugged her son in delight. "Chris, that's just wonderful. Are you sure?"

"Course I'm sure."

"Is Amanda sure?"

"No problem. I phoned her earlier and she's just as thrilled about the OBE as I am. She couldn't come with me but she sends her best."

"It won't be long now will it?"

"Another fortnight at most, the docs say. We're both getting nervous."

"That's only natural with your first. Your Dad and I were the same with you – and you were a week early. Do you remember, Howard?"

Howard pocketed the telephone company's latest attempt at legalised extortion and poured more champagne "How could I forget!" He laughed as he recalled the birth of his son all those years ago. He and his newsroom colleagues had celebrated in The Swan with Two Necks and there was no way he would ever forget the hangover. They'd given him cigars, as was customary then, although he had never smoked.

He wondered if he should buy cigars for Chris but thought better of it. His son didn't smoke either. It was one of the few characteristics which his father admired. They could never discuss politics, international affairs or commerce without the discussion ending in heated disagreement. Howard realised it was natural for sons to oppose their fathers' ideals and beliefs for the hell of it – to assert their own manhood. Hopefully, Chris would grow out of it, though his father wasn't prepared to bet on that.

Try as he would, Howard could barely believe that the tiny bundle he'd held in his arms all those years ago had grown into the prematurely balding, self-assured capitalist with the beginnings of a middle-aged spread who was knocking back champagne in his kitchen. It was a complete mystery where the years went. You were simply too busy trying to make a living and keep the bailiffs from the door to notice your children growing up.

It was the same with his daughter, Sally. There had been some anxious moments with her as a teenager with a taste for all-night raves and the unhealthy activities that went with them. But she'd matured at university where she achieved a first in fine arts and was already making a name for herself as an artist. An aunt had left her a part share in a gallery in Kensington although she spent most of her time at her rented studio in the foothills of the Sierra Almijara in Andalusia. There were rumours of a romance with a Spanish art dealer but, now in her thirties, she was leaving it late to have children. If she wasn't careful, the years would melt away and it would be too late.

But there was time for William. His younger son still lived with them and was studying sports medicine at college. His ambition to become a footballer had suffered a major setback when he sustained ligament damage while playing at school. But he still hoped to find work in the sport. For some inexplicable reason the lad was crazy about Crystal Palace, despite advice from people who knew about such things that a physio's job with such a club might not rank among the most lucrative. He would learn about life's realities soon enough and all you could do as a parent was hope the lesson wouldn't be too painful.

Barbara, a practising Catholic in contrast to Howard's agnostic/nominal C of E, would remind her husband that you also prayed for your children but that was another story. Howard had not yet discovered the power of prayer and, at 64, reckoned he never would. He knew that Chris, though a baptised Catholic, rarely went to Mass. A shared scepticism over the place of religion in a secular, high-tech world was one of the few things they had in common. But his son and his equally agnostic wife were still keen to have Howard junior christened. It was rather like taking out an insurance policy in case you were wrong and, in fact, the Almighty did have some say in the destiny of the world in general and your children in particular.

Barbara seemed to read his thoughts. "We're so looking forward to the baptism, aren't we, Howard?"

He did his best to appear enthusiastic although if truth be known he did not feel old enough for grandfatherhood. But he was chuffed about them naming the lad after himself. That had come out of the blue. Nobody had even mentioned the possibility until word got round about his OBE. He could hardly refuse the award now. Or could he? An element of psychological pressure seemed to have crept into proceedings. He detected the hand of Barbara plus, of course, Chris and Sally. The unworthy thought occurred that he might just possibly have been stitched up.

Slightly mellowed after the champagne, Chris was persuaded to stay for tea and buttered crumpets before driving home. Round the kitchen table, conversation turned to the parlous state of the economy. The Great Recession had left a legacy of chronic hyperinflation due to the Bank of England flooding the country with debased currency unsupported by gold or other assets.

"So much for your capitalist system," Howard told his son. "The moment they started printing 'Monopoly money' it was discredited. What have they achieved? Inflation running at 14 per cent and unemployment worse than the 1930s."

Chris still had a job although he hadn't had a rise for two years. Some of his agency colleagues had just been made redundant and he knew his luck could run out at any moment. But he clung to his child-like faith in capitalism with the tenacity of a shipwreck survivor hanging on to a piece of the wreckage. "It's *controlled* inflation, Dad. There's spare capacity in the economy to take care of it. Prices will soon start to come down again."

"That's what they've been saying for years. But prices are still going up. And as long as the money supply goes on expanding they'll *keep* going up. Meanwhile, millions of old people are being fleeced...trying to survive on a fixed pension. And they won't even have *that* much longer if New Phoenix have their way."

"The Maturity Contract, you mean? It's just a White Paper, Dad."

"A very murky White Paper if you ask me...produced by murky capitalists targeting the weakest members of society. That's the trouble with capitalism...always the weakest who come off worst."

"It's still a better system than socialism, I don't care what you say."

"Come on, Chris...at least socialism knows how to look after elderly people. Look at China...they're treated as honoured citizens there."

His son was quick to quote George Bernard Shaw: "Socialism will not work until human nature changes; and when human nature changes, socialism will not be necessary."

"For socialism, read capitalism," Howard fired back. "If GBS were alive today, he'd have to change the wording. It's usury and human greed that undermine the capitalist system. When human nature changes, capitalism will not be necessary."

But, for once, they parted on friendly terms. Chris gave his father a bear-hug and reminded him that his grandson would still be called Howard, in spite of the old Leftie's misguided views. "Cheers, granddad," he grinned. "See you at the maternity hospital. And no more nonsense about refusing your OBE – okay?"

He climbed into his high-powered status symbol, blew a kiss to his mother and gave his father a broad, knowing wink. Howard got the message.

*   *   *

"How have I allowed myself to be talked into this?" Howard asked Bernard, his fellow hack and confidant, during one of their snooker evenings at the Liberal Club soon afterwards. He'd just cleared the table with a break of 27 which showed he could still pot a good ball, although in the old days he'd scored the occasional century break.

He ...cked Bernard for a beer in the bar. His former newsroom colleague had been astonished but generous in his congratulations when he'd phoned him earlier to tell him of the award. But congratulations were the last thing Howard needed. As they sat with their drinks he told him: "I don't believe it was intended for me in the first place – and I certainly don't want it. But I seem to be stuck with it whether I want it or not ..."

... had not yet ... frame shook ... permanently avuncular ... hair was as grey as Howard's and Bernard on top but there was no diminishing ...umour that had relieved tough campaigns ...ared in the past.

"Women," he intoned in his thick Halewood accent, "can talk you into anything. As Confucius said: 'Show me a woman and I'll show you trouble'."

Howard took a swig of his special brew. "Did he say how to get out of it?"

"No, but the usual method is to find out what they want and give it to them."

Bernard's marriage had been one of Fleet Street's many casualties. The long hours of night work and the heavy drinking took their inevitable toll in the divorce courts. He'd experienced little difficulty in finding out what his wife wanted but had rarely been able to give it

to her. Without ... children to ... the relationship,
it gradually fell apart ...

The pair finished their drinks and ordered another
round. They watched the bar's TV screen in ...
Scunthorpe were playing newly-relegated Manchester
United in a Championship match. The score was 0-0
and the game looked boring.

After a few minutes, Howard said. "I'm going to be
a ...

names like ...
all of a sudden, they ...

"That's brilliant!"

"But there's some small print invo..."

"How do you mean?"

"They know how I feel about the 'honour' but ...
situation seems to be that I'd better accept it or else…"

"Or else, it'll be back to Sebastian or Jeremy?"

"Correct."

Bernard thought for a long time between gulps of
beer. Then he reminded Howard: "You told me you
didn't think the award was intended for you…who *do*
you think it was intended for?"

"Hugo Michaelson."

Both veteran hacks fell about.

"That's made my day, Howard," Bernard spluttered.
"If anyone qualifies for the ONEBE it's old Hugo.
You're right, there must have been a mix-up…and
you're going to the Palace instead of him!"

"Be serious, Bernard. How *can* I? The whole thing's
just a charade…a circus to keep the plebs happy."

"I know, but you've got to go now. Think about
it…with all his contacts in high places, Hugo's bound

to know what's happened. Someone in the Cabinet Office is sure to have mentioned it, congratulated him off the record and everything..."

"And Hugo's hopping mad..."

"Exactly. And so are the jobsworths who've cocked it up. This'll be one of the few times when heads will roll."

"Do you think they might try to claw the medal back, admit they made a mistake...blame the computer...damage limitation?"

"They're hard-nosed enough. They might just live it down. But not once you've accepted. There'd be hell to pay. It'd bring the whole honours system into disrepute."

"Isn't it discredited already? I mean, since the old commonwealth ditched the Crown, the empire's become a quaint back number."

"It's a joke, I agree. But an investiture's still a great day out for the punters. They've worked hard all their lives for their gongs..."

"Not the fat cats...they've bribed their way in."

"No, but most of them. They still believe it's a real honour that counts for something."

They supped their ale and brought their collective wisdom to bear on the issue. Howard could wait for the Cabinet Office to realise their mistake and retract their offer since he had not yet accepted it. That would let him off the hook as far as the family were concerned but he might have to wait a long time, and they would start asking awkward questions.

Or he could send back the acceptance slip with some rude words scrawled across it, which had been his initial reaction. But that option had been overtaken by events. It would inevitably result in prolonged family aggro which, at Howard's time of life, was something he could do without. The only other option was to accept the 'accolade' for a lifetime of dedicated service to journalism, and grin and bear it.

No man could have contemplated the acceptance of an honour so gloomily. The former writer of countless human interest stories sighed as he tried to untangle his own. "What do you advise, Bernard?" he asked as they finished their drinks and the barman phoned for taxis.

"I'd say accept it, Howard. Everyone would be pleased, except Hugo…"

"And me!"

"Just look on the positive side. You may not regard it as an honour but most people still do. Okay, you're retired, but maybe you could use it in some way to change things. God knows there's plenty of things in this country that need changing."

As they sat watching the football – Scunthorpe had scored and were leading 1-0 – while waiting for their taxis, the match was interrupted by a newsflash. In the last few minutes, the announcer said, the government had indicated acceptance of the White Paper incorporating a maturity contract for state pensioners. The measure would be enshrined in a radical Health of the Nation Bill to be introduced urgently in parliament.

Bernard gave Howard a knowing wink. "See what I mean, my old mate!"

Howard marvelled at his friend's impeccable timing. "You'd been tipped off, hadn't you?"

"I did hear a whisper…nothing official. But it's official now. Like I say, there's plenty that needs changing."

The move had been ominously quick, Howard thought, as his cab rattled homeward. It could only mean one thing: the legislative process would be even quicker. On reaching home, he hurried into his study and found the letter from the Cabinet Office. He extracted the acceptance form and signed it, before placing it in the reply-paid envelope for posting next morning. He would use the 'honour' to change things, as his wise old friend had suggested. A highly original method was already taking shape in his mind. Could this be his ultimate mission? Barbara had told him his time would come. Maybe it had just arrived.

SIX

The faint tick of the antique wall clock was the only sound that broke the silence of the editor's inner sanctum on the third floor of *The Announcer's* central London building. Editorial departmental heads, men in shirtsleeves, women dressed more smartly, pored over the night's news list – a list of prospective stories for the following day's paper. High on the book-lined wall behind Hugo Michaelson's desk a large oil painting of His Lordship surveyed the assembled hacks with the aloof disdain of an aristocrat who wouldn't dream of soiling his hands on their labours but was happy to profit from them.

After several minutes, Hugo, wearing an off-white linen jacket almost matching hair that appeared to have been styled by a demented barber, leaned forward, brows furrowed. The vacuous expression and unkempt appearance were carefully cultivated trademarks of a harmless Right-wing buffoon when he appeared on TV chat shows, but here in his impregnable lair he was no fool. And as head of one of the world's most powerful news organisations he was far from harmless.

"Well, ladies and gentlemen," the languid Hampstead drawl began, "no prizes for telling me which of these stories will make tomorrow's splash."

It was a case of 'no contest' really. The government's decision to fast track its Health of the Nation Bill, subject to a rigid three-line whip, made it the obvious choice. The measure was a seminal development in politics, crossing the line on euthanasia from voluntary to obligatory. In terms of newsworthiness, it represented a quantum leap above the usual diet of death, destruction and disaster. Even the national obsession with petty rules and regulations, and bizarre attempts to enforce them by PC pedants, jobsworths and the mentally unsound, didn't stand a chance.

It was that blinding moment when the editor of *The Announcer* finally saw the light. "We need to make a campaign issue of this," he declared with unaccustomed intensity that startled his executives. "We've been silent too long on euthanasia. I'll be writing an editorial on this population control menace. Our golden oldies've suffered enough. It's time we stood up for them…after all, I'll be one myself soon."

Within a couple of hours, Irene Thomas, *The Announcer's* social affairs editor, had completed a scathing dissection of the Health of the Nation Bill, which scrolled down on the splash sub's screen below the inspired banner headlines:

THREE SCORE YEARS AND THEN?
'Health of Nation' Bill spells
doom for the elderly

The paper employed several leader writers, Hugo Michaelson being the most prolific. He took the old-fashioned view that editorials, at least on major issues, should be written by the editor. And the Health of the

Nation Bill was clearly a major issue – not just in terms of newsworthiness but also on a personal level. Years earlier, he and his young bride had returned from honeymoon in the Maldives – the happiest time of his life – when she told him she was pregnant. It was 'unplanned' and, in line with the received wisdom of the times, she intended to have an abortion. The child had been a boy. He'd always wanted a son, planned or otherwise.

They'd divorced soon afterwards but the pain still lingered, and alcohol proved an analgesic of limited strength. The 'culture of death', long accepted by the unquestioning masses, had robbed him of his son. Now it threatened to return in the form of social euthanasia and was likely to pass just as uncritically into the national consciousness.

Not if Hugo Michaelson had anything to do with it.

He removed his jacket, unfastened his onyx cuff-links and rolled up his shirt-sleeves to just below the elbow. Anything higher would conflict with his Eton background. He might be a hack but he was a gentleman hack. Enemies regularly branded him a public school elitist and sentimental old reactionary (to name the more polite epithets) but he was past caring. Less of the 'old', he would quip. A thick skin was essential in journalism. All that mattered was: can you write and can you meet your deadlines?

There was no denying that, after a couple of stiff malts, Hugo *could* write. And nothing motivated him more than a tight deadline. A glance at the Rolex told him there was an hour before the Leader Page went to press. He reached into his desk drawer for the bottle and turned to his keyboard:

Weakest to the wall

It is said you can judge a nation by the way it treats its older people. In which case, yesterday's announcement of obligatory euthanasia as a tool of population control amounts to an indictment of our civilised society. The government have used a flawed United Nations directive as an excuse to drive their weakest citizens to the wall.

The theory is our islands are bursting at the seams, that there are too many people and there will soon be insufficient food to go round. None of this is true. Despite a tsunami of immigrants, Britain is still not overcrowded. Only the cities are overcrowded. Take a walk in the Scottish Highlands or the Yorkshire Moors and you may not meet another person all day. Urban areas comprise 6 per cent of the land mass. They just need to spread out.

It is true that droughts and floods across the Third World have decimated food stocks but panic over dwindling resources is misplaced. There are huge surpluses of food throughout Europe crying out for redistribution. Improved GM technology offers the prospect of dramatically increased grain and rice crops if our leaders were far-sighted enough to develop it.

Unforgivably, they prefer to hide behind a discredited United Nations resolution they should have rejected out of hand. History is littered with UN resolutions routinely ignored by such regimes as Israel, Burma, Russia, Zimbabwe, America and even the UK when it suited us over Iraq. Why not this one? Because our bankrupt government need a scapegoat to blame for their dereliction. They did not have to look far.

We are told the Bill is too important to allow MPs to follow their consciences. It is too important *not* to. The *true* health of the nation demands a free vote on this sinister measure – when it will surely be defeated at Third Reading.

*   *   *

It was Barbara who took the call from the hospital in Cheam. Susan Mitchell had been admitted with a suspected stroke. She was conscious but there was some numbness in an arm and leg. Her speech was only slightly affected. She could receive visitors later that evening. Barbara told Howard the news before she hurried off to the afternoon shift at her own hospital. She was already late.

"Don't worry," she called over her shoulder. "It doesn't sound too bad from what I can gather. I'll phone you later."

Howard had been digesting the implications of the Maturity Contract as detailed in *The Announcer* and his relief that its editor had finally spoken out over the issue now turned to anxiety over his mother. Since he'd retired they could only afford one car, and Barbara had taken that to work. So he set off for the railway station to catch a train to Cheam, calling in at a florist's for the mandatory bouquet.

He waited over an hour at the station as a biting wind blew clouds of litter along tracks overgrown with weeds, forming drifts on the neglected platforms. All pretence of a regular timetable had long been discarded.

When the ancient, graffiti-daubed rolling stock arrived it was almost empty. Few could afford the fares since their recent 20 per cent increase. In the grimy, unheated carriage he found a seat that hadn't been vandalised, pulled his cap lower over his forehead and dug his gloved hands deep in the pockets of his sheepskin.

His thoughts as the train trundled the few miles towards Cheam were as depressing as the windswept scene slowly unfolding outside. His little old mother, who'd always been there for him as a feeble and defenceless child, was now feeble and defenceless herself. She needed him now just as he'd needed her then. And her need was all the greater since the welfare state, having neglected her welfare throughout her advancing years, no longer had any further use for her.

Susan Mitchell's bed was curtained off when he entered the geriatric ward but the sister told him it would be all right to sit with her. He shouldn't stay too long. Talking tired her. She'd suffered a mild stroke. Her speech was only slightly affected and there was some paralysis down one side. It might wear off with physiotherapy but at her age the prognosis wasn't optimistic. She was going to need long-term care in a residential nursing home.

A weak and weary smile greeted him when he pulled back the curtain. Her pale face was a mask of fatigue and her hair now seemed a lot greyer but she looked better than he'd expected. He kissed her gently on her hot, dry cheek and held her scrawny hand, with its plastic identity band flopping from her slender wrist. "You look just the same, Mother!"

He presented her with the flowers, slightly bedraggled roses and carnations. The clouded blue eyes brightened. "I'm all right, Howard. I just want to go home but they won't let me. Doctor said I had to stay in. Stuck-up young madam. Can't stand being pushed around by snooty young women." The words were clear and unslurred, if slower than usual.

He sat on a plastic chair pushed tightly against a bedside locker. "You're not all right, Mum. You've had a cerebral haemorrhage. It's only mild but they've got to do more tests. Can you remember what happened?"

"Not really…one minute I was watching *Songs of Praise* and the next I was lying here in bed. They told me the warden found me on the floor when she did her evening rounds. She called the ambulance. They're used to doing that where I live. Somebody pops off nearly every week."

"Is there anything I can get you?"

"A glass of water would be nice."

There was a jug of water on the locker but no glass. He went in search of a nurse and eventually found a young trainee in a small office. She was calling her boyfriend on her videophone and uttered an expletive when Howard asked politely for a glass. After a long search, she found a plastic cup and rudely slapped it in his hand.

When he returned and poured his mother the water, she drank nearly all of it. "That's better," she sighed. "You're a good boy, Howard." She sank back on her stacked pillows. "They don't take much notice of you in here."

He took the cup and settled her comfortably. "Do you need anything else?"

She shook her head wearily.

"What about something to read…a book, your *Saga* magazine?"

She closed her eyes and sank back on the pillows. "Too tired to read...just want to go home." After a while, her eyes still closed, she murmured: "Not much point in keeping me in here really...they just want to get rid of me...might as well get on with it now..."

"Don't be silly, Mother. You know I'd never let them..." for a moment he was lost for the right words..."do anything like that."

"No chance of my telegram from the Palace now." Her voice had dropped to a whisper. He didn't want to tire her further so he stroked her hand and stood up. "Better be off, Mum. I'll see you tomorrow. And stop worrying...you're in good hands here." He wished he could believe it. "Bye now, my darling." He embraced her gingerly and she held on to him for a long moment.

"Bye, Howard. You're a good boy. You've always been a good boy."

He fought back tears as the train rattled homewards. How times had changed. Not that long ago, patients of all ages were treated with respect and dignity. Today there were widespread reports of the elderly being subjected to degrading treatment; of food and water placed out of reach, of basic needs neglected and even of abuse by bullying staff. He would need to visit his mother every day to check on what passed for her care. Hospitals were supposed to be sanctuaries for the sick. Now, with good reason, his mother's generation feared them.

*　　　*　　　*

Howard and Barbara waited throughout spring and into summer for the official invitation to the investiture. Over the years, what was laughingly described as the postal service had shrunk from two deliveries a day to two a week, if you were lucky. Then, as postal jobs were progressively axed and the price of postage stamps rocketed, the 'service' finally reached its nadir of once a week. Even this delivery, previously expected at around 8 am, began arriving later in the day, sometimes in the early evening and occasionally, by torchlight, at supper time.

However, an alternative system had been thoughtfully provided. If you wanted your mail on non-delivery days, you could visit your local sorting office between the hours of 5 am and 6 am when, on payment of a fee, you could ask a communications co-ordinator (formerly known as a postman but, hey, why use two syllables when you can use 10?) to perform a search. He would then disappear, never to be seen again.

Many plausible reasons were advanced for the shambles, which almost matched that of renewable energy in terms of the vast sums of money poured into it in return for imperceptible gain. But the main one was the idiosyncratic leadership of the organisation's chief executive, a gentleman promoted far above his ability and who was missing his way as a stand-up comedian. When pressed by the media to explain why thousands of parcels were going missing every week, he would declare that a great many more parcels were *not* going missing.

While this philosophy was of little comfort to aggrieved parties, it appeared to satisfy him that everything was running smoothly. He was at pains to point out that ongoing economy measures were necessary in order to "streamline the organisation" and "meet the new challenges of advanced technology", and you had to admire the guy for delivering these well-worn clichés as if he really believed them.

Fearing that her husband's investiture invitation might have been swallowed by a black hole in the labyrinthine postal system, to remain there until the end of time, Barbara decided to take her chance at the local sorting office. She set her alarm for 4 am and managed to reach the dilapidated building at 5.15 am. Much to her surprise, she was successful. Probably due to the official Crown imprint on the envelope, the missive had qualified for priority dispatch. A young man with a 'communications co-ordinator' badge assured her it would have been delivered next day.

She excitedly woke Howard two hours earlier than usual to present him with the long-awaited invitation. After his customary protestations, they examined the gilt-trimmed card together. The date of the ceremony was only six weeks away. A covering letter from the Ceremonial Secretariat was dated three weeks earlier.

"We should be grateful for 'priority dispatch'," Barbara laughed. "Otherwise we might not have received the invitation until after the big day.

"If at all," her husband added drily, but he was mightily relieved that his award had been confirmed. If the Cabinet Office had withdrawn it, with a grovelling letter of apology and blaming their computer for the mistake, it would have put paid to the ambitious mission he was secretly planning.

His wife was delighted he'd accepted the award after all. She attributed it to her own powers of persuasion, while acknowledging the part played by Chris and his new son, who had come into world at a healthy 8lb a few days after the champagne celebration in their kitchen. Plans had already been made for their first grandchild's baptism at her church, St Chad's, and the names Howard Sebastian agreed by all concerned. They had a distinguished ring to them, Barbara thought. Howard Sebastian Mitchell...the boy would surely go far in life, perhaps even as far as her husband, whose career had finally received the official recognition it deserved.

Top of Barbara's immediate agenda was the pressing need to inform all the family of the date of the investiture which, in view of the short notice, did not give them much time to prepare. Secondly, was the equally vital task of persuading Howard to hire a morning suit for the occasion. A visit to Buckingham Palace to receive an honour as illustrious as the OBE happened only once in a lifetime, she told him. There was no way she would go with him if he wore his old jacket with the patched elbows. The shame...she would never be able to live it down.

Howard may have changed his mind over the investiture but he remained adamant about what he should wear on the day, so a period of strained negotiations followed. If his wife continued to insist on fancy dress he was ready to call the whole thing off – despite the hassle and family recriminations it would cause. The threat was a bluff, of course, but it effectively concentrated Barbara's mind.

"All right – a suit then. A dark lounge suit with a nice cravat."

It was the first crack in her resistance. "I don't have a dark lounge suit."

"We can buy one."

"I'm too old to start buying new suits. I can't afford one anyway."

Barbara's still youthful face creased into an impatient frown which made her look older. "This is an important occasion, Howard. It's worth buying a new suit for. They're not all that expensive if you know where to shop."

Howard relented. "Oh, very well then. But no poncey cravats...I'm a journalist not a ballroom dancer."

SEVEN

Howard Sebastian Mitchell took a dim view of proceedings at his baptism in St Chad's a couple of weeks later. He hollered throughout the ceremony until the moment of his christening, when holy water was poured on his hairless head in the name of the Father, Son and Holy Spirit. Then, as if by magic, he promptly fell asleep. Father O'Hagan, the elderly parish priest, said that was a good sign and even Howard senior and fellow sceptics among the family gathering were impressed.

Howard, urbane in his new dark blue suit with his iron-grey hair neatly trimmed, was also touched by the reverent and emotional nature of the service. The baby in his long white christening robe, cradled by Amanda, with his father and all his loving family gathered in front of an altar bedecked in lilies, formed a perfect tableau for photographs at the end of the Mass.

Barbara, her embroidered lilac outfit recently chosen for her husband's investiture, was close to tears as always on such occasions. Sally wore a figure-hugging dark green satin two-piece to highlight her flowing blonde hair and William, his dark hair almost as long as his sister's, managed to look untidy in a new light grey suit. He had been entrusted with the camcorder and took his duties far too seriously to show emotion. Which didn't mean he didn't feel any. He was an uncle now and it felt rather strange. Perhaps there was more to life than football and girls after all.

Later, as both families mingled at the christening party in the Mitchells' home, the conversation was all about the beauty of the service and the respectful devotion of the congregation. It had been a regular Sunday Mass packed with parishioners of all ages, which was what impressed the C of E/agnostic contingent, more accustomed to near-empty churches. They also noticed the large number of two-parent families – children with fathers as well as mothers – in stark contrast to the secular world outside with its proliferation of single mothers, feckless absentee fathers and feral children.

Catholics regularly came under fire in the secular media on account of their unchanging moral values in a rapidly changing world yet, after young Howard's baptism, Howard senior was grudgingly prepared to allow them some credit. But there was no way he could go along with the ritual, the incense, the holy water, the candles and the trans-substantiation. You didn't need all that in order to worship God, assuming you believed in Him in the first place.

Barbara, on the other hand, was convinced that Christopher, Sally and William had benefited from being baptised Catholics, although they'd all since sadly lapsed. When she raised the matter with Father O'Hagan after Confession, he agreed it was a great disappointment but assured her all would be well in the long term. Her efforts to give their lives a sound ethical and moral foundation would not be in vain.

She prayed every day for her whole family – her children, her husband, her new grandson and her mother and father, Fred and Lilian. Both well into their eighties, her parents lived in sheltered accommodation in Brighton. For their age, they were a sprightly couple but on the day of their first great-grandson's christening they'd both been stricken by a virus and were unable to travel up to London. Like Howard's mother, now bedridden after her stroke, they had to settle for William's DVD of the occasion.

There were a lot of misty eyes around when Chris and Amanda took their son to see his great-grandparents soon afterwards. Lilian prepared a special tea with a cake covered in blue icing and the name Howard in fancy white piping. Fred fussed and fiddled with his video camera, reminding everyone that it seemed only yesterday that he had done the same at Chris's birth.

Howard junior was not on his best behaviour when introduced to his other great-grandmother, now hollow-cheeked with a leg and arm slightly wasted. On her discharge from hospital, Howard senior had found his mother a residential care home near Cheam that still upheld standards of human dignity. Despite her illness and the hassle of moving home, she seemed content to be in her own cosy room, complete with her beloved telly and the old remote control she could understand. Now, with the arrival of a great-grandson, her happiness was complete.

The moment she took him in her wrinkled arms and held him close to her frail body, ancient and modern formed an instant bond. "What a lot of noise from such a little man," the family's grand matriarch chuckled, and the cries turned to gurgles. The faces of the family round the old lady's bed beamed with delight and the baby's nose wasn't the only one that needed blowing.

But behind Susan Mitchell's indulgent smile lay the grim realisation that her days were numbered. She knew Howard would arrange her Maturity Contract 'opt-out' when it became law, as it surely would. But she had less confidence in New Phoenix to honour it. Politicians were all the same. You couldn't trust any of them. It probably wouldn't be long before all the happy people round her bed were queuing up to 'say goodbye to Granny' – before she was wheeled off along the death pathway.

*   *   *

"Joshua Matthews."

The young nurse emerged with her clipboard from a treatment room in the Ear Nose and Throat clinic and announced in a whisper the name of the next patient to be seen. A waiting room full of deaf people remained solidly impassive. She looked round and tried again, raising her quiet voice slightly.

"Joshua Matthews."

The patients, mostly elderly, many of whom had waited hours to be seen by a doctor or audiologist, turned to each other questioningly. But otherwise nobody moved. The nurse nervously made a third attempt, this time more loudly. Patients in the front rows shook their heads while others behind them stirred uneasily but Joshua, wherever he was, did not respond.

With a sigh, the nurse turned on her heel and went back into the consulting room, presuming the patient had not attended. Moments later, however, a burly male doctor with his own clipboard emerged and boomed:

"JOSHUA MATTHEWS."

A grey haired gentleman seated at the back of the room sprang to his feet.

If medical professionals treating deafness don't really understand the condition, the general public can't be blamed if they don't either. Deafness is probably the most misunderstood of all disabilities. You can't really mistake the blind, with their white sticks and guide dogs, or the physically disabled hobbling on their crutches or scattering pedestrians on their supercharged scooters. But the deaf, or hearing impaired to give them their politically correct designation (why use four letters when you can use 15?), are impossible to identify unless they're wearing a hearing aid. Even then, many people can't come to terms with the fact that the deaf are not ignorant or stupid, they just *cannot hear.*

"Howard Mitchell."

Howard made sure he sat near the front of the waiting room but still had to strain to hear the young nurse's tiny voice. He'd been going deaf in his left ear for years. The condition was hereditary and, as with most sufferers, it crept up on him so gradually that he hardly noticed. He just wondered why people spoke more quietly these days than they used to and why the volume of his videophone needed frequent adjusting. But when he heard some population control freak say on TV that human beings needed to stop breathing in order to save the planet, he finally accepted that he needed a hearing aid. Barbara told him the guy had said "stop breeding" not "stop breathing." Although she added: "But that as well".

Rather than pay money he could ill afford to private hearing aid cowboys, he'd put his name down for one of the latest digital aids on the NHS and now, two years on and several hearing tests later, he was about to have it fitted. He entered the small soundproof room with its electronic gadgetry and sophisticated earphones to be greeted by an unsmiling young male technician with slicked back hair done up in a ponytail.

"Name?"

"Howard Mitchell."

"Address and date of birth?"

Howard felt his reception would not have been out of place if he'd just been remanded in prison but supplied the required data without comment.

"Put this in."

The technician handed him the tiny instrument to fit in his left ear, bringing its sound volume in line with his good right ear. He then carried out a few perfunctory tests, at the end of which Howard found the aid made a big improvement to his hearing.

"Right," the ponytail said, handing him a small plastic case, an instructions booklet and a supply of miniature round batteries. "Full instructions in the booklet. We'll see you again in three months. Make an appointment at the desk on your way out."

"Thanks very much," Howard said as he was ushered through the door. "Good afternoon."

There was no reply from the technician. It would have been unrealistic to expect one. Basic conveyor belt treatment was all you received. The coarsening of society had long since squeezed out common courtesy. They were doing you a favour to treat you at all, Howard thought as he drove away from the hospital in his battered Rover saloon.

But he was impressed with his digital hearing aid. If anything, it was almost too efficient. It amplified the car's engine noise to the level of an aircraft's jet engine. As he had not yet mastered the instrument's fine tuning, he switched it off to save its battery. Then, without thinking, he removed it from his ear and replaced it in its plastic case.

Barbara had been busy planning her own, Sally's and Amanda's wardrobe for the investiture when he'd left home for the hospital. Hats, shoes and handbags seemed to be the targets of a major shopping expedition. Howard would never understand women's obsession with clothes. What did it matter what you wore, as long as it was something comfortable? Surely that was what charity shops were for. His wife, daughter and daughter-in-law were unlikely to avail themselves of these admirable outlets, however, preferring a day trip to the West End. So he'd been instructed to buy something for dinner on his way home.

As he pushed his trolley into the Co-op supermarket, he paused to glance at the day's newspapers with the tabloids' unintelligible punned headlines on the sex lives of pop stars and TV soap performers. Only a few months earlier he'd been instrumental in forming the opinions of millions as an editorial executive with the country's leading quality daily. It's come to this, he thought, rummaging through Reduced to Clear baskets along with a crowd of other pensioners in search of Bogofs before their sell-by dates expired – the Bogofs' sell-by dates, not the pensioners', although by the look of some of them it could be a close-run thing.

He trundled along the tinned foods aisle and stopped to check the price of asparagus spears. It had risen by over 30 per cent since his last visit a month ago. He decided to stop buying the brand on principle. So much for the official inflation figures, he thought. The Consumer Prices Index claimed the rate was in single figures. If you believed that you'd believe anything. The government's manipulation of food price increases was almost as cynical as its massaging of the crime statistics – a crime in itself.

After choosing a packaged steak and kidney pie for dinner along with a cauliflower and parsnips he headed for the checkouts. There were six of them, only one of which was operating, with a long queue of customers. It grew even longer when it was Howard's turn to pay using his debit card. On trying to recall his PIN number his mind suddenly went blank. All the pin numbers and passwords he had to remember were boggling his brain. The harder he tried to remember the debit card number, the more a sense of panic prevented it. Since he had insufficient cash to pay for all his purchases, he was obliged to jettison those he couldn't afford.

Watched by the pitying checkout girl and the increasingly impatient customers behind him, he began to unpack the supplies he had just stowed in a recyclable bag. Could he do without the cauliflower, he asked himself. What about the parsnips? Did Barbara like parsnips? He couldn't remember. The checkout girl attempted to deduct the discarded items from his bill but this involved a special technique which she had not fully mastered. It was necessary to call a supervisor. After several unintelligible announcements were made on the store's tannoy, a supervisor finally appeared.

As she reversed the till's electronic process Howard suddenly remembered his PIN number, so it was a matter of restoring the machine to its normal function.

To the mounting irritation of everyone in the queue, (you could read their thoughts: 'Silly old fool'... 'Why are they always in front of me?') he then repacked all his purchases in the bag before, to everyone's relief, the transaction was completed. Well, almost.

In the confusion, he'd left his debit card in the validator slot and the checkout girl called after him. But Howard didn't hear. He'd almost reached the adjoining Post Office before the girl caught up with him and handed him the card. His abject apologies seemed to mollify her. There was always one, her expression suggested. A less charitable sentiment was probably shared by the waiting customers, now rapidly losing the will to live.

At the Post Office, he queued for 15 minutes to pay his road fund licence. Two counter clerks were on duty but when it was Howard's turn, one put up a 'position closed' notice and disappeared into a back room. The customer being served by the remaining clerk seemed to be conducting a small business from an improvised office at the counter, dispatching a large pile of parcels to destinations around the globe, each needing to be stamped and registered on Post Office files. After a time, the scene acquired a certain existentialist quality but Howard's sense of passive resignation was rudely broken when the customer behind prodded him in the ribs and said: "Oi, I'm talking to you, mate. Are you deaf or something?"

Howard turned to confront a long-haired and bearded bear of a man dressed in a T-shirt with the message: 'I'm here – now what were your other two wishes?'

He had to smile. "Yes, I am deaf actually." His hearing aid was still in his pocket. "What did you say?"

The irresistible charmer waved a tattooed arm towards the other counter which had reopened. "It's your turn."

Howard rarely lost sight of the fact that you were as old as you felt but as he trudged towards the car park with his tax disc, his Bogofs and his breathlessness, he began to feel rather less young. Then he reminded himself that life could only get better now he was the proud owner of a state-of-the-art, digital hearing aid.

All he had to do was put it in his ear and switch it on.

EIGHT

The sun that never went down on the British Empire, before the empire itself sank without trace, shone brightly on Buckingham Palace the day Howard called to collect its long-defunct Order. Flags fluttered in the light summer breeze. The band of the Grenadier Guards played a rousing patriotic march on the forecourt. Soldiers in quaint red tunics and black bearskins falling over their eyes strutted up and down in front of American and Oriental sightseers pressing against the tall iron railings. Electrically-powered, open-top buses carrying day trippers from Lancashire, Yorkshire and other remote points of the realm cruised round the Victoria Monument, directed by sullen bobbies, their handguns barely visible under bullet-proof jackets.

Security was all-pervasive and deeply paranoid. What in the early years of the century was termed a surveillance society had developed into a full-blown Orwellian police state. Cameras and microphones were everywhere, even in public toilets as public figures of a certain predilection had found to their cost. The SSS (State Security Service) controlled everything under the brooding command of its own Cabinet Minister, Sir

Justin Beryan, known to everyone as Beria, Stalin's secret police chief.

Somehow, nobody quite knew how though there were dark murmurings of subliminal TV techniques, parliamentary democracy had survived a decade of unprecedented corruption almost unscathed. But there was a downside. Exploiting a populist backlash against foreigners taking British jobs, the BNP emerged from the political wilderness to form the main party in a fragmented Commons Opposition – fractionally ahead of the Tories with Labour out of sight behind the Scot Nats.

To complete the change from the old order, the party in government, New Phoenix, had elected fervent feminist Dame Jessica Sykes as their leader, now Prime Minister. Nothing revolutionary about that since most positions of power were occupied by women. But a lesbian, living at No 10 with her partner? And most startling of all, an Australian lesbian? Just how cutting edge could you get?

But some things never change. While governments could come and go, dictators topple and even capitalism itself crumble like a squashed meringue, it was one of life's reassuring certainties that Britain's ruling class and its honours system would outlast them all. For those who had made a notable contribution to society – and for those who hadn't but were prepared to pay – an award, no matter how outdated, represented the ultimate status symbol. Almost as prestigious was to be able to boast that they had actually shaken the limp hand and breathed the same air as a majestic owner of Britain's numerous royal palaces.

During the early part of the century, some awards ceremonies had been held at Windsor Castle and others at Balmoral, in the Crown's modest 50,000-acre Aberdeenshire estate. But the experiment was not a success. Nowhere, it was felt, quite matched the splendour and the decadent opulence of Buckingham Palace. It was into this red and pink carpeted, crystal chandeliered and gold encrusted ambience of pomp and privilege that Howard, his family and a throng of formally-dressed fellow guests were ushered by deferential flunkeys.

Under the watchful eyes of visible and covert CCTV cameras, their invitations were scrutinised by polite but solemn security officers with close-cropped hair, some wearing shades. Then after passing through metal detectors, more flunkeys led the Very Important Persons across the Grand Hall, up the magnificent marble Grand Staircase and along the Grand Gallery en route to the Grand Ballroom and their long-awaited Grand Gongs.

Howard had insisted on wearing his red NUJ tie with his new lounge suit for the investiture and this, plus the fact that he was the only man in the queue not resembling a penguin, attracted hard stares from its uniformed escorts, continually speaking out of the side of their mouths into their jacket buttonholes. But it wasn't the security goons' suspicions that made him feel uncomfortable. As the long line of supplicants filed slowly past the trappings of faded imperial power – the priceless Rembrandts, Poussins and Canalettos, the Gobelin tapestries, the ornate gilt-framed mirrors and the French antique furniture – Howard recalled the thoughts of Henry James on "the black and merciless things behind the great possessions".

All his initial distaste for the charade in which he was participating returned and he felt like throwing up on the shocking pink carpet. What was he doing here with these people, many of them worthy citizens no doubt but others so desperate to prove their importance they'd paid wads of cash to dodgy politicians? His socialist instincts demanded that he turn round and walk out immediately. But he couldn't do that, however appealing the idea. He'd forced himself to come this far as part of an audacious project now approaching a climax. There could be no going back.

When his turn came to receive the Most Excellent Order of the British Empire, Howard resisted a sudden impulse to perform a clenched fist salute for the benefit of the assembled photographers and TV cameramen. The decision owed much to the presence of two minders built like front row forwards on each side of the head of state. But he made sure there was not even a hint of a bow, a scrape or a cringe.

The Special One did not appear to notice. Nor did he as much as raise a noble eyebrow over his subject's informal clothing. But as he mechanically pinned the gold medal and pink ribbon on Howard's jacket, he caught sight of the scarlet NUJ tie. Turning to the aide whose task it was to hand him the awards and certificates, he spoke a single word. The minion smirked. Although Howard had made sure his hearing aid was switched on, it failed to capture the refined utterance. But he had developed some lip-reading skill and believed he knew what the word was.

It was: "Naff."

*   *   *

Barbara, Sally and Amanda in their summer finery with hats fit for Royal Ascot, Christopher in his hired fancy dress, and a grey-suited William all insisted on staying for refreshments afterwards. Howard's gleaming medal, an exquisitely crafted cross *patonce* with the motto: 'For God and the Empire' and its portentous citation were admired at great length by his proud family. Everyone realised the empire had passed into history last century but they were prepared to pretend that it was still alive and well – just for a day, anyway.

But for Howard the whole pantomime remained baffling. 'God and the Empire'? As far as most people were concerned, neither existed. Yet hundreds had just lined up for similar medals to feed their delusions of grandeur. Some had even paid a fortune in readies for the privilege. You had to hand it to the Establishment's public relations experts for their iron grip on mind control. Clearly you could fool most of the people all of the time.

But not him.

The ordeal was prolonged while they all lined up again for the silver service buffet reception. After tea, smoked salmon and, yes, cucumber sandwiches, served on delicate monogrammed porcelain, he unpinned his embarrassing medal and placed it in his jacket pocket in its red leather presentation case. Then, shrugging off the congratulations of fellow guests, he hustled his protesting family towards the door. They needed to pose for photographs outside.

As they were about to leave, a young woman servant reminded his party that all investiture guests were allowed travelling and accommodation expenses. How much did they wish to claim? Howard felt he was taking enough liberties with the honours system without putting in a claim for expenses, however modest. "Don't worry, my dear," he told the servant as she produced a notebook and pen. "We shan't burden the privy purse with our bus fares from Wimbledon."

Everyone laughed. They were still laughing as they posed for the traditional photographs in the palace quadrangle with scarlet-clad Beefeaters wearing medieval ruffs and cute black hats festooned with coloured bows that both Barbara and Amanda took quite a fancy to. It had all gone so well, they told themselves. The sun was still shining, the band was still playing and there was time for a stroll by the river...

*　　　*　　　*

"Why are all these people following us, Dad?" William wanted to know as Howard set off with his family along Birdcage Walk towards the Thames, pursued by the boisterous media.

"They're the Press," his father answered.

"I know. I thought we'd done all the photos."

"Yes, but I didn't want to give an interview then. When we get to the Parliament building I'm going to hold a Press conference."

Howard briskly led his entourage along pock-marked streets of a city in the throes of terminal capitalism. Former up-market fashion showrooms had been incongruously converted into greengrocers, their wares spilling across littered pavements. Sandwiched between steel-shuttered banks and jewellers, takeaways and lap-dancing clubs rubbed shoulders with drop-in abortion clinics and state-licensed brothels. Once-famous department stores, their plate glass windows permanently boarded up, now housed hundreds of squatters. Some people said it would not be long before the Palace itself was occupied by squatters. Others maintained it already was.

"How much further is it?" William asked, after about half a mile.

"Nearly there now."

"Why aren't you wearing your medal?"

"You'll see."

Barbara had stopped smiling the moment they'd set off on their unscheduled jaunt. Her husband had said nothing about an extra photo call. It wasn't part of the script for their big day. But after more than 40 years married to a newspaperman nothing came as a surprise any more. As she tagged along dutifully, chatting to Sally and Amanda, a familiar sinking feeling grew stronger. She knew instinctively that things were about to stop going so well.

When the group and its stragglers reached The Embankment alongside Westminster Bridge, Howard Mitchell OBE, jumped on to a stone step and turned, holding up his hand. The Press gathered round, jostling for position, microphones, cameras, notebooks and voice recorders at the ready. Hardened hacks, they expected the usual platitudes from a recipient of a royal honour. They were in for a shock.

Howard took the presentation case out of his pocket, extracted the gold and pink decoration and held it aloft. Raising his voice above the rumble of the traffic, he declared: "This is a very special occasion for me – but not in the way you might think. As you all know, I've been awarded the Order of the British Empire for services to journalism. As you also know, the British Empire does not exist. The award is therefore meaningless and an insult to my intelligence."

The silence that greeted this statement was not so much deafening as eerie. All eyes were fixed on the scholarly grey-haired figure and the medal glinting in the sunshine. A small crowd of passers-by and tourists who had quickly gathered were too shocked to say anything. Camera shutters stopped clicking and the sound of the traffic seemed to fade. For a long moment, time stood still. Then he cleared his throat and spoke again:

"Even if this award *meant* anything, there's no way I could accept it from a government who want to kill me off and grab my pension on the pretext of 'saving the planet'. In this supposedly enlightened year of twenty-eighteen our leaders have finally crossed the line on euthanasia. They're making it obligatory instead of voluntary. The elderly have become a burden our bankrupt state can no longer afford. They want rid of us. *Every year* three hundred and eighteen thousand, one hundred and eighty-two of us must do the decent thing and opt for assisted suicide. That's the figure they've plucked out of the air. If we refuse, they'll cut our pensions by half."

Howard paused for breath. He could feel tightness in his chest but was determined to carry on. He gestured towards Big Ben and Parliament in the background. "For years they've robbed us of our human rights because there's no government minister or trade union to defend us. Now we face losing our lives when they decide our time is up. They think we're too old and feeble to fight back. Big mistake!" He raised his Order of the Non-Existent British Empire high in the air, where it gleamed in the bright sunshine. "It's time for action. The fightback starts here!"

To the astonishment of the journalists, the horror of his family and gasps from the onlookers, he hurled the medal high into the air. It hung there for a moment, the splendid pink ribbon acting rather like a parachute, before plunging into the murky water with a faint plop and sinking slowly, ignominiously from view.

The clamour from the journalists was instant and insistent. How old was he? Wasn't he a grandfather? Was it true he had a heart condition? Arthritis? Deafness? Did his wife and family approve of his campaign? Howard knew what they were driving at. They wanted to typecast him as 'past it' – an old codger, a sad has-been trying to make a comeback in an age that had left him far behind. That was the prevailing culture of modern journalism. Ageism was back in fashion. Youth was the name of the game. You were over the hill at 40 so he was clearly a fossil.

The tightness in his chest had turned into a dull pain. He needed to use his angina spray but to do so now would only play into the journos' hands. He pushed his way through the media scrum towards his wife, son and daughter, ignoring all the personal questions.

"Show us the empty case, Howard," a snapper shouted, and he obliged, holding up the presentation case while doing his best to look pleased despite the increasing discomfort. After more badinage the media melted away to meet their deadlines. At last, a couple of surreptitious puffs under the tongue from his nitrolingual spray worked their magic.

William, who hadn't been all that keen on the investiture since it involved having his hair cut, was impressed by his father's dramatic display of grey power. But now he noticed the covert action and realised stress had taken its toll. He made him sit on a bench to recover and Barbara and Sally came and sat on either side and held his hands. But Howard was soon back on his feet none the worse for wear, the episode quickly forgotten.

Support from Christopher and Amanda was conspicuous by its absence. They had disappeared in the confusion and Howard realised that their reaction would be less sympathetic, to put it mildly. As for Barbara, his wife was suffering from delayed shock, mixed with suppressed anger. How dare he ruin their long-awaited day of celebration? There was no limit to his natural talent for upsetting people. Yet deep down in her heart of hearts, where no-one except her husband ever reached, she knew he was right. She just wasn't prepared to say so right now.

In her best nursing sister manner, she salvaged what she could from the ruins. Part of the day's schedule was a television interview with Howard that evening. She'd assumed it would be of the usual back-slapping nature. But clearly more fireworks lay ahead. So after handing her husband two painkilling tablets and taking two herself for a headache that had started over 40 years ago, she marched her family off to one of the city's few remaining French restaurants for lunch. She was determined to extract at least some pleasure from their big day at the Palace.

NINE

BBC TV's peak time evening news programme, *Newsline*, led with the moment when Howard and his Most Excellent Order of the British Empire parted company. When the opening synthesised music faded, more than 8 million viewers watched a clip of the dramatic sequence as the programme's glamorous presenter, Philomena Riley, announced:

"Tonight on *Newsline* we bring you an exclusive interview with Howard Mitchell, the pensioners' new champion, who today sent this signal to the government over the proposed Health of the Nation Bill..."

Reading from an autocue, the high-profile presenter described events on The Embankment that afternoon as "unprecedented and historic". Viewers would decide for themselves whether the former *Announcer* journalist had insulted the Crown as well as other holders of the distinguished Order by his actions – or whether he was justified by what he saw as the government's inhuman Maturity Contract.

"A Palace spokesman declined to comment," Ms Riley continued, "but we have been joined in the studio by Professor Gerald Smythe, an expert on constitutional affairs and an adviser to the Ceremonial Secretariat, the government body that controls the honours system. First, however, Mr Mitchell's one-man protest and his controversial ditching of his OBE..."

There followed a replay of Howard's "historic" performance, his rousing speech and a skilfully enhanced close-up of the gleaming gold medal plunging into the Thames from a great height, the widening ripples and the startled spectators. In the background, two figures were seen hurrying away, both wearing Ascot-style hats.

"Look, there's Chris and Amanda," William shouted, as he, his mother and sister watched on monitors in the hospitality suite. Barbara pulled a wry face. "They couldn't take any more, poor dears. I know just how they felt...I almost ran away myself!"

"But you're glad you didn't, aren't you?" Sally asked.

"Of course, dear. Once I'd got over the shock, I knew your father was right. He usually is."

"But people are going to give us some funny looks when we get home."

"Let them!"

"Chris'll go berserk. You know what he's like."

"Too bad. He'll have to learn self-control sooner or later."

When the film clip ended it was back to Ms Riley. "We showed the same footage to members of the public earlier this evening and asked for their views. This was their reaction."

What journalists describe as a *vox pop* followed – several snapshot comments from people in the street presented in a quick-cutting sequence.

"It's like sacrilege, innit," a middle-aged woman market worker declared. "It's an insult to the Crown."

"Good luck to him, I say," a taxi driver told the interviewer. "If I had an OBE I'd do the same."

A young woman shopper said: "He's right. Human life is more important than gongs."

Other comments from people approached at random included:

"He should be arrested for polluting the Thames..."

"A lot of people will send their medals back now. The system's just a joke..."

"What empire...?"

"His action was disgraceful – disrespectful to people who've worked hard for their medal..."

"An OBE? Yes, I've had one...Oh, sorry, I thought you meant an Out of Body Experience..."

"If he'd paid good money for his OBE he wouldn't have thrown it away..."

And finally, an aged lady with a walking stick offered: "He'll do for me. Someone needs to make a stand before they wipe us all out."

In the studio, Ms Riley thought opinion seemed to be equally divided. What did Prof Smythe think?

The professor, bow-tied, bespectacled and with an impeccably trimmed goatee beard, left nobody in any doubt what he thought. "Frankly, I have to say I am appalled. What we have seen was scandalous, outrageous...grossly offensive to all right-thinking people. It was a blatant insult to the monarch and to all the worthy citizens of this country who have devoted their lives to serving others and been awarded the OBE which they richly deserve – which cannot be said for Mr Mitchell, I regret to say."

Follow that, Howard thought. Not for the first time, he'd really upset the Establishment. But he kept his cool. "I cannot accept an honour from a dishonourable government. Prof Smythe talks of insults to the monarchy but this nation's pensioners have been deeply insulted for years. They've had their state pension frozen, their winter fuel payments cut and even been robbed of their bus passes. Now they face a crude ultimatum: choose terminal sedation or have your pension cut by half. What could be more insulting than that?"

The erudite professor didn't intend to be sidetracked by minor issues like life and death. He was more concerned with Howard's unforgivable breach of protocol. Wagging a podgy finger at the insolent upstart, he fumed: "You have defiled a distinguished honour dating back to Queen Victoria. Thousands of OBE holders will feel their achievements count for nothing."

The professor was starting to bluster. Howard grew in confidence. "Times have changed since Victoria's reign. No-one disputes the worthiness of many OBE holders. Not all of them, of course. As we know, money often changes hands…"

The champion of ancient chivalry winced at this but refused to be deflected from Howard's heinous offence. He wanted blood. "You have brought our nation's illustrious honours system into disrepute," he spluttered. "You should pay for it!"

The righteous indignation left Howard unfazed. "It's not me who's brought the honours system into disrepute…it's done that itself."

Ms Riley interjected: "Do you really think your protest will change government minds on the Maturity Contract?"

It was Howard's chance to launch his agenda. "It's got to! We have no union to defend us, no voice to speak for us in Parliament. We desperately need a Cabinet minister for the elderly to protect our human rights. An official tsar, as they're called. You have tsars for children, tsars for animal welfare, tsars for racial equality and sex discrimination…you even have a tsar for fish – to conserve stocks – so let's have a government tsar for pensioners, the most persecuted and exploited group of all."

Cutting them both off with an apologetic smile, Ms Riley said: "I'm afraid I'll have to stop you there. Howard Mitchell, Professor Smythe…thank you both for coming in." Turning to the rostrum camera, she invited viewers to vote interactively on the issue. "Was Howard Mitchell right to stage his protest on behalf of pensioners or was he wrong?" The result would follow at the end of the programme.

"And now from grey power we turn to girl power…"

As deafening rock music filled the studio to accompany the sensational break-up of an all-female vocal group, Howard rejoined his family in the Green Room.

"How did it go?" he asked.

Barbara embraced him. "You were brilliant, Howard," she said, and she meant it. "You've definitely started something. Money can't buy that sort of publicity."

They relaxed with their cheap hospitality alcohol and waited for the result of the interactive vote. When it came, it was screened for 20 seconds but the message was loud and clear. The figures read:

Right: 89 per cent.

Wrong: 11 per cent.

"We're on our way," an upbeat Howard assured his exhausted family as they headed for their taxi and home. It had been a long and eventful day…and the fun had only just started.

TEN

Press coverage of Howard's one-man demo surpassed all expectations. As he and Barbara spread the morning newspapers on the kitchen table next day, they found that every front page featured the story:

GOING, GOING GONG *(Sun)*

GREY POWER FIGHTS BACK *(Mirror)*

A SHOCK TO THE HONOURS SYSTEM
(Mail-Telegraph)

STUNT INSULT TO MONARCHY *(Times)*

OBE DITCHED IN DEATH BILL PROTEST
(Guardian-Independent)

HOWARD MITCHELL SPURNS AWARD
(Announcer)

TRACY BEDS SOAP HUNK MICK
Granddad ditches gong – Page 4 *(Star)*

'Granddad' and his wife had a good laugh over the *Star's* treatment, with its salacious picture of a topless Tracy (apparently a TV reality show winner) almost eclipsed by an enormous close-up of an OBE, a black cross scrawled over it but with its inscription, For God and the Empire, still visible. Realising that devoting the entire front page to a genuine news story would offend their core readership, the rag's executives had settled for an uneasy compromise, relegating the man of the moment to the inside page.

"They've still done us proud," Howard observed, turning to Page 4. It carried a full report of events plus the flying gong picture that was rapidly assuming iconic status. He wasn't unduly surprised that, after the *Times*, the coverage of the *Announcer* was the most restrained. For all its descent into down-market territory, the paper still clung stubbornly to its delusions of grandeur. Although frequently outraged by the award of honours to rock singers and conceptual artists, it remained a staunchly committed mouthpiece of the Establishment. As such, it regarded the antics of its former employee as deeply embarrassing.

Since the merger with the *Daily Mail*, surviving *Daily Telegraph* executives had been obliged to modify their elitist perceptions of society, with a view to attracting readers from outside the Home Counties. As a result the new paper, the *Mail-Telegraph,* took a more balanced view of what its *Telegraph* half would have previously dismissed as a distasteful publicity stunt.

As for the recently-merged *Guardian-Independent* and the red-tops, they enthusiastically backed any campaign to abolish an honours system that millions of readers regarded as corrupt and irrelevant. They had waited a long time for a high-profile champion of their cause and now that he'd arrived he was welcomed with open arms. Their new-found hero even offered a double whammy by calling for a pensioners' minister – something for which they had crusaded for years without the slightest success. If their editors and executives actually said any prayers, which was unlikely, Howard would surely be considered the answer to them. It was a classic case of 'Cometh the moment, cometh the man.' Superman himself could not have timed his entrance better.

The overnight sensation and his wife were still basking in the glare of publicity when the telephone rang. It was Kath Benson, news editor of *The Announcer* and Howard's former colleague from way back.

"How's the old folks' saviour this morning?" she wanted to know.

"Dazed but happy."

"You've made all the front pages, even the *Star!*"

"I know, we're just looking at them now. Has there been any reaction yet?"

Kath gave a hollow laugh. "You could say that, Howard. People all over the country are threatening to throw their gongs away. They're asking for your phone number. You don't want me to give it to them, do you?"

"You must be joking."

"Your email address then?"

Howard had finally activated the state-of-the art laptop in his study but barely used it apart from emails on the investiture and his grandson's christening. "Okay, I'll settle for that." He reeled off his electronic address and promised to phone her in time for that night's first edition to report on feedback.

Moments later the phone rang again and Howard answered. It was the call he and Barbara had anticipated with some misgivings. They'd been justified. Christopher was immediately in full, uninhibited flow. Was his father prepared to reimburse him for the valuable time he'd taken off work to attend Buckingham Palace for a ceremony that turned out to be a complete shambles?"

"I..."

"And are you prepared to refund the cost of hiring an expensive morning suit and top hat..."

"Listen, Chris..."

"As well as the horrendous expense Amanda went to in buying half the stock of that boutique in Bond Street? To say I'm surprised at you, Dad, is the understatement of the year. You let us name your grandson after you while all the time you were planning this...this blatant publicity stunt behind our backs."

"It was no stunt, Chris. Somebody had to make a stand on behalf of..."

"I'm not just surprised at you, I'm ashamed...ashamed of my own father! You not only turn down the sort of honour millions would be proud to accept but you treat it with contempt. Why didn't you just say you didn't want it?"

"I tried to but..."

"But you were more interested in your precious news stories. Why don't you accept the fact that you're retired now? Call it a day. Enjoy what's left of your life. Maybe you'd be a lot happier."

"I'm quite happy as I am, thank you."

"All that grey power nonsense...it's just so embarrassing. I don't understand how you could do this to your family. What about Mum? You must have upset her. Have you given any thought to her feelings?"

"As a matter of fact your Mother supports what I'm trying to do."

"Well, you do surprise me. There's no way *I* support you. Amanda's suffering from post-natal depression and doesn't want to know me. You've made me a laughing stock at work. What with all this and the hassle of the baby crying every night…"

His son tailed off miserably and despite the insulting tirade, Howard felt a pang of sympathy. He remembered the sleepless nights he and Barbara had to deal with all those years ago when their children were babies. "Chris, calm down. Just relax and be reasonable. Why not come round this evening and we'll talk about it?"

"There's nothing to talk about. I just wanted you to know how Amanda and I felt. We've changed our minds about naming our son after you. In future we'll use his middle name. He'll be called Sebastian."

There was a click and he was gone.

Howard sat down heavily at the kitchen table. He'd expected a harangue from his volatile son but not this bitter hostility. His own father had died when Howard was in his early twenties. There was no way he would have ever spoken to him like that. It would never have occurred to him to offer his father or mother advice on how to live their lives. You treated your parents with respect in those days.

But now the generation gap had widened to a point where respect had flown out of the window. The old and the young had grown so far apart they were almost out of each other's sight. The social dichotomy had reached the stage where young people, brainwashed by popular ageist dogma, were prepared to consign their own parents to the scrapheap almost as a matter of routine. Worse still, they were arrogant with it.

Perhaps he was just getting old, he reflected. Becoming a grandfather for the first time had made him soft. What had happened to that thick skin he'd acquired over four decades as a newshound? "I've been insulted by the best in the business," he would quip when newsroom colleagues complained about the abuse they endured as part of the job. Nothing could hurt him any more. Yet Christopher's bombshell over his grandson's name left him deeply wounded.

Barbara had gathered from the one-sided nature of the conversation that the old animosity between father and son had resurfaced. She brought him a cup of tea and held his hand. "Was it as bad as all that?"

"Worse. He's very angry. They're going to call the boy by his second name, Sebastian."

"I'll talk to him."

"If you get a chance."

*   *   *

Unlike some of his retired ex-colleagues and friends of a similar age, Howard wasn't a natural 'silver surfer'. A chronic computerphobe, he knew he'd barely scratched the surface of his lap-top's myriad functions but had no interest in exploring them further. He rarely received more than half a dozen emails a week, which suited him perfectly. So when he switched on the device that evening and logged on to incoming mail, he was totally unprepared for the bizarre spectacle that confronted him.

95

Since talking to Kath less than five hours earlier, he had received a total of 139 emails. As he stared at the cluttered screen in disbelief the number rose to 143 – at which point he realised he had a problem. How on earth was he going to deal with the mountain of correspondence unfolding before him and climbing by the minute?

He called Barbara to come and inspect the scale of his new-found popularity. She shared his incredulity but was late for work, as usual. There was only time to select a few messages at random from the growing list. The first read:

Saw you on TV last night and in papers this morning. Couldn't agree with you more. I hold the MBE and have decided to sell it. As you say, it's meaningless. Pensioners being robbed and abused with impunity. High time for action. Anything I can do to support your campaign, let me know.
Hubert

Another read:

Dear Howard
Dont have a so-called honour. No way would i accept one, if offered. Worked all my life as a miner and for what? A pittance of a pension i can't live on. i suffer from emphysema and chronic bronchitis. Cant afford 2 heat my flat. Cant afford own computer. Have used friends. With u all the way.
Stan

Another:

> At last someone with the courage to stand up to the shysters and chinless wonders running the country. Count me in on your campaign. Can't start soon enough. Don't have much money but I'd be happy to make a contribution. Let me know. Best of luck.

Another:

> Dear Mr Mitchell
> I'm 82 and have serious illness. They want me to go in hospital but too scared. Lost husband and son in two wars. They gave their lives for this country, what a waste. More power to your elbow, son. My daughter is sending this. She agrees with me. God bless.
> Florence

Barbara was searching her handbag for her car keys. "I'm in a hurry. I'll help you sort it out this evening."

"It can't wait till then, darling. They need a follow-up story for the first edition."

"You don't work for *The Announcer* any more – remember?"

"Not just them – all the papers, the TV, everyone…"

"William might help," she said over her shoulder.

"He's not here…I thought he'd gone to college."

"He's off this week. Try his mobile."

But when he phoned his younger son, there was no reply. Then he thought of Bernard Baxter.

*   *   *

"You can't keep a good man down," were Bernard's first words when Howard opened his front door to admit his closest friend and snooker partner. As always, his old colleague was unstinting in his praise. "Congratulations on another great story, my old mate. I was just about to call you when you phoned."

"Am I glad to see you, Bernard," Howard said, ushering the former *Announcer* news sub-editor straight into his study and pointing to the daunting sight unfolding on the computer screen. "Feedback," he said simply. "Quite a challenge, eh?"

Bernard peered through his thick glasses at the still-expanding catalogue of emails and his permanently genial expression gave way to a prolonged wince. "Some challenge!" he said in his thick Scouse accent.

Howard knew there was nothing his friend liked better. That made two of them. "I realised I'd touched nerves but I'd no idea the reaction would be so strong – and so quick. I gave Kath Benson my email address this morning and this is what happened. They're still arriving…look, there's over 150 now!"

Bernard seated himself at the keyboard and started calling up the email messages. Some of the methods for disposal of unwanted gongs were gems of news stories in themselves. One correspondent had fixed his medal to his dog's collar. Another was using his to stop a conservatory table from wobbling. Others intended to sell their 'honours' or give them to children and grandchildren as souvenirs. Several planned to have their gold medals melted down and reworked as rings for their wives. As one put it: "That would mean more to her than the medal does to me".

Many correspondents intended to return their awards to Buckingham Palace, with letters telling them in no uncertain language what they could do with them. "No doubt they'll polish mine up and recycle it for some other mug," one wrote in disgust.

After sampling dozens of other messages at random, Bernard said: "It's just like old times, Howard. I know it's a hoary old cliché but this story really *will* run and run…"

"So you'll help me with the follow-up?"

"You bet."

"Cheers, Bernard. I'll make some coffee."

With only hours to go before the media's early deadlines, they needed to get organised. It was necessary to plan a campaign strategy. For a start, a name for their pressure group, an address and a website were necessary as soon as possible. A bank account would also be required but that could wait. First off was a name…

"Grey Power's a bit dated don't you think?" Bernard said. "And Pensioner Power's a bit hackneyed."

Howard nodded. "They're labels. We need something more active and witty. Like Not Dead Yet. That would have been great for us but, of course, the disabled have beaten us to it."

"How about Save Our Seniors? It's active enough…and urgent."

"Hmm…it's good but not terribly original. It lacks that special twist…"

"Life Before Death?"

"Clever…but…"

"Not easy is it?" Bernard sighed, draining his coffee cup.

"Why not *Life* With Dignity?"

The veteran sub and headline writer thought for a while. "I like it...but it's got a pro-life ring about it. Not that there's anything wrong with pro-life as such...just that it suggests their whole ideology...you know, abortion, sterilisation etc."

"You're right," Howard conceded. "There's plenty of groups fighting their corner. Our concern has to be the golden oldies...the need to keep them breathing and drawing their pensions despite the efforts of our great rulers to stop them."

Bernard was beaming from ear to ear. "That's it. What you said...Keep Breathing! What do you think?"

They knew instinctively that they'd cracked it. They were like cub reporters again with their clenched fists and high fives. "Keep Breathing...just the job," Howard enthused. "It's got the lot. It's active, it's positive..."

"It'll catch on!"

When the euphoria had subsided, it was back to business. "Okay. What's next?"

"An address," Bernard said. "We're going to need a postal as well as an email address. We could use a box number mail collection service to start with."

"Right. How soon can that be fixed up?"

"I can sort it out tomorrow, no problem."

"A website?"

"That could take longer, several days at least. And it's likely to cost a bit. I know someone, a bright young designer, who could do it for us at a special price."

"How much, roughly?"

Bernard did a mental calculation. "Well into five figures. But it would be a professional job with a menu of options and everything."

"Installed on the internet, up and running in, say, three or four days?"

"Hopefully. It'll depend on how much data you want on it. Have you seen the NPF[1] website?"

"Yes, it's quite impressive. They do a good job but they're a bit old-fashioned. We need to be more militant, take more direct action..."

"Like throwing our medals around."

"Dire threats call for drastic action, Bernard. We both know that."

"Do you want me to go ahead with the website?"

"Absolutely. Every confidence."

"Okay. Next up you're going to need an urgent Press release."

"I'll take care of that, if you'll prepare an acknowledgement to all these emails. Tell those with novel ideas for gong-disposal to contact the media for maximum publicity. Tell all of them about the name, the postal address and the website – upcoming soonest, as we used to say. Would you like a Scotch?"

Bernard grinned. "Thought you were never going to ask."

*　　　*　　　*

By the time the nationals had started telephoning and a young reporter from the local paper had successfully door-stepped him, he'd drafted the necessary Press release. The statement said he was overwhelmed by public reaction to Keep Breathing's campaign. Messages of support had been pouring in over the last

---

[1] The National Pensioners' Forum

24 hours. Pensioners all over the country who had received honours for distinguished service to the community were prepared to follow his example and either throw them away or sell them. Some had already done so. He thanked everyone who had offered advice and even financial contributions. Most of them were elderly but many principled younger people were keen to join the struggle. They wanted justice for their parents and grandparents. All would receive personal replies.

Bernard was still working on the computer when Howard completed his Press release. After dispatching the statement to the Press Association for onward transmission to all the national media, he checked the emails again. The total had reached 209. Keep Breathing was on its way – at a breathless rate of knots.

There was no time for snooker any more. They set up their postal address the following day and within 48 hours more than 100 letters had been received. Many pensioners still did not own a computer, either because they couldn't afford one or they didn't trust them. They were obliged to put their faith in a postal service that proudly claimed it delivered more letters than it lost. So a vast volume of mail addressed to Keep Breathing could still be out there somewhere.

The website was set up soon afterwards. It boasted a full menu offering advice on pensions, social security benefits and health issues – reproduced courtesy of the NPF – as well as a guide to the Maturity Contract and how to register a legal opt-out certificate. During its first 24 hours of operation the site attracted a total of over 2,000 'hits'. Hundreds of emails arrived by the day. Within two weeks, membership totalled 15,000, many offering to withhold income and council taxes in protest at the Maturity Contract. They were ready to go to jail if necessary in defence of their human rights. Howard, Bernard, Barbara and William were shell-shocked by this demonstration of the power of the Press.

The tabloids in particular kept the pot boiling and rang him up every day for an update on his campaign's progress. This was in itself remarkable as there could not be the slightest suggestion of a sex angle in the story. Although *The Announcer*, *Times* and *Guardian-Independent* soon lost interest, the *Mail-Telegraph* and *Express* both ran features on Howard and his family. The *Express* managed to track down his ageing mother in her care home and had wrung the optimum level of human interest from the discovery. Its headline ran: **The mother behind the man of the moment**. This feature alone captured the sympathy of millions.

Howard also appeared on a TV afternoon chat show hosted by an equally sympathetic couple themselves on the verge of retirement, but his most challenging assignment awaited in the form of an appearance on the weekend edition of *Pandora*. This was the BBC2's showcase current affairs series acclaimed for exposing dark secrets and national scandals. The producer had assured him the whole issue of elder abuse in an era of shameful mistreatment would be explored in depth (as far as it was possible to explore any issue in depth on television, of course).

Meanwhile, Keep Breathing had acquired its own bank account with a fighting fund. Bernard, who was now coming in every day, was appointed treasurer and updated the fund daily on the website. Membership was free and donations were not requested. If people could afford to make a contribution, it was gratefully received on the understanding that nobody would profit from it or, indeed, receive a salary or any other money apart from legitimate out-of-pocket expenses.

The idea behind the fighting fund was that when members refused to pay fines imposed on them for their 'crimes' and were handed short prison sentences, the fund would immediately 'spring' them by paying the fines on their behalf. The prisoner would then be released, giving Keep Breathing two bites at the publicity cherry. The prison authorities would soon tire of this strategy. They had enough problems finding accommodation for real criminals in their overstretched system without veteran 'politicals' using it as a media circus.

Members of an adventurous nature suggested stopping traffic by monopolising pedestrian crossings – a continuous stream of pedestrians exercising their right of way – and sit-down protests in public places such as the centre circle at football matches, although no-one offered to streak. All shared an unshakable belief that their defiant stance placed them firmly on the high moral ground. Their generation had been systematically exploited by hostile regimes for decades. The state pension was the lowest in Europe and now the government wanted to mug them for half of it.

If you kept kicking your dog you shouldn't be surprised if it turned round and bit you.

ELEVEN

"This is a party political broadcast on behalf of the New Phoenix Party."

Howard, Barbara and William were video recording the government's allotted five-minute TV propaganda slot on the basis that it was important to know your enemy. Howard's forthcoming appearance on *Pandora* made it vital to keep abreast of developments.

The slick production opened with footage of the familiar Westminster scene, superimposed with the caption: LONDON 2011. To the derisory strains of *Land of Hope and Glory*, the camera panned from Big Ben to street level to show petrol-powered vehicles with exhausts belching smoke and pavements crammed with pedestrians scurrying along in fast-motion. Then, as the music track faded, the film cut to the studio and a well-known soap actress, Meg Meredith. Surprisingly, although glamorous, she was not young. In view of the gravity of their message, the producers had resisted the temptation to front it with a bimbo. What was needed was a more mature figure to explain the party's caring population policy in a kind and understanding manner.

"Good evening," she said smiling her famous, engaging smile and reading from an autocue in professionally imperceptible style. "If you remember the way we were seven years ago, you'll probably agree that things have changed a bit since then. But have they got any better? In some ways they have…"

To the accompaniment of happy rock music that swelled and diminished between scenes, the film then cut to the British coastline ringed as far as the eye could see by gigantic windmills all rotating furiously (a windy day had wisely been chosen for the filming) as Meg, the mother-figure, continued:

"…almost a fifth of the nation's electricity is now provided by wind farms…" (cut to huge dam across the River Tay) "…while hydro-electric power generates eight per cent of Scotland's energy."

To close-ups of smoke-free car exhausts, she continued: "Most road vehicles are now electrically-powered or run on clean bio-fuels, cutting carbon emissions and helping to save our precious planet…" (cut to familiar view of the Earth shot from space) "…from man-made greenhouse gases."

"But there is a downside to the success story. Since 2011, the United Kingdom population has increased from 60 million people to 70 million – that's a rise of over 16 per cent. At the same time, the total drawing the state pension has risen from 11.6 million to almost 15 million, a staggering increase of over 30 per cent and the number's still growing."

Clips of very old men and women, some hobbling with the aid of Zimmer frames and others clearly demented, filled the screen as Meg continued in voice over. "The sad truth is that world economies, including ours, can no longer sustain this level of population growth. Global warming has decimated the planet's food and energy resources to critical levels. So desperate is the crisis that our United Nations partners have ordered a cap on world population. Britain has been set a target of a 10 per cent reduction and if we don't achieve it we'll face sanctions."

Turning to a second camera, the actress's concerned expression relaxed into a reassuring smile. "New Phoenix believe our compassionate Health of the Nation Bill provides a realistic answer to the problem. It helps those for whom life has become an unbearable burden to end their pain and suffering in comfort and with dignity. There is no compulsion, however. For those unwilling to co-operate, the Bill offers cast-iron safeguards, including a legally binding opt-out clause. But those who consent would not only do so in their own interests but nobly serve those of future generations across our endangered planet."

There followed a brief scene of happy children of different races enthusiastically waving national flags before a final close-up of the soap star's smiling face. "I can't think of a better way to be remembered than that…can you? Good night."

"What did you think of it, William?" Howard asked as the rock music faded along with the caption: 'A party political broadcast on behalf of the New Phoenix Party.'

"Quite persuasive actually," his son answered. "I'm thinking of putting both your names forward as volunteers."

"We're in our prime!" Howard protested

"You could go on their waiting list. I'm sure Chris would agree."

"You're right, he would…the patriotic thing to do!" They all laughed, while realising it was no laughing matter

When they checked the computer for reaction to the broadcast afterwards, the wordsmith found himself lost for words.

William came to his assistance. "Gobsmacked!"

In the short time since the broadcast, over 400 messages had been received and more were arriving by the minute. Some were from existing members of Keep Breathing but most were newcomers terrified by the prospect of 'noble' euthanasia and begging to be allowed to join. The task of dealing with them would stretch throughout the night.

The mountain they had to climb kept growing and so far they'd barely reached base camp. But William seemed to understand his new role in the team. "Relax, Dad," he said. "I'll take care of it. But I demand double time for night work."

Howard clapped his son firmly on the back. "You can have double sausages for breakfast."

*   *   *

They had a new parish priest at St Chad's. Father Fitzgibbon was rather different to Father O'Hagan, who had gone back home to County Wicklow and well-earned retirement. While the much loved cleric had offered his flock the comfort of traditional Catholic doctrine in an immoral world, Father Fitzgibbon's ministry turned out to be more of the Catholic-Lite variety. Though ordained as priest of a universal church whose *raison d'etre* was unswerving allegiance to immutable truth, he remained his own man, with his own interpretations of truth sometimes bordering on heresy.

When not celebrating Mass, the hirsute cleric preferred to reject clerical attire in favour of a leather jacket, jeans and trainers in order, as he put it, to relate more closely to the community. It was noticeable that he used the word 'community' more often than the word 'God' and that the social life of his new parish took precedence over its spiritual welfare.

From the start, regular members of his flock suspected that their new shepherd's theological instruction might be less than 'sound', as they charitably put it, and their suspicions were soon confirmed. What made matters worse was the fact that Father Fitzgibbon was a Yorkshireman and had a particularly blunt manner, which some regarded as offhand. Young, long-haired and trendy they could just about handle. But young, long-haired, trendy, heretical, and blunt with it…that was something else.

Barbara had done her level best to like Father Fitzgibbon. He was a young man of God transplanted into a new parish far from home and it was her Christian duty to welcome him without reserve. But as successive homilies chipped away at Church teaching, she began to have doubts about him. What particularly upset her were his attempts to rationalise the miracles of Jesus. He would rattle them off in the Gospel readings followed by such statements as: "Whether or not you believe in the literal interpretation of this passage…" suggesting that some other kind of explanation might be equally valid. "What the passage really tells us is…" and there would follow a rambling lecture on the need to protect the fragile balance between humans, animals and the ecology.

Some of his interpretations of the miracles were harder to believe than the miracles themselves. It was possible, he felt, that the feeding of the 5,000 only took place because the 5,000 brought their own packed lunches. With a priest like Father Fitzgibbon it was hardly surprising that the congregation began to shrink. Barbara never wavered in her faith, however. You went to Mass to meet God. The homilies you could take or leave. But when the young reverend declared that it was no longer necessary to fast before receiving Holy Communion, she felt he'd pushed his luck too far.

She pointed out that canon law stipulated you must abstain from solid food and liquids other than water for one hour beforehand. Unless he had somehow managed to acquire a Papal dispensation overruling canon law, his pronouncement could only be regarded as heresy. Father Fitzgibbon had replied, none too politely, that there were two ways of observing the law – either its letter or its spirit. He believed that, "in this day and age" (another of his favourite stock phrases) the spirit of the law was what mattered.

"That was simply no answer," Barbara told Howard after returning from Mass in a less-than-uplifted state of mind. "Christians have fasted before receiving Holy Communion since the third century."

"They must be feeling pretty hungry by now," Howard quipped.

"I might have known you wouldn't take this seriously..."

"Sorry, darling, but I'm afraid I can't rid you of your turbulent priest." Howard was amused by the ongoing tales of controversy at St Chad's. They'd never had these problems in the Anglican church as far as he could recall. No-one had ever mentioned fasting as a preliminary to Holy Communion.

"What's fasting for?" he asked innocently.

110

"What for?" Barbara was incredulous. "Out of devotion to Jesus, of course. In the Middle Ages they used to go without food for over 12 hours before Mass. Now we're told we needn't even fast for one hour – in case we might get a bit hungry," she snorted. "Health and Safety would never allow that!"

Howard thought he understood where she was coming from. Father Fitz, as he called the young priest, seemed to be saying that as long as you *felt* like fasting it would be okay? Surely the whole point of fasting was to resist the pangs of hunger not imagine that you were doing so. Humpty Dumpty's dictum in *Alice Through the Looking Glass* came to mind: "Words can mean what you want them to mean."

"Either you respect the rules or you don't," he said at length.

She smiled fondly at him. "You're picking it up, Howard. We'll make a Catholic of you yet."

"No way," he exclaimed. "You'd need a miracle to do that!"

*　　　　*　　　　*

Sally Mitchell perched like a golden eagle on her favourite spot half way up the Sierra Almijara and watched the world go by 750ft below. It wasn't the most demanding of tasks since the only things moving were a farmer slowly leading his horse along a goat track, accompanied by two dogs. As the tiny figures reached a narrow dusty road snaking up the mountainside, a solitary lorry like a toy passed them, climbing the steep gradient at a snail's pace, its wheels perilously close to the unguarded edge and a sheer drop of several hundred feet.

She had travelled along the same road by taxi many times. It always felt like a white-knuckle ride even though drivers assured her no-one had fallen over the edge in living memory. But whenever she reached her studio, part of a small hotel complex surrounded by an olive grove at the end of a stony track, the fears melted into insignificance. This was her private retreat, where she could sketch and paint in the perfect light and meditate in the vast, encircling solitude; where the air was pure and pollution-free and the silence spiritual. It was a place of breathtaking scenery, the massive grey slab of Mount Maroma towering over green and brown slopes dotted with olive trees and terraced *pueblos blancos* clinging to vertigo-inducing cliffs.

These quaint, white-walled villages, mostly dating from the 13th century, acted as a perfect foil for the grandeur of the Andalusia landscape. It was a combination that attracted a steady flow of British and American artists over the years. Colonies had sprung up in the Moorish village of Canillas Albaida and in nearby Competa, where some shops now boasted English names.

When Sally drank coffee with Eduardo, her art dealer boyfriend, and her fellow artists in the small square's only pavement café, she sympathised with the local population. They told her in voluble Spanglais that the remoteness of the area would protect it from the full-blown tourism blighting the coastal towns. No coach parties would ever venture up the unfenced mountain roads, barely wide enough for two vehicles to pass without their more religious occupants – and even their non-religious occupants – breathing a silent prayer.

In her lofty eyrie Sally watched the toy lorry disappear from view round a rocky outcrop. She hastily unfolded her sketch pad. Although still early afternoon, the clouds were darkening above Mount Maroma and, if she hurried, she might capture one of nature's mysterious mood swings to match her own. Very faintly, carried on the breeze from the ancient village of Archez far below, came the tiny sound of its church bell chiming the hour and she realised that a shift in wind direction heralded a change in the weather.

As heavy clouds rolled over the Sierra and the air grew chilly, she hastily applied a few finishing touches to her sketch and retraced her steps along the stony track to her air-conditioned studio with its futuristic furniture and avant garde artefacts. She brewed a cup of herbal tea and reclined on a couch to assess the sketch dispassionately. It took less than a minute to decide it was not good enough. With a sigh, she crumpled the paper and threw it away.

Emotional problems weighing on her mind were beginning to affect her work. Time was passing and she was still no nearer resolving the dilemma over Eduardo and their future together, if there was going to be one. He was a dear and she'd known him for years. With his extensive contacts he'd been able to arrange lucrative commissions for her as well as exhibitions in prestigious galleries. She knew he loved her and she loved him almost as much as she loved her work. But they were both well into their thirties and there were times when she felt the prospect of motherhood slipping away for ever.

Pencil slim thanks to a diet of humus, lentils and lettuce, the years had treated her kindly but there was no guarantee of continued altruism. She knew you didn't push your luck with the forces of nature. On the rare occasions when she and Eduardo discussed marriage they always hit the same brick wall: he would marry her only if they lived permanently in Spain afterwards. Business considerations demanded it.

Sally, equally adamant, bridled at the word 'permanently'. England was no longer the green and pleasant land she remembered from childhood but it was still her home. All her family were there and right now they needed her more than Eduardo did. Her grandmother had suffered a stroke and her father was fighting a desperate battle to protect her and her entire generation from a predatory state. From their frequent telephone calls, it seemed his own health was suffering as a result.

She sighed again, pushing her unruly blonde mane back from the strong, handsome face and intelligent grey eyes. Why was everything so difficult? Even out here in the wilds of Andalusia there was no escape from life-altering decisions. Listlessly, her mood still downbeat, she squatted on an art deco patterned rug and began the daily routine to clear her mind of all the worldly hassles.

It was time for her t'ai chi meditation.

TWELVE

With a few flicks of a powder puff across his nose from the make-up girl and a touch of eyebrow pencil, he was ready, at least facially, for his appearance on *Pandora*. "Have you been on TV before?" the girl wanted to know.

Howard wasn't exactly a regular face on the nation's screens although he'd appeared twice recently. But in his early days as a reporter he'd done occasional spots as a freelance contributor. "I was on television in the days before *EastEnders*," he told her.

She was suitably impressed. "Wow…you don't look that old!"

He found the remark strangely reassuring. As usual, he was feeling nervous before going in front of the cameras. He kept forgetting the compelling arguments he'd been rehearsing in his mind all day and was worried that the programme's supercilious presenter, Adrian Lennox, would make him look foolish, a talent he regularly employed at the expense of guests who'd neglected to do their homework.

Barbara had made sure he'd done his, and insisted on coming with him to keep reminding him of his lines, like a human tele-prompter.

When the programme's guests and their supporters were led into the hospitality suite to meet the great man, the arch inquisitor and scourge of Cabinet ministers and bishops did not seem quite so intimidating. In his late fifties, his face was long and lugubrious, shaded by unprepossessing designer stubble, and he wore a dark brown rug. It was a masterpiece of the wig-maker's art but if you looked carefully you could see the join where the hair colour did not quite match his dyed sideboards despite the best endeavours of the make-up department.

Fashionably dressed in a dark suit with an open-neck shirt, the contrast with Howard, wearing his old jacket with the elbow patches and his NUJ tie, could not have been more marked. After cordially shaking hands with his guests, he offered them all a drink, knocking back a large gin and tonic himself in seconds.

"Always better to have a drink first," he grinned amiably. "Can't go out there alone!"

Everyone laughed and, put at their ease, relaxed in the leather armchairs with their drinks. As always, only cheaper brands were available. Howard wanted his usual beer but had to settle for an inferior brew. Barbara, who was driving, stuck with Coke and ice. The show's producer, an intense young woman with close-cropped hair and dressed all in black, advised Howard to switch his hearing aid to the loop position to match the studio's sound system.

Then she introduced the guests to each other. There were four of them and as the programme's sub-title was Health of the Nation? (a question mark having been judiciously added to stimulate debate), they were divided along pro and anti lines. Leading the pro-death contingent was New Phoenix MP and *Guardian-*

116

Independent columnist Sylvia Pullar, the controversial Bill's spokesperson. A devout feminist and former student of the Mary Warnock Charm Academy, she was fifty-something, small and shrivelled, with little round spectacles and dark hair in a short boyish cut.

Her sidekick was Dr Darren Sharma, young, wispy-bearded and idealistic-looking. Both were smartly dressed — she in the regulation leather jacket of the liberal intellectual and he in a trendy, polo-neck jumper — and both radiating confidence.

The pro-life team consisted of Howard and the NPF chairman, Owen Evans. Although Howard had conferred by telephone with the softly spoken Welshman several times, he had no idea his colleague was quite so ancient. Owen was a gentleman of the old school down to the waistcoat of his three-piece suit and his bow tie. He had white hair, carefully combed from a side parting, a full beard and walked with the aid of a stick. But his alert expression belied the frailty and there was a look of quiet determination in the tired old eyes.

Over the years, *Pandora's* output had acquired a reputation for stage-managed controversy and Howard suspected they had set him up. He was about to be hung out to dry but it was too late to do anything about it. The guests were already being led into the studio, with its cameras, dazzling lights and profusion of trailing cables. He and his frail partner were gently helped to their seats at a long table bearing their name plates, personal microphones, jotting pads and ballpoint pens, and Howard strove to collect his scattered thoughts. But then, with four minutes to go before the programme went out live, Owen confided that he had a pacemaker and was experiencing some chest pain. There was no cause for alarm but his breathing was also affected and he might not be able to contribute much to the programme.

This information caused Howard's own breathing to tighten and he asked a production assistant for two glasses of water, one for Owen and one for himself. He took a swift puff of his angina spray and realised he was sweating profusely under the arc lights. Another production assistant noticed and dabbed his brow with a tissue. Then the cameras were rolled into position, the synthesised music swelled and the countdown began.

Despite his fearsome reputation, Lennox was an intellectual only in the loosest, television sense of the word. The carefully cultivated image of a deep and erudite thinker was strictly for the cameras. In reality, he belonged to that breed of shallow-minded satirists spawned decades earlier who excelled in corrosive iconoclasm but wouldn't know where to start if asked to create an icon themselves. As such, he relied heavily on his autocue and the prompts in his earpiece for most of his celebrated soundbites.

When the programme's opening sequence of large boxes spinning round the screen faded along with the strident music, he aimed his trademark smirk at the rostrum camera and intoned his familiar greeting: "Good evening, and welcome to tonight's edition of *Pandora*. What have we got in our magic box for you tonight? Well, remember this?"

Immediately, a replay of Howard's now-famous fling on The Embankment filled the screen. Once again, his ONEBE flew through the air and hovered for a moment before plunging into the muddy river. It was a scene repeated on television and in the newspapers almost as often as the winning goal in the Cup Final, but Lennox knew there was plenty of mileage left in it.

"Don't we all!" he smirked, turning to his autocue. "Howard Mitchell's unprecedented gesture of defiance launched a new style of political protest. It was more than an act of rebellion against the Establishment, it was pure innovation. It created a template for a pensioners' protest movement that continues to grow and gather strength. Tonight we have with us the founder of that movement, the creator of the iconic scene that captured the nation's imagination, leader of the Keep Breathing pressure group…Howard Mitchell. Also in the studio are the MP Sylvia Pullar, spokesperson for the government's Health of the Nation Bill, Dr Darren Sharma, a specialist in geriatric medicine, and Owen Evans, chairman of the National Pensioners' Forum."

As the cameras panned to Howard, Lennox went on: "The ripples seem to be spreading far and wide from your spectacular action that day, Mr Mitchell."

Howard smiled. "Yes, you could say it's caused a bit of a stir."

"That's putting it mildly. As I understand it, people all over the country have been inspired by your protest. You must be very happy at the response."

"Overwhelmed actually!"

"How many have signed up as members of your campaign?"

"Well, at the last count, more than 35,000…we can hardly keep up with it."

Lennox was visibly impressed. "That's phenomenal. Why are they all so keen, do you think?"

"Well, they want to keep breathing, basically…"

"Don't we all!"

"Yes, but our leaders have got other ideas…"

119

"You mean the Health of the Nation Bill going through Parliament?"

"That's right. Healthy it isn't! It's a monstrous, inhuman measure…"

Lennox interrupted: "Can I stop you there, because those are serious allegations and I'm sure our other guests would challenge them." Turning to the measure's advocate, the presenter continued: "Ms Pullar, I imagine you'd have something to say about that…"

In the gallery, the programme's director switched to the camera focused on the MP and initiated a sequence of talking heads as the population control expert adjusted her spectacles. She appeared pained by Howard's words while adopting the patient manner of a teacher addressing a backward pupil.

"As you say, Adrian, it's a serious charge and one which I categorically refute."

As soon as he heard the word 'refute', Howard knew he was dealing with a semantics scholar. It was a favourite word of politicians, lawyers and other shysters trying to pull the wool over your eyes. It meant 'disprove'. She couldn't disprove the charge. She could only deny it. The name of the game was sophistry.

And right now it was in full spate. "The Health of the Nation Bill has been drafted in response to an urgent United Nations directive on population control. Many other countries are affected as well as us. Our Bill is based on the principle of pensioner autonomy. It's a strictly compassionate measure offering people of advanced age, for whom life has become an intolerable burden, the option of ending their pain and suffering with dignity."

"Whether they are terminally ill or not?" Lennox asked.

"You don't need to be terminally ill to be suffering. Medical research confirms that, in the final quarter of our lives, physical and mental degeneration accelerates."

The presenter turned to Darren Sharma. "Dr Sharma, as a specialist in geriatric medicine, do you have any scientific evidence to support this theory of accelerating deterioration?"

The dynamic young doctor had plenty. "It's a phenomenon widely recognised by physicians of all disciplines and fully documented in several major clinical studies. Orthopaedic surgeons, cardiologists, oncologists and, of course, psychiatrists all accept the principle of accelerated degeneration."

The presenter persisted with his line of questioning. "Can you produce evidence of the acceleration among your patients?"

"Absolutely. Numerous analyses of individual case histories have proved beyond all doubt that wear and tear intensifies with each year over the age of 60. Then problems multiply dramatically."

"And your Bill offers a sure way to solve them?"

The irony was lost on the young medic. "Progressive physicians believe that when human life ceases to be tolerable, doctors have a moral duty to intervene. Many older patients tell us they long for closure but lack the courage to end their lives themselves. They just need someone to respect their autonomy and do it for them."

"Why does patient autonomy only apply if you want to die?" Howard asked. "I'm campaigning for the autonomy of patients who want to live and at the same time hang on to their pensions. From the response I'm getting it seems they are in a large majority."

"They're the lucky ones," Ms Pullar snapped. "We're campaigning for the unlucky ones – those whose lives have become intolerable."

"Doesn't it all depend on what is meant by 'tolerable'?" Lennox asked.

She sighed patiently. "You've only got to go into any care home for the elderly to see the quality of life for many of them is intolerable. Where is the dignity in being dependent on others for eating, drinking, washing and all your basic needs? I for one wouldn't want to live like that – not if I'd been offered dignified terminal sedation."

"But that's your own subjective judgment," Howard managed to squeeze in. "You can't form government policy on personal preference. Thousands of pensioners are quite happy despite severe infirmities and handicaps. They learn to adapt and lead useful lives."

The prospect of older people leading useful lives was not one that suited the MP's argument. She changed tack. "You're ignoring the fact that the Bill's Maturity Contract incorporates a cast iron safeguard. Everyone will have the opportunity to decline terminal sedation. All they'll need to do is sign an opt-out form and register with a solicitor. It will be a legally binding."

"In return for a fee?" Lennox asked.

"There will be no fee."

"And then they have to take a cut in their pension?"

"A modest reduction, yes."

"Five per cent a year is hardly modest. The pension's already frozen...people can no longer live on it...you're putting them under subtle pressure to end their lives."

She glared at the presenter through her John Lennon spectacles. "No-one will be put under any pressure. There's no question of coercion. People will simply be offered help to end their suffering in a civilised, compassionate manner."

Howard soldiered on in the absence of any support so far from Owen. "They talk about compassion but what they really want is to kill us off. We're told the opt-out clause is a cast iron safeguard but we've heard it all before. Ten years ago you could sign an opt-out if you didn't want to donate your vital organs for transplants. But the opt-out's legality was later overturned by the European Court. So much for 'cast iron safeguards'. Now when you die, your organs are up for grabs by anyone prepared to pay for them."

Sharma cut in: "No-one would want to pay for a 70-year-old's organs."

Howard recognised the red herring. "It's not our organs you're after this time, doctor. It's our pensions."

"I utterly refute that." The medic had also done the crash course in semantics.

"You can deny it all you like but we suspect the opt-out clause will wither on the vine if this Bill becomes law. The door will then be open to the situation that exists in Holland – where some old people are being put to death against their wishes."

"This isn't Holland," Sharma said helpfully.

"Thank God for that!"

"Let's not bring religion into this," Lennox quipped.

For a brief moment there was silence. Then Owen stirred. "I agree with Mr Mitchell," he said in a quavery Welsh voice. "Safeguards are worth less than a politician's promise. But they won't need to renege on the opt-out this time. The Maturity Contract will squeeze the life out of our generation in a couple of years. There's no way we can live on a reduced pension. The politicians know that. They say they're only doing it to meet the UN target but that's just a cynical excuse. The real reason is money. It all goes back to 1980, when Thatcher cut the vital link between earnings and pensions. She didn't like us either."

"The link has since been restored," Lennox reminded him.

"Yes but if she hadn't broken it in the first place, today's state pension would be about 25 per cent of average earnings. Even that's inadequate but at least it's above the poverty level, and it's poverty – the indignity of poverty as well as the hardship – that'll drive us to ending it all with so-called dignity."

"Not intolerable pain?"

Owen laughed quietly at the presenter's naivety. "People of our age can handle pain. What we can't handle is humiliation. Ms Pullar and her cronies know that. Sooner or later, we'll crack and we'll all be lining up for terminal sedation. That's what they're depending on."

In a dramatic gesture, the venerable figure turned painfully to the rostrum camera and addressed the nation's viewers directly, much to the director's dismay.

"The National Pensioners' Forum have organised a petition to fight this evil Bill and I urge you all to sign it…and support Howard Mitchell's campaign…in the service of humanity…"

His voice, which had grown steadily weaker, tailed off in a bout of coughing and he reached for his glass of water. He never made it. The white head fell on his chest and he slumped forward across the table. There were shocked gasps all round the studio and panic swept the gallery. Cameras swung away from the scene except the rostrum camera focused on the presenter. Dr Sharma sprang forward and tried to loosen Owen's collar and tie, while two production assistants levered him to an upright position.

Lennox, ever the seasoned trouper, kept his cool. The show had to go on. As frenetic action unfolded off camera, he told viewers: "I'm afraid we'll have to leave it there. But the debate goes on. Is the Health of the Nation Bill a compassionate answer to patient autonomy or a cynical form of population control? This question needs to be answered as the controversial Bill faces a tough passage through Parliament. Good night."

The familiar *Pandora* theme music returned and the programme titles scrolled as Howard, Sharma and the studio floor manager carried the frail old man to the Green Room. They laid him carefully on a sofa. His eyes were closed and his face had turned an alarming shade of purple.

"It looks like a heart attack," Sharma said, feeling his pulse. "Is there any oxygen anywhere? Defibrillator? Somebody find me a defibrillator. And somebody call an ambulance."

Barbara identified herself as a nurse and mopped Owen's perspiring brow with her handkerchief. Howard had already phoned for an ambulance. Now he could do nothing but grip Owen's hand. A trolley equipped with oxygen and a defibrillator arrived from the medical centre but before he could be lifted on to it, his body shook and he opened his eyes. "I told you I...wouldn't be...much use."

Howard felt acute pangs of guilt over his earlier misgivings. "You were magnificent, Owen. You were the star of the show!"

The gaunt features creased in pain. "Death is never...dignified...is it?"

"You're staying with us, Owen...we need you for the campaign..."

Owen's last words were very faint: "Keep breathing..."

His eyes closed and Howard felt his hand go limp.

They tried to revive him with the defibrillator but gave up when there was no response after the third attempt.

Owen Evans wouldn't be doing any more breathing.

THIRTEEN

Of course, the front pages were full of it next day although, for some strange reason, *The Announcer* preferred to relegate the story to an inside page. But Owen's dramatic demise, watched as it had been by millions, was perfect for the tabloids. They knew Adrian Lennox could sometimes frighten his guests half to death but no-one could remember anybody actually dying on his show – or on any other live TV chat show for that matter.

Since red-top readers were mostly telly addicts who lapped up anything to do with the medium, and as *Pandora's* producers would agree there was no such thing as bad publicity, the story represented a natural splash. And the headlines almost wrote themselves:

**DEATH WITH DIGNITY – ON
PANDORA...***Express*
DEATH ON LIVE TV...*Mirror*
A CAUSE TO DIE FOR...*Sun*

Apart from *The Announcer* the quality Press also gave prominent coverage to Owen's sad death, although no-one seemed to know much about him. He was 84, a widower with no children, and had been chairman of the NPF for more than a decade. But because the forum shunned direct action apart from the occasional polite petition to MPs, its profile and that of its courtly leader had remained low key.

Howard was unable to offer much in the way of guidance for the reporters who telephoned him. He told them the old man had proved an inspiration in the short time he'd known him. In tribute to his memory, moves were afoot to affiliate the Keep Breathing campaign with the forum. Together, they would represent a formidable alliance in the fight for justice. While Owen's death would be a great loss to the forum's thousands of members, positives would follow. Their late chairman would surely emerge a martyr of the pensioners' movement – words that were to prove uncannily prophetic.

Both he and Barbara were shaken by Owen's death but Barbara was satisfied that nothing more could have been done to save him. He was suffering from ischemic heart disease which had reached an advanced stage and, in line with Dr Sharma's clinical data, had started to accelerate. He must have been in great pain towards the end of the programme but had managed to deliver an eloquent message to millions of viewers. As he'd said, the older generation could handle pain. They'd survived the war. They were a different species to younger people.

Before settling down in his lounge with the morning papers, Howard had checked the computer for feedback following the *Pandora* programme. Once again, the emails were scrolling off the screen, thanks to his Press contacts giving his email address at the end of their stories. Bernard would later bring the incoming letter post, which would swell membership still further. The campaign was on a roll. Once joined by the Forum's 100,000-plus members there would be no stopping it.

The gathering strength of the movement had become apparent to almost all national newspaper editors yet it seemed that, on this occasion, *The Announcer* had given it the cold shoulder. It had led with an admittedly disturbing account of a BMA decision to abandon all resuscitation for terminally ill patients. Howard shook his head in disbelief over that – as he did with another front page story about an oddball judge who ruled that to deport a serial murderer would infringe the killer's human rights. Everyone, even murderers, had human rights. Everyone, it seemed, except older humans.

Searching for at least some mention of the day's main news story, he turned inside and read: 'Our pets are just like us, say owners'. Some dog-owners were prepared to pay thousands if their pet needed a heart bypass. After a two-year, publicly-funded study, scientists had cracked the genetic code of the fungus causing dandruff. And the public 'watchdog' responsible for policing MPs' expenses had been caught with his own snout in the trough he was supposed to be guarding.

Finally, he spotted it: 'Pensioners' leader dies on TV show.' Three short paragraphs followed, reporting that Owen Evans, chairman of the National Pensioners' Forum, collapsed and died while appearing on *Pandora* on BBC2. Mr Evans was said to have been leading a debate on the government's proposed Health of the Nation Bill. Others taking part in the debate included Sylvia Pullar, the New Phoenix MP and leading supporter of the Bill. The programme's producers were shocked by the death of Mr Evans, who had led the protest group for over 10 years, and offered sincere condolences to his family and fellow members.

Not for the first time, Howard was staggered by *The Announcer's* treatment of an obvious front page news story. The fact that his name had not been mentioned didn't concern him. After all, its subject matter was the death of Owen Evans on a live TV broadcast. What was intriguing was the absence of any mention of the Keep Breathing campaign, currently carrying all before it, which Owen had been endorsing when he died.

Then it dawned on him. Someone in the Cabinet Office, no doubt a crony at his drinking club, must have tipped Hugo off about the OBE cock-up. It was bound to happen sooner or later. The editor would have been doubly enraged. Not only had the prestigious honour been awarded to Howard instead of himself but the ungrateful hack had then proceeded to defile it. The most effective revenge would be to play down the Keep Breathing campaign, keeping it tucked away on inside pages.

At least we know where we stand, Howard thought, tossing the paper away without bothering to complete the crossword. There would be little point in briefing *Announcer* reporters on his campaign's progress in future. But there were plenty of other print and broadcasting journos eager to report every development.

The latest Press release being prepared for the nationals by Bernard and himself featured the growing number of members willing to go to prison for non-payment of fines. One rebel, a diabetic with a triple heart bypass, was due in court for refusing to pay an inflated council tax demand in full. He'd paid the bill plus a percentage in line with inflation, leaving a small balance that he refused to pay. He expected a heavy fine plus costs, which he wouldn't pay either. "This is all a matter of principle," he said in an email. "I've stood by my belief in justice and fair play all my life. I'm too old to abandon it now."

Howard knew that his member's protests of unfair play would carry no weight with magistrates hearing his case. They had no discretion in the matter. Ironically, justice was no more than an onlooker in their courts. All they could do was apply the law, which meant something else entirely. It also meant that the frail defendant would end up being led to the cells, strip-searched, fingerprinted, DNA tested and subjected to other indignities before being incarcerated with killers, crooks and paedophiles for seven days. Such was the severity of the 2018 police state.

There was no way Howard could allow it – hence the 'anonymous donor' in the form of the fighting fund. The payment would be relatively modest but there was a downside to Keep Breathing's charity. More members were lining up for their day in court and the total cost would be heavy. Donations were still pouring in and Howard had contributed his own TV appearance fees and Press tip-off income but there had also been substantial outgoings for the website and subsequent updates, postal and travelling expenses, not to mention horrendous telephone and electricity bills. To be on the safe side, he decided to check the current bank balance with the treasurer.

"You're not going to believe this," Bernard told him, "but we've just reached six figures."

FOURTEEN

The grey stone chapel nestled in a Brecon Beacons valley of unforgettable beauty, close to a village with an unpronounceable name. It was early autumn and clusters of ash and oak round the cemetery had taken on a yellow tint. But the surrounding hills, lit with patches of bright sunshine, were still a lush green, dotted with a regular pattern of sheep.

By the time they had squeezed in local villagers, NPF officials, an immaculately attired male voice choir who had arrived by coach from Hay-on-Wye, Owen's ageing sister and slightly younger brother-in-law, there was barely room for Howard and Barbara. Lack of space might have been a reason why no TV cameras were present, although the customary scenes of guests arriving, followed by the coffin could have been shot outside the chapel.

The least the broadcasters could have done out of respect would be to send a camera crew from their Cardiff studio. But then their guest who'd provided millions of viewers with unprecedented unscripted drama had been an octogenarian and, as such, a second-class citizen. So the question of respect didn't arise.

You could almost hear the young, elderphobic executives' reasoning: Owen's death was 'old news'. Geriatrics were *expected* to die. It was what they did. The fact that the old-timer fell off his perch on their programme had admittedly boosted ratings but coverage of his funeral wouldn't boost them further. Viewers had already forgotten him. A new sensation was occupying their minds – an alleged heroin addict among junior members of the royal family. Adrian Lennox had promised to unmask the delinquent one night soon and the nation was holding its breath.

To the strains of *Jesu, Lover of my Soul,* on a wheezy organ but sung with emotional gusto by the choir, Owen's light oak coffin was carried into the austere building by dark suited pallbearers and placed on a trestle in front of an aged pastor. This being a Presbyterian chapel, there was no altar, just a small cross and bunch of flowers on a plain table. Howard had been in pubs with more atmosphere but once the choir began singing *Guide me, Oh thou Great Jehovah,* that all changed.

The passionate tenor voices soared above their bass counterparts, their harmony and intonation rapturous. What was it about Welsh male voice choirs that brought Howard out in goose bumps? Perhaps the answer was that they were more than singers, they were vocal musicians. There were no hymn books but the hymns' verses were printed on a four-page order of service, the front bearing a picture of the druid-like Owen with the dates of his long lifespan.

In his eulogy, the pastor recalled how Owen had lived in their community for most of his life. He had roamed the hills and valleys in his youth and had courted his wife, Ellen, there. They had been married in that same chapel. The couple were known and loved throughout the area before his wife sadly passed away 10 years ago. The minister paid tribute to Owen's lifetime of public service, first as a solicitor and town councillor, and later as leader of the NPF. He would long be remembered as a champion of the elderly and vulnerable, a generation now marginalised by an increasingly callous and uncaring society.

A glowing tribute was also paid by the forum's vice-chairman, Dr George Armstrong, who described his late colleague as "one of nature's true gentlemen". During his leadership, their group had gone from strength to strength and now represented a powerful voice in the life of the nation. It was at present organising an online petition against the Health of the Nation Bill which had already attracted thousands of signatures. Owen would be a hard act to follow but it was vital to carry forward his work at a time when senior citizens found themselves under pressure as never before.

After the rousing final hymn, *Praise my Soul, the King of Heaven,* they lifted Owen and gently carried him out into the sunshine to join his Ellen in the grave overlooking their beloved valley. No-one, Howard and Barbara agreed, could have contemplated eternity from a more sublime resting place.

As the coffin was lowered into the ground, the sun glinted one last time on the brass nameplate:

Owen Bryn Evans

...almost as if the old man had winked at the mourners gathered round. Then they scattered the ritual dust, finally obscuring the name. But not before Howard felt a frisson of inspiration.

As they settled with their drinks at the wake in the village pub, Howard told Barbara of the spooky moment at the graveside. "I've had an idea," he whispered. "Owen Bryn Evans...O...B...E! We'll produce an alternative OBE – in memory of Owen. All our members jailed for their beliefs will be awarded our special OBE – for services to the elderly."

"Brilliant, darling." Barbara was still carrying her order of service and checked out the full name above Owen's picture. "Well spotted." She really meant it. Not for the first time during their long and eventful marriage, she had to admire her husband's serendipity. It had marked him out from the run of the mill as a journalist and it still hadn't left him. "Nothing escapes your eagle eye!"

He grinned, doffed his cap and did a mock bow. "It's a gift," he replied modestly.

She downed her red wine and soda. "This calls for another drink." They'd come by car and he was driving back. So they relaxed and chewed over the idea along with the crisps and peanuts. It was not long before practicalities took over. Could they be sued for copyright?

"Not when the initials stand for something else," Howard said. "Their OBE stands for Order of the British Empire. Ours will stand for Owen Bryn Evans. Anyway, there's no way they would sue. It would only give us more publicity."

"Can we afford all those gold medals?"

"They might have to be silver. It depends on how many we're going to need."

"It shouldn't look tawdry – like a cheap imitation."

"It won't look tawdry. It'll look dignified...with Owen's head embossed on one side and his full name with the initials highlighted in some way."

"And what on the reverse...an inscription?"

Howard scratched his head. "We'll need to think about that."

Barbara finished her wine. "How about: 'For God and long life'?"

"Why God? This should be a strictly secular honour, surely."

"I was comparing it with a real OBE – for God and the Empire."

His indignation was not totally affected. "*Ours* will be the real OBE. The other's just a meaningless bauble."

"Well, we can't just say 'for long life' can we?"

"No, that doesn't sound right. We need something more..."

"Dignified..."

"Something Owen would approve of..."

"Do you remember his last words?"

"Only too well, they were 'Keep breathing.' We can't really put that on the medal..."

"No, his last words on air...on *Pandora*..."

"Something about humanity, wasn't it? I couldn't hear him very well, his voice was so faint."

Barbara thought back to the traumatic moment. "In service to humanity...I'm pretty sure those were his words. That would be ideal for the inscription, wouldn't it?"

"Absolutely. We could make it 'For services to humanity'."

"Yes, Owen would approve of that."

When they put their ambitious plan to George Armstrong he agreed immediately.

"Splendid idea," the acting NPF chief enthused. He was a sprightly retired GP who lived in Hay-on-Wye. Considerably younger than Owen, he was solidly built with a round, honest face, the sort of old-fashioned country GP you unreservedly trusted with your life. His dark blue eyes lit up when conversation turned to a merger of their two groups.

The move would need to be ratified by their memberships but he was confident it would go ahead. "What our people need is a shot in the arm," he said as he sank a pint of best bitter. "We've been a bit laid back of late. It's played into the hands of the mercy killers, I'm afraid." He added with a twinkle: "But at our time of life, militancy can be a bit tiring. You know what they say – when you're young, you don't have the experience and when you're old you don't have the strength!"

*   *   *

"I know exactly what George meant about lacking strength," Barbara said as they drove back to London along the M4. "Retirement can't come a moment too soon."

"You young people…you've no stamina," Howard teased.

His wife lowered her windscreen sun visor and gazed intently into the vanity mirror as she applied a touch of lipstick. "I'm starting to look as old as I feel…"

"You always look like a first-year fresher to me."

She leaned back and closed her eyes. "You're a journalist, Howard. You should be ashamed of telling fibs."

"It's the truth!"

The juggernaut in front braked and he was forced to slow down. Traffic was building up ahead, the sky was darkening and a hazy crescent moon peered over the horizon. They trundled along in third gear for miles. Then in second gear. Then first. Then standstill.

Barbara opened her eyes and took her videophone out of her handbag. "We're going to be late home. I'll phone William."

It was Bernard who answered. He looked tired. William had just left. There'd been a prolonged power cut and the computer's batteries had failed. A backlog of Keep Breathing registrations had built up. Bernard would need to stay the night in their spare room, if that was okay.

"Of course, Bernard, you're one of the family now," she told him. "I really don't know what we'd do without you. You deserve a medal. One day you might be awarded the OBE."

Bernard laughed but when she explained what the initials stood for and the proposed link-up with the pensioners' forum, he congratulated Howard on his brainwave. "Tell him he deserves the medal, not me."

"Where's William gone, do you know?" she asked.

"I thought he deserved a night off, he's been working so hard. He's got tickets for a pop concert. Then he's staying over with Louise...I think...don't quote me on that. Cheers."

The car inched forward in first gear. "They'll be living together soon," Howard said. "She's a nice kid I know and it's the modern way but I don't care for it.

Living together is for people who haven't the bottle to get married...make a proper commitment to each other."

"I agree," Barbara said. "But they often get married eventually."

"More often than not they break up. We're always told about the rising divorce rate but unmarried couples are five times more likely to split up than married ones."

"Which is tough on the children..."

"Who don't have a proper surname..."

The desultory conversation rambled on to match the pace of their progress until it was time for the latest news bulletin on the car radio. He may be retired but news was still his business. There had been updates since his last check. Two UK soldiers had been killed by 'friendly fire' in the American-led invasion of Sri Lanka. (Since the island was found to be sitting on an oilfield with a potential yield of 60 billion barrels, coalition forces had taken a sudden interest in protecting the natives from Tamil 'insurgents').

The Prime Minister, Dame Jessica Sykes, had flown off with her actress partner for a fact-finding visit to the Bahamas; 18 per cent of teenagers were suffering some kind of sexually transmitted disease; inflation was up again and England were still losing in the Test match. The familiar depressing catalogue ended with a similarly bleak weather forecast and a warning from the Highways Authority of severe congestion on the M4 between Junctions 16 and 17; drivers being advised to find alternative routes with adequate battery-charging points for electric vehicles. (Many garages on minor roads still sold only petrol and diesel.)

"Now they tell us," Howard sniffed.

Even as the broadcast ended they could see a traffic tailback of red lights stretching miles ahead. Progress was still no more than a crawl and the forecast rain suddenly began lashing the desolate scene. "It's not looking good," he observed unnecessarily. "Can you dig out the road atlas?"

Barbara searched the cluttered glove box. Electric cars boasted navigation devices but they were plagued by glitches – like her videophone's GPS function. An atlas was good enough for their old Rover. It was more reliable and a lot less expensive. She found the book and switched on the map light. "After Leigh Delamere turn on to the A350…head for Chippenham…then pick up the A4 to London."

It seemed like a good idea. The only problem was that scores of other motorists and drivers of street-jamming, diesel-powered trucks had also thought of it. Negotiating Chippenham turned out to be a no-win scenario. After trying for an hour and ending up completely lost, Howard decided he'd had enough. He turned into the car park of a thatched inn.

"I need a drink," he said.

"We both need a drink." His wife replaced the atlas in the glove compartment. "I've no idea where we are."

"Lost in the wilds of darkest Chippenham," he grinned, as he helped her across the pitch black car park in the swirling rain towards the inn's brightly lit doorway. Above, hanging baskets swayed in the wind along with the sign, The Owl and Pussycat.

Inside it was warm and welcoming, with low beams, polished brass and the familiar red patterned carpet Howard had found in almost every country pub on his travels throughout the British Isles. There was the usual stone fireplace with a roaring fire, as the evening had turned cold, logs stacked on either side, horse brasses and softly-shaded lamps. The walls were hung with autographed photographs of famous sportsmen and other celebrities who had visited the pub over the years, including Joe Davis, the father of professional snooker, and Lester Piggott, hero of the Turf with nine Derby winners.

A few agricultural types leaned against the bar in quiet conversation and the ubiquitous Jack Russell terrier lay at their feet, its large brown eyes raised at the approach of a stranger. The elderly, bewhiskered landlord greeted him warmly. "Good evening, sir. Nasty night," he said in a resonant West Country burr.

Howard smiled. "Too right. Must be all the global warming."

The farmers laughed and politely stood aside for him. The bar boasted an impressive array of pumps, including local ales, farm ciders and, to Howard's surprise, his own favourite brew. He ordered half a pint and a red wine and soda with ice for Barbara, who'd found a seat at a cosy corner table.

"Have you come far, sir?" Mine Host asked, as he served the drinks.

"From Powys. We're heading for London but the roads are impossible. It could be next week before we get there."

As he carried the drinks to their table, he passed the entrance to a small restaurant. In contrast to the bar area it was buzzing and a glance at a blackboard menu offered several reasons why. "Cheers," he said, taking a seat alongside his wife on a comfortable sofa. "We seem to have struck lucky finding this place."

"Cheers. Makes a change for us!" and they clinked glasses.

Seduced by the blackboard menu, they ordered a gastro pub dinner – Porterhouse steak with garlic prawns and chips for Howard, roast guinea fowl with braised red cabbage and cranberries for Barbara – washed down with a glass of excellent house red. Neither could face a pudding.

After coffee, Howard gave their charming Hungarian waitress his debit card to settle the modest bill and then a surprising thing happened. Moments later, the landlord appeared and placed the silver plate bearing the debit card on the table with a sweeping ceremonial gesture. For a moment, Howard wondered if the card had been declined and the guy was being sarcastic but his broad smile suggested otherwise.

"It's Howard Mitchell, ain't it sir? Seen you on telly and in the papers. Thought I recognised you when you came in...and I was right. Please accept dinner with my compliments. Honoured to have you with us – and you also, madam." He shook both their hands vigorously.

The weary but well-fed travellers sat back in their seats, startled by the fulsome bonhomie. "That's most kind of you," Howard said. "The meal was excellent."

"Delicious," Barbara added.

"I very much admire your work," Mine Host enthused. "To throw your medal away for something you believe in...that takes great courage these days if I may say so. Everyone I've spoken to round here supports your campaign, sir. So this is the least I can do."

"You're very kind," Howard said again and Barbara beamed in approval.

"If there's anything else... a Cognac, perhaps? Maybe our best room for the night?"

They glanced at each other. It was getting late. The weather was still atrocious. Both were tired and probably over the drink-drive limit. Suddenly, London seemed a very long way away.

"I have to admit that sounds like a good idea," Howard said.

Barbara agreed. "Me, too. It's been a long day."

Their proud host hurried away to make the arrangements and Barbara phoned Bernard to let him know their change of plan.

*   *   *

The Owl and Pussy Cat's best room was clearly its landlord's pride and joy. Elegantly proportioned and furnished with antiques, it boasted an enormous double bed with squashy pillows and a multi-coloured patchwork duvet. There were two winged armchairs, large screen TV, hospitality tray with tea and filter coffee. Even a supply of chocolate biscuits. The en-suite bathroom had a king-sized bath and separate shower, and everything worked.

Barbara stretched out on the bed and yawned. "We have no night clothes."

He subsided next to her with a befuddled sigh of contentment: "Who needs night clothes?"

"We do."

"Not if we're going to get round to some serious nooky." His voice was all innocence. "It's been a long time, after all."

"You are joking, of course."

"Never been more serious."

She reached out for his hand. "Aren't we a bit too old for that kind of thing?"

143

"Speak for yourself. I'm still in my prime!"

They had to laugh. His arthritis had become so bad it took him ten minutes to get dressed in the morning. He couldn't play more than a couple of frames of snooker without pain; that's how serious it was. Then there was his angina. He hadn't had any attacks recently but stress or over-excitement could bring one on. In his condition, sex didn't seem like a good idea. Barbara had gone off it herself anyway. She was invariably exhausted after her shift on the wards.

"I thought you asked your doctor whether it was okay to have sex."

"I did."

"Well…what did he say?"

"He said: 'Only with your wife. I don't want you to get excited'!"

The remark might have upset her once but not now. "You men…you're all the same," she chided him with mock severity.

"Seriously though, he told me what he called 'coital relations' were no bad thing in moderation. You just need to relax and take things more easily…it helps the heart to pump a bit faster and improve your circulation."

Barbara knew that was true but remembered the last time they'd tried it almost six months earlier. In aeronautical terms the flight never got off the ground.

"You know what happened last time…"

"I'd drunk too much wine, remember?"

"You've had too much to drink tonight."

"Maybe, but it's good, honest English ale."

"Plus red wine at dinner, don't forget. You know what they say about grape and grain."

Howard painfully eased himself off the bed and opened the coffee jar. "The remedy is to mix them both with coffee. Come on, I'll be the owl and you can be the pussycat."

She groaned theatrically. "Very funny...I just hope we don't regret this, that's all." And she staggered off to the bathroom.

Later, as they lay semi-clothed on the bed, he marvelled at the smooth contours of her shoulders and breasts. Her face may have acquired a few frown lines and the untamed fair hair more than a few strands of grey – for which he knew he'd been mainly responsible – but she still had the body of a teenager. How strange it was that women showed their age on their faces not their bodies, while with men it was the other way round.

This time the flight had managed to take off but couldn't stay up for long, before suddenly crash landing. He covered her with the duvet and kissed her gently. His mind went back to a night long ago at uni when a breathtaking vision had teased him about clones. He was still pleased with his boyish reply: "I wouldn't mind if they were all like you." He'd been a budding wordsmith even then.

He kissed her again and stroked her hair. "I still wouldn't mind if they were all like you," he whispered. But she was already asleep. The frown lines had turned into slight smile lines, whether of emotional satisfaction or amusement could only be a matter of conjecture. Probably the latter, he thought. What was it George Armstrong had said? When you're old you don't have the strength. But it could be fun trying.

After a breakfast as sumptuous as the previous night's dinner, the landlord insisted on posing for photographs with the couple. "To go on the wall with the other celebrities," he explained. While protesting his status as a celebrity, Howard was secretly pleased that his mug shot might appear alongside that of Joe Davis, pioneer of the beautiful game, not to mention the legendary Lester Piggott who, if he remembered correctly, had been a bit of a rebel himself.

It was late morning before they were allowed to tear themselves away, thanking their host for his lavish hospitality and assuring him that, if they were ever in that part of the world again, they would definitely call in for a free drink.

"Keep Breathing!" the sprightly figure called after them, waving cheerily in the Rover's rear view mirror as they drove off.

Howard turned on to the A4 and headed for London. "I told you we'd struck lucky. Not a penny on the old expense account."

"Maybe we should award him our special OBE," his wife suggested.

He affected outrage. "That would be blatant corruption. Think of the cash-for-honours scandal it would cause!"

FIFTEEN

Howard, Barbara, Bernard, William and his girlfriend, Louise, were videoing the state opening of Parliament – the annual ceremony when the monarch was conveyed to the House of Lords in a gold-encrusted bullet-proof coach to announce the legislative programme for the coming year. The programme was prepared ostensibly by the Cabinet but the real authors were the shadowy Powers that be. For them it presented the illusion of an omnipotent emperor handing down enlightenment to a servile and touchingly grateful nation, not to mention his fantasy empire.

Apart from giving foxes, deer, hares, birds and fish a hard time, there was nothing the ruling class liked better than an opportunity to dress up in medieval robes and wigs to demonstrate their God-given superiority over lesser mortals – which was exactly what the day's ritual offered. It was one of the few days in the Parliamentary year when MPs, with their bottomless expense accounts, lavish pensions and inflation-busting salaries whether they worked or not, were actually required to attend their place of employment.

Led by the portly, middle aged Prime Minister, Dame Jessica Sykes, her dyed mid-brown hair swept back in a bun and wearing a sombre black suit a size too small, they shuffled into the suffocating magnificence of the House of Lords chamber. Its membership may have shrunk but tradition still demanded that the upstarts stood submissively and, in certain cases, crawled before the throne. The unedifying spectacle was regarded as symbolic but hardly meaningless since, as Bernard pointed out, if that were the case they wouldn't have done it any more. He was prepared to bet that, to people raised from birth on the staples of privilege and elitism, it still meant plenty.

As the Mitchells' extended family watched the glittering occasion unfold on the TV in the lounge, comments tended to be at some variance with the hushed and reverential tones of the commentator. "What pathetic arse-lickers they all are," Bernard observed as the robed Lord High Chancellor grovelled at the feet of his unelected master to hand him 'his' Speech, watched by fawning pages and liveried lackeys.

"You wouldn't credit it in this day and age, would you? Grown men – if you can call them that – cringing in front of a drip like him. He probably needs a footman to help him get his leg over."

William and Louise burst out laughing but Bernard was quite serious. "It's true. They have hundreds of servants who wash them, dress them, comb their hair, cut their nails, clean their shoes, fasten their shoe-laces…just like children. Lackeys do everything for them. Except for one thing, that is, and it really brasses them off…when they go to the lavatory they have to wipe their own arses."

Louise pulled a face. She was a bright 19-year-old with fashionably tousled dark hair, torn jeans and scruffy trainers, heavily into the novelties of her generation. But Bernard's remark quite put her off her jam and peanut butter sandwich. They all focused on the screen as their great leader, his imperial crown gleaming under a spotlight and his splendid military uniform draped with rows of medals he hadn't earned, started to read his solemn declaration.

He began with: "My government's proposals on climate change and population control." In a thin, hesitant voice, he outlined plans for cutting carbon dioxide emissions by 50 per cent. Since this wildly ambitious target showed no sign of being reached, powers would be extended to tax households that failed to reduce their carbon footprint at the required rate. This new and imaginative method of robbing citizens would be called the Energy Levy. It would be calculated by local government inspectors and applied as part of council tax. All royal palaces and residences would be exempt from the levy.

The cultured tones continued: "Sadly, even measures as radical as the Energy Levy will be insufficient to comply with our legal and moral obligations to protect the global environment. The United Nations, of which Britain is a permanent member, has emphasised the urgency of reducing world population if our poor overcrowded planet is to survive. It is our duty to the international community to play our part.

"Accordingly, the Health of the Nation Bill has been tabled to reduce the population of our overcrowded islands by 10 per cent by the year 2040, as required by our United Nations partners. This vital target will be realised through the restructuring of the state pension system and the introduction of the Maturity Contract – offering citizens in the evening of their lives a unique opportunity to preserve the health and prosperity of future generations.

"It is imperative to expedite this legislation, which has now reached the committee stage after its Second Reading, by applying a guillotine procedure at Third Reading. I am mindful of the fact that its proposals have proved controversial and unpopular but it is a duty which all of us who serve our great nation cannot afford to shirk. There is no alternative."[1]

Howard and Bernard both winced at the well-worn cliché. During their time as working journalists, they'd associated it with cynical politicians who knew there were plenty of alternatives but would lose face by admitting it. The royal waffle droned majestically on…the reform was a compassionate means of relieving suffering…if offered safeguards for people to opt out…but loyal mature subjects would welcome it…in their own interests as well as the nation's and the planet's.

They switched off the doom-laden agenda. "At least they're not cutting the state pension for all of us," Barbara pointed out.

Bernard laughed. "They won't need to – there'll be hardly any of us left! They're fast tracking the Bill, just as we thought. We'd better get a move on."

While Barbara poured coffee, William handed round sandwiches and Bernard opened a bottle of beer, Howard phoned George Armstrong. The newly-elected

---

[1] Long before the Millennium, Margaret Thatcher, later Baroness Thatcher, used the expression so often in debate that she became known as Tina.

NPF chief had watched the programme and picked up the same alarm signals.

"Patriotism's the name of the game now," he told Howard. "They're playing the old Thatcher card. Give your life to save your country in its hour of need. Young people would never fall for it but it could fool the older generation. Patriotism used to mean something to them, probably still does."

Howard recalled Samuel Johnson's definition of the word: "The last refuge of a scoundrel."

"We've got a whole Cabinet full of scoundrels," George exclaimed. "When I was a practising GP, geriatric patients used to tell me they feared becoming a burden on their families. Now the spin merchants have gone one better: not only will you be a burden on your family if you opt out of assisted suicide, you'll also be a burden on your country. That should have us all queuing up for terminal sedation."

Howard realised the government's PR machine would soon implant the patriotism theme in the national psyche. Tried and trusted methods would include its incorporation in TV soap storylines, popular radio series and features in Establishment-controlled tabloids. The technique had worked perfectly in gaining public acceptance of drug-taking, abortion, political correctness, homosexuality and prostitution. Obligatory euthanasia in the national interest and to save the planet would soon join the list.

"They've thought of everything, haven't they…with patriotism the ultimate clincher."

"Every trick in the book…and a few yet to be included. But that's only to be expected. They've hired some of the best brains in the country."

151

Howard reminded him that Keep Breathing and the Forum were not without high-powered brains themselves. With a joint membership of more than 150,000, increasing by the day, and with growing media support, they were emerging as a potent force. The government, with their slim majority, had been quick to recognise the threat. They were determined to force the Bill through on party lines before the public had time to recognise its dangers.

With Christmas only weeks away, the Third Reading could be expected to take place in early February. If the guillotine were implemented, the Bill could become law in less than three months. It was vital, therefore, that Howard and George launched a joint protest campaign immediately.

They agreed on a twofold counter-attack:

1: An urgent email circular to members of their groups informing them of the developing emergency and urging them to contact MPs, demanding a free vote and a select committee to consider the Bill's contentious issues. They were advised to suggest amendments before its truncated Third Reading. These would be unlikely to succeed as any committee would be biased in the Bill's favour. But at least the move would act as a delaying device.

2: All sympathisers urged to join a mass lobby of Parliament during the Bill's Third Reading, and present their online petition in documentary form. George would organise the placards, banners and leaflets, while Howard would take care of the publicity.

*   *   *

It's an ill wind that blows nobody any good – a saying hijacked in recent times by manufacturers of wind turbines but one adopted by the legal profession since the dawn of capitalism. Once plans to fast-track the Health of the Nation Bill were announced on the internet, the thoughts of lawyers all over Britain lightly turned to their investment portfolios and flotilla sailing in the Caribbean on their next vacation.

The planners assumed the Bill's approval was a foregone conclusion. So confident were they that they included a template of its opt-out clause. It would be legally binding in advance of the legislation if signed, witnessed and registered by a solicitor.

Although the plans had yet to become law, the rush of mature, middle-aged and even younger people clutching template printouts and demanding registration began almost overnight. As models of integrity and good standing in their lodge – and mindful of their central role in a humanitarian crisis – the legal eagles responded to the challenge in keeping with the noble spirit of their calling. They drew up a standard fee – below their normal eye-watering hourly rate but still potent enough to make a pensioner's eyes water more than usual.

Not for the first time (or, indeed, the last) the government had misled the public by claiming no fee would be charged for opting out. What they really meant was that, in cases of financial hardship, pensioners could apply for legal aid. Since most suffered financial hardship, the backlog of applications would be guaranteed to blow a few fuses in the Maturity Contract's already dysfunctional computers.

Not requiring legal aid himself, Howard paid the standard fee up front but still faced an uphill struggle before he could register his aged mother's opt-out. Despite her affliction, she was fully compos mentis and understood that the ongoing polite debate between unworldly academics, utilitarian doctors and unscrupulous politicians was, for her, a matter of life and death. When Howard last visited her at her care home he'd promised to secure the all-important document as soon as possible. "Next week?" she had pleaded and he'd tried to convince her it wasn't that simple.

The first problem had been convincing his solicitor's receptionist that his parent fell into the most vulnerable age group. Fortunately, the care home matron held her birth certificate. Then there was the need to prove his own identity despite the fact that he'd been a client for over 20 years. After his passport and utility bills had been solemnly scrutinised, he was finally confronted by the main obstacle: the Data Protection Act. In the interests of patient confidentiality, opt-out certificates could only be issued directly to patients who had themselves requested them.

For an extra fee the solicitor, Aubrey Kerr, agreed to visit his bed-bound client to complete the formalities but it would have to wait until a week before Christmas. When the day of the visit dawned grey and frosty, Howard arrived in his old Rover and Kerr in a top-of-the range, all-electric Jaguar. Howard carried an extra large bouquet and the solicitor, balding, stolid and grey suited, an imposing brown leather document case containing Susan Mitchell's legal lifeline, among several others.

She was sitting up in bed in her old cardigan watching a game show on TV. Her hearing aids were switched to the loop system and she didn't immediately notice her visitors. Howard had phoned earlier to say he was coming but she'd obviously forgotten. He felt a sudden surge of emotion for the frail stroke victim who had never done anyone any harm throughout her long life, now relying on a dodgy piece of paper simply to survive.

When a commercial break appeared she turned her head shakily, smiling in surprise. Howard bent to kiss her haggard face and gently held the once-dainty hand now blotched and gnarled. She adjusted her hearing aids and, without shouting, he raised his voice: "We've brought you an early Christmas present."

The lawyer snapped open his case and extracted the all-important document with a flourish.

"An early what?" Her voice was tremulous and her words slurred. She seemed apprehensive, not recognising the solicitor.

"This is Mr Kerr, my solicitor, Mother. He's brought you your Maturity Contract opt-out…you know, what you asked me to get for you…"

She squeezed his hand. "I remember now. It's very kind of both of you."

"You just have to sign it and get Matron and Mr Kerr to witness it. Then Matron will keep it in her safe and nobody will be able to touch you…I promise."

"You're a good boy, Howard, to go to all this trouble."

"Don't be silly, Mother. It's the least I could do. It may all come to nothing but we've got to be on the safe side."

She took the official-looking document and searched for her magnifying glass. Matron found it and handed it to her.

The document was headed in a flowery script:

This Is To Certify

...followed by several paragraphs of legal jargon to the effect that the undersigned Susan Mitchell, being of sound mind, hereby refused consent to any or all provision or provisions for terminal sedation under Health of the Nation legislation. For additional protection, Kerr had added that she further refused consent to 'mercy killing', assisted suicide, assisted dying through withdrawal of food and fluids and any other form or forms of euthanasia under the said Act or any other Act of Parliament, Regulation or Order thereof. She also stated that, under no circumstances whatsoever, did she agree to the termination of her life prematurely, but wished to die a natural death.

It was all watertight, the lawyer assured them. But then, so was the Titanic. If the Bill became law, the declaration would at least buy Mrs Mitchell time and at her age every day was a bonus. She read the certificate, nodding approvingly before taking Kerr's gold pen and signing in a wobbly hand. Matron signed as a witness and the lawyer added his own signature.

The vital task accomplished and the legal eagle having sped off in the Jag, Susan Mitchell rested her head wearily on her pillow. "I've passed my expiry date...my 'best-before' date...haven't I?"

"It's your best-*after* date, Mother!" her son admonished. "You're like a fine wine that improves with age."

She laughed at that. "His Majesty says we've all got to make sacrifices...it's our duty...for the sake of the nation."

"Let him make some himself. He could start by handing back the Crown estates his predecessors stole from the British people. That would help the nation no end."

She sighed and closed her eyes. "I had such a weird dream last night. Remember what I told you about the fear we felt during the Blitz...you know, that men were up there in those planes trying to kill us?"

"I remember, Mother. I can't imagine what you went through."

"Well, in my dream, I saw a plane flying overhead and I felt the same fear...like a knot in the pit of my stomach, just the same as all those years ago. Then, all of a sudden, I could see inside the plane...those men...they weren't German airmen. They were doctors in white coats...and they were British! That's when I woke up sweating."

Howard shivered and found he was sweating himself. He'd already had a similar dream. In it he was fighting with unsmiling, robot-like attendants carrying clipboards with computer printouts as they tried to drag his mother away from him for terminal sedation...but he'd had an angina attack and was too weak to stop them.

He bent forward and stroked her hair. "You've got your certificate, Mother. You're safe now, my darling." He wished with all his heart that he could believe it.

SIXTEEN

One of the most serious consequences of Britain's decline from an imperial world power to the European equivalent of a banana republic was the total collapse of public confidence in authority in general and computerised systems in particular. So it was not surprising that life-and-death legislation involving politicians, civil servants and computers should arouse deep suspicion among the older generation. They'd seen it all before. Institutionalised chaos and incompetence had become a way of life – something you learned to live with along with power cuts, political correctness and the self-righteousness of 'green energy' campaigners.

Potential victims of the Health of the Nation Bill made sure they signed their legal opt-outs after protracted struggles to secure them. But those who could afford it also began exploring an altogether safer option: emigration – quit a broken, derelict country for somewhere more civilised while they still could. Fred and Lilian Craig were among them.

"They're talking about emigrating next spring." Barbara hung up the kitchen telephone after a long call to her mother and turned to Howard, wiping a tear from her eye. "Mother says they've both had enough of this country. They're looking at cottages for sale in Normandy and Brittany."

Howard was preparing afternoon tea and crumpets for themselves and Bernard, still hard at work in the study. He put a consoling arm round his wife's shoulders as she dabbed her eyes with a handkerchief. "Along with thousands of others, I expect…you can't blame them."

"I understand why but it's just, you know…a shock." She replaced the handkerchief in the pocket of her jeans. "Dad says they need to escape while the going's good. Time isn't on their side. They've signed their opt-outs but he says they're not worth the paper they're written on."

"He's almost certainly right there."

She sat down and stirred her tea absently. "They want out but they don't want to leave us. Wish we could all go with the poor dears."

"They won't be all that far away, darling. We can pop over to see them any time – probably more than we do now."

"That's what I told Mother but she's still upset about the whole business. She can't believe what's happening around us…drugs, guns, mass abortion and now mass euthanasia. They were both horrified when you threw away your OBE. But now they believe you were right. They say the country's going to the dogs…"

"Long gone, I'm afraid"

"But there's something else…Dad's showing early indications of Alzheimer's. He can't always choose the right words. He's very forgetful. He's unsteady on his feet and gets mood swings…from depressed to angry and aggressive." She took out her handkerchief again.

159

"That's just not like him, he's always been a very gentle man. Mum's upset because he can't get the drugs he needs…"

"I know, those NICE people say they're too expensive."

"But he could get them in France. They're more enlightened there, he says."

Howard poured tea for Bernard. "He's right. They take care of their old people. Here they just want to get rid of them."

As a nurse, Barbara knew all about that. "Especially Alzheimer's patients. Most people at hospital think they should be helped to end their lives."

The solemn mood changed abruptly as Bernard came in for his well-earned tea break. He'd been drumming up support for the online petition against the deadly Bill, which now boasted over half a million signatures, as well as dealing with the usual mountain of emails. Before he'd switched off the computer he'd checked the BBC's Front Page on the internet and taken a printout of a newsflash. Now he waved it in front of Howard with a theatrical flourish, beaming through his thick spectacles.

"Take a look at that, my old mate. It seems the doctors might be getting cold feet."

Howard took the printout and read:

BMA split over euthanasia Bill
The British Medical Association's medical ethics committee is reportedly divided over the role of the association's 160,000 doctors in the proposed Health of the Nation Bill, currently being debated in Parliament. At a meeting in London today they voted to ballot the association's full membership on

details of the controversial measure before a final ruling on the issue from its governing body. The result of the ballot is expected to be announced early next year.

Howard passed the printout to Barbara. "Let's not get too excited. They're not backing out of the deal, they're just protecting themselves. You know what doctors are like."

Bernard, munching a crumpet, thought he knew. "Put three of them in a room, tell them your symptoms and you'll get four opinions!"

Barbara reached for the phone: "I'll let Mother know..."

"Tell her not to cancel their emigration plans just yet," her husband advised.

But she couldn't wait to pass on the good news. This was the breakthrough she'd been praying for.

*   *   *

Had the first crack appeared in the enemy's seemingly impregnable citadel? Despite his outward scepticism, Howard couldn't help feeling secretly excited. Decades earlier the Berlin Wall had started to crumble. Could this be another such seminal moment? The analogy might seem far-fetched but there were clear parallels. The Wall had been the symbol of inhuman communist oppression but the UK government's social engineering was equally inhuman. It symbolised capitalist oppression. There was little difference between the two tyrannies.

He hastily prepared a Press release, setting out his group's response to the BMA development. It read:

Keep Breathing welcomes the decision by the BMA medical ethics committee to reconsider its position on the Health of the Nation Bill. In association with the National Pensioners' Forum and other senior citizens' welfare groups, we repeat our demand for the inhuman Bill to be scrapped immediately.

We also renew our demand for the urgent appointment of a Parliamentary Commissioner for the Elderly, to protect our most vulnerable citizens from any future threats of similar lethal legislation, and to represent their interests at all levels of political decision-making.

He resisted the temptation to enlarge on the extreme vulnerability of Alzheimer's sufferers under the proposed Bill since it was always advisable to keep Press releases succinct. Long, rambling expositions only antagonised hard-pressed sub-editors. Bernard had gone home so he emailed the statement to the Press Association. As he was about to return to the kitchen and help Barbara prepare dinner, the study telephone rang. It was Dr Armstrong.

"Hi George. We've just been discussing your devious BMA colleagues."

The NPF chief laughed loudly. "What a bunch of pussyfooters! Hippocrates must be turning in his grave."

"Do doctors still take the Hippocratic Oath?"

"Not in its original form, more's the pity. If they did they'd never have got involved with the Bill in the first place."

"Let's get after them while they're having second thoughts," Howard suggested.

"You're right." George's gentlemanly voice became urgent. "Strike while the iron's hot. Could we get a mailing shot out to every doctor before Christmas…urging them to come to their senses? We could split the cost, if you're agreeable."

Howard did a mental calculation. There was still a healthy credit balance in the fighting fund. Many tax rebels were insisting on serving their prison terms as a matter of principle, rather than letting the fund pay their fines.

"Okay, let's go for it."

"It'd give them something to think about when the pressure's off over the holiday period."

"Good thinking, George. I'll work on a rough draft and get back to you tonight."

*   *   *

It was a wild, stormy evening and St Chad's was deserted when Barbara pushed open the heavy studded door and crossed herself with holy water from the stoup in the porch. Walking slowly and silently along the carpeted aisle, she reached the altar and genuflected reverently. Then she knelt in a side chapel adorned with flowers and lit a candle before offering prayers of thanksgiving to Saints Cosmas and Damian, patron saints of doctors, for the BMA's change of heart.

Although Howard had advised her not to read too much into the surprising announcement, it was the sign she had been praying for – that God in His wisdom would intervene to halt the evil Bill. She realised it was only a tiny step forward but it was a ray of light in a murky world, a world which the Pope had described as "in the hands of fallen people".

How right he was. At every turn she was confronted by them. From her hospital's management downwards, she was routinely victimised and abused for refusing to take part in abortions. If patients asked to see a priest, management would invoke the politically correct bureaucracy of the Data Protection Act to prevent it. She would have to smuggle a priest in regardless. This had involved her in disciplinary action more than once, when atheist colleagues reported her. Each time, the matter was quietly dropped by the health authority. The knowledge that her husband was a journalist likely to expose its members' machinations and jeopardise their overpaid sinecures might have had something to do with it.

Anti-Christian bigotry was everywhere. There was no escape. She was appalled by the depraved images you could access on the internet, which she regarded as an instrument of evil. Television was almost as bad. Even her favourite soaps seemed to be all about drug-taking, promiscuity, violence and, creeping in recently, the demonising of old people, with dark hints of euthanasia. If you could escape the foul-mouthed chefs, you'd find aggressive atheist professors denouncing the Vatican and tin-pot satirists abusing their freedom of artistic expression to vilify Christianity. For as long as she could remember it had been the same...always Christians under attack, never Muslims or other religions. The fanatical academics and grubby satirists were too concerned for their own skins. Basically, they were cowards.

Even here at St Chad's, unbelievable though it seemed, disturbing forces were closing in. Some parishioners – liberal Catholics, they called themselves – told her they supported euthanasia and assisted suicide, challenging Church teaching on the sanctity of human life from conception to natural death. They referred her to 'end-of-life assistance' sites on the internet all of which, she found, advocated physician-assisted death as a compassionate means of ending unbearable suffering. But her nursing experience told her that sophisticated palliative care offered a more compassionate end for terminally ill patients than killing them.

That's what assisted suicide would lead to. People would be pressured into killing themselves. If that failed, they would be forced into it. Which was the same as killing them. Her internet research threw up the alarming views of weirdos like Mary Warnock, Jack Kevorkian and Philip Nitschke, Australia's gruesome 'Dr Death'. She unearthed the bizarre Hemlock Society, an Exit International group urging compulsory euthanasia for the over-80s, and the Church of Euthanasia, led by a self-confessed Satanist.

The more digging she did, the more chilling it became. In states where euthanasia had been legalised – Belgium, The Netherlands and Oregon – there were horror stories of elder abuse by relatives with a financial interest in a patient's death, of depressed teenagers being encouraged to kill themselves and of demented old people being 'terminated' without their consent.

When she reported these unexpected results to the liberal Catholics, it silenced them – but only for a time. They came back at her again with the same blinkered arguments. It was like swimming against the current, though at least she was still afloat and one day the tide would turn.

Right now she had her own mission – to pray for a successful outcome to the BMA's crucial ballot on the euthanasia Bill. On her way out she genuflected and glanced at her candle among rows of others, glowing symbols of hope in a dark and troubled world. Each represented someone's silent prayer for divine intervention.

It was better to light a candle than curse the darkness.

*   *   *

There is nothing quite like a deadline to concentrate the mind, as any journalist facing that intractable, ruthless enemy will tell you. Within a few days, the BMA would be balloting the nation's doctors on their response to the Health of the Nation Bill and it was vital that Howard and George got their feet in the surgery door first. By telephone and email they worked throughout the night on their joint mailing shot and as dawn arrived, with the coffee pots drained, they felt they had achieved a powerful briefing.

It took the form of a personalised letter and was headed with the first canon of the Hippocratic Oath, no longer sworn by doctors but still their unwritten credo:

DO NO HARM

Bearing in mind that all physicians were busy people who received a high volume of mailings from drug companies and with little time to read them, it was agreed that while the message had to be compelling, it should be kept simple. It read:

Dear Doctor

Our government faces dire financial problems and is turning against its old people to solve them. To comply with a misconceived UN resolution and to reduce demand on the welfare budget, its Health of the Nation Bill calls for assisted 'terminal sedation'

166

for your patients when their 15-year pension provision expires – *whether they are terminally ill or not*. In other words, social euthanasia, regardless of your clinical judgment and professional care.

What did the old Hippocratic Oath tell you about this intrusion of totalitarian politics into your special area of expertise? It instructed:
Never do deliberate harm to anyone for anyone else's interest;
Keep the good of your patient as the highest priority;
Avoid violating the morals of your community.
The misconceived Bill represents a direct assault on human life, personal autonomy and basic morality in a civilised society. Those who do not consent to end their lives 'to save the planet' are offered a cynical opt-out by way of a reduced pension they cannot hope to live on – a repugnant form of coercion.
But our greatest concern is for your dementia patients whose understanding of the Bill is negligible. This most vulnerable group would become the Bill's prime target. As their caring physician, you are their last hope. We appeal to you not to fail them.
Please vote against this monstrous legislation in the BMA ballot.
Yours sincerely
Keep Breathing and NPF Coalition

Bernard, their willing workhorse, would help Howard process the letter as an urgent priority through a leading direct mail agency after William had cooked everyone's breakfast. All that remained now was to ask Barbara to pray that the postal service delivered at least most of the mailing on time.

Then take his medication and go to bed.

SEVENTEEN

Five million for a knighthood...Adrian Lennox couldn't believe it. What was the Phoenix Party *doing* with all the money? Last year the going rate had been three million. The *Pandora* anchor man had been tempted then and they'd even given him their secret Swiss bank account number for his 'donation'. But the deal fell through at the last minute. A son by one of his mistresses had got into trouble with the Drugs Squad. Supplying, they claimed. It had cost him an arm and a leg to get them to drop the charges.

That was his problem basically, he reflected, as a smiling air hostess brought him more vintage champagne and he admired her shapely legs. Too many mistresses. Which was why he wanted a knighthood – not for himself or his services to broadcasting, such as they were, but for his long-term, long-suffering partner, Rose. Rosie had shared his life and a series of relatively humble homes for 30 years as he'd struggled to make a name for himself as a TV satirist.

The couple now enjoyed all the trappings of wealth, including the obligatory neo-Georgian stately pile in Oxshott, with celebrities and professional footballers for neighbours. But acceptance by the 'old money' – the genuine gentry who regarded them as vulgar *nouveau riche* from the murky world of television – still eluded them. What was needed to seal their social status was a title, if only for Rosie's sake.

Rosie knew about his affairs but realised they meant nothing; it was just the testosterone talking. In all their years together she'd never said a word about them – not once even hinted at marriage. If anyone deserved the title of Her Ladyship, she did. Lady Rose Lennox…there was a sophisticated ring to it that suited her style and elegance, albeit slightly fading now in middle age.

But five million! That was the price a Westminster insider had told him, strictly off the record, just before his flight had taken off for the Bahamas. He gazed down from his seat in first class at the featureless Atlantic far below. Maybe he should settle for a lesser honour. An OBE perhaps. As a thrusting young iconoclast the idea of a medal glorifying the defunct British Empire would have earned scornful mockery but the years and a burgeoning bank account had mellowed him. If you couldn't beat the Establishment, what you did was join them. Adrian Lennox had joined with enthusiasm.

An OBE might do to be going on with, he mused. Posing in top hat and tails with Rosie in her finery outside Buck House would certainly enhance his celebrity status. But that's what it would have to be – an interim measure until he could afford the ultimate status symbol. The going rate for the 'God and Empire' medal was down to less than a quarter of a million since that decrepit old hack, Howard Mitchell, had defiled his by tossing it into the Thames. How ungrateful could you get? After they'd given it him for free!

It was hardly surprising that OBEs, CBEs and other minor awards were still struggling to recover from the severe image problem that Mitchell's much-publicised act of vandalism had caused. Oiks all over the country were sending them back to the Palace, attaching them to their dogs' collars or melting them down into rings and lucky charms. No, he decided, the OBE had become forever tarnished. It had lost its prestigious shine, even as an interim measure. Nothing less than the kosher knighthood would do.

The ageing multi-millionaire satirist reclined in his luxurious leather armchair and adjusted its headrest, careful not to dislodge his hairpiece, and savoured the champagne. He was going to need all his charm in the forthcoming interview with the Prime Minister. If he played his cards right, she might nominate him for the precious prize, if not for free then at least at a decent discount.

Dame Jessica was officially visiting the playground of the super rich on a fact-finding mission, although the precise nature of the facts she was supposed to be finding remained a closely guarded secret. The Australian feminist-turned British politician liked to keep even her closest advisers guessing – a trait she exploited to great advantage since becoming Prime Minister. There were rumours she was about to meet the American Secretary of State, which was as high as any UK prime minister could aspire in the White House hierarchy these days.

Speculation was rife that she would be ordered to increase British military support for the US invasion of Sri Lanka if she wanted a share of the area's vast potential oil revenues. The meeting theory seemed unlikely, however, since she was with her long-term partner, Meg Meredith, the soap star and euthanasia activist, whose high profile would be sure to upset the Americans. They had passed a law in 2015 barring all homosexuals from public office. It was more likely that the pair were just enjoying another freebie holiday at the taxpayer's expense – the prerogative of prime ministers, deputy prime ministers and their paramours since time immemorial.

Lennox had been sent with a film crew (all of whom, including the producer, were languishing in economy class) to interview Jessica in her exotic Nassau location because of the controversy the Health of the Nation Bill was generating back home. The BBC's hierarchy had detected a swing in public opinion since the BMA's decision to return the issue to the melting pot. Could it be possible that Phoenix's progressive reforms were in danger of defeat? This unthinkable prospect called for no less a celebrity than Adrian Lennox to redress the balance in a 'keynote' interview with the Prime Minister on *Pandora*.

Once the decks had been cleared and Meg packed off to the beach, surrounded by bodyguards, the interview was set up on the terrace of the pair's luxury apartment, with exotic plants and palm trees in the background. Lennox went through his 'running order' with Dame Jessica. The programme would go out live, with a seven-second time lapse to delete inadvertent expletives. The deal was that their discussion would be limited to the Health of the Nation Bill. Under no circumstances would he ask her about Sri Lanka. If he did, she would terminate the interview immediately.

After pina coladas and rum and Cokes all round with the crew and the usual warm-up banter off camera, they were finally set to roll. On cue, Lennox adopted the

171

sardonic smirk he reserved for all politicians he was about to hang out to dry but this time it would be different. He would go easy on her. He had his reasons.

"Welcome to this special edition of *Pandora*, direct from the Bahamas," he intoned in the fruity baritone familiar to Britain's viewing public. "Tonight we talk to the Prime Minister, Dame Jessica Sykes, about the storm brewing over the Health of the Nation Bill – her controversial scheme for euthanasia on the NHS."

He turned to the portly politician, seated opposite in her holiday attire of open neck floral blouse with a chunky coral necklace and tight white skirt a size too small. "Prime Minister, at this time of growing crisis in Britain, it seems doctors may be having second thoughts about your Bill. What's your view on the BMA's decision to ballot their members?"

Dame Jessica wouldn't see 60 again. Even though she'd had her roots dyed, the severe, swept back brown hair and hard, piggy eyes slightly too close together, served to emphasise the fact. But her image consultant had told her she looked younger when she smiled. She beamed indulgently at Adrian as if he were her favourite son.

"It's their democratic right, of course. I'd be the first to defend it. But I have to say that they're not helping to move our vital reform forward." Her voice was light, with a slight Queensland twang. "They need to be absolutely clear of the importance of our Bill. I'm confident they'll make the right decision in their ballot."

Lennox wasn't so sure. "Sceptics are saying the Bill makes no distinction between patients who are terminally ill and those whose symptoms are controlled. They're concerned it can apply to elderly people who are in no pain at all."

172

The Dame's smile changed to an expression of caring solidarity with the suffering. "Modern medical research indicates that most pensioners are in pain of one kind or another. Many will tell you they've reached the end of their natural lives...that they're tired of life and would be happy to end it themselves but don't have the courage. When I reach that stage, I'd be only too willing to fade away in pain-free peace and comfort...wouldn't you?"

Her inquisitor had been around too long to be distracted from the point that easily. He pressed on: "These doctors say the Bill is at odds with the principles of the Hippocratic Oath...to do no harm...to regard their patients' welfare as their highest priority."

"The Hippocratic Oath went out with the Ark but our Bill is in no way at odds with it. In fact, it *does* place patients' welfare as the highest priority. It offers compassionate closure to their painful lives. How can that be doing harm?"

"It all depends on your definition of harm, doesn't it," Lennox observed. "Doctors say they still follow the Hippocratic law that prohibits the taking of life."

As ever, she'd done her homework. "They're quoting the original Greek version, which dates back to 400 BC. There happen to be other versions of the Oath, more relevant to modern medicine. The American version, that of the great physician, Louis Lasagna, actually sanctions taking life if it's considered to be in patients' interests."

"That's a subjective judgment, surely."

"Yes, but based on the latest advances in medical science. The original Hippocratic Oath prohibited abortion, for example. Nowadays most doctors have no

173

problem with that. In 400 BC there were no anaesthetics, antibiotics, heart bypasses, organ transplants...but this is the 21st century. We take these things for granted. I'm all in favour of medical ethics as long as they keep pace with medical science."

Lennox glanced at the notes on his running order. "Medical science is not the same as euthanasia. You're using euthanasia as a tool of population control. Can that be morally right?"

"The situation is not of our making. Our hand has been forced by the United Nations. They've alerted us to a worst case scenario if global warming continues to decimate crops. In Britain we import half our food and energy. Supplies are already starting to dry up. We've had to prepare contingency plans for food rationing as well as more power cuts. There's only one logical solution – to reduce the number of citizens in our overcrowded islands..."

"But isn't that a form of social engineering?"

"It's *civilised* social engineering by way of enlightened reforms such as our Health of the Nation Bill."

"I accept the need for drastic measures but why target frail old people?" Lennox asked. "Why not tackle birth control instead of death control...step-up contraception or even abortion if necessary?"

"Contraception and abortion would be counter-productive. They would reduce the number of future taxpayers. We need to reduce those taking money *out* of the system – not those paying in. The Health of the Nation Bill does just that." The Prime Minister paused and took a sip of water from a glass on the cane table between them. At the end of round one she was clearly ahead on points.

Lennox also took a sip from his own glass (gin looked identical to water) and ploughed on: "This is the first time obligatory euthanasia has been considered in Britain…religious leaders say it's unethical and immoral. Doesn't that bother you?"

"There's a first time for everything. Religious leaders don't have to grapple with the government's economic problems. They should refrain from interfering…we don't interfere with their prayers and their hymns. The Maturity Contract is a first, as you rightly say. But it's neither unethical nor immoral. It's a logical, compassionate measure with a cast-iron safeguard. People can opt out if they wish. They have the right to choose."

"If they can afford to lose half their pension."

"The reductions are five per cent a year. They're given ample time to adjust their financial circumstances."

"Most elderly people rely on their meagre state pension…they have no other means of support. They say it's not enough to live on *now*…by cutting it still further you're effectively squeezing the life out of them. You're bleeding them dry before you kill them off!"

"You're using very emotive language, Adrian. The harsh reality is the state can only do so much to support its ageing population." She spread her hands in a gesture of helplessness. "The bottomless well has run dry. Families will have to accept their fair share of responsibility."

"And those without families…?"

"There are many admirable charities devoted to the care of the elderly. They can be relied on to help in cases of genuine hardship."

"You talk about genuine hardship...what about those suffering from dementia, Alzheimer's...people unable to get their heads round the Maturity Contract?"

"The Mental Capacity Act of 2005 covers terminal health care for the cognitively impaired. They are protected by a Lasting Power of Attorney – an LPA as they're called. The same safeguard will apply to the Health of the Nation Bill."

Lennox knew all about 'safeguards'. He suspected many vulnerable patients in NHS psychiatric wards would inevitably slip through the safety net. He was about to ask what would happen to them when the producer hissed in his earpiece: "Meg's just told us...the old girl's only here for her tax-free property investments. Get after her."

He had his orders. Forget the softly-softly approach and his forlorn hope of a reduced-price knighthood. It was time to cut to the chase. Dropping the bland, fawning interview[1] style he switched on his more familiar intimidating manner: "Let's get down to basics, Dame Jessica...isn't *money* the real reason for the Health of the Nation Bill – not a worthy desire to save the planet? Aren't you just using the UN resolution as a convenient excuse to save millions on state pensions?"

If she was startled by the abrupt change of style she didn't show it. "I would absolutely refute that..."

As she paused for breath, Lennox cut in: "Critics are saying your last loan from the IMF is running out...that you've been told there's no more cash in the pipeline."

Her piggy eyes narrowed indignantly. "I can assure you..."

---

[1] Known as the 'Parkinson technique' after a long-forgotten chat show host.

But the street fighter was in full flow: "…so you're turning on your weakest, most vulnerable citizens because you're desperate to raise additional revenue…"

"Utter nonsense…"

"…to fund the war in Sri Lanka."

He'd decided to call her bluff. It was a calculated risk. If she walked out, so be it. The show thrived on controversy. It would boost ratings. But he didn't think she would. He was right.

Her face had flushed under the make-up and as she took another drink of water, her tanned and manicured hand shook imperceptibly. For a moment it was touch and go. Then the wobble subsided and she said: "As I told you before we started, I'm not prepared to discuss Sri Lanka. All I will say is there is ample support for our boys there…we'll provide them with all it takes to restore peace and stability in the region."

Dame Jessica was aware of the almost nightly TV ritual of British soldiers returning home in coffins. She knew most had joined the army because it was the only job they could find. There were moments when she actually shared the nation's despair. But they soon passed. It would not be long before the heroic self-sacrifice of 'our boys' would be rewarded with the ultimate prize – a share of the abundant oil revenues soon to flow the country's way. Obviously, she couldn't say as much publicly so it was time to return to the 'threat to mankind' posed by over-population.

"As I was about to say before you interrupted me, we're talking about a global emergency here – a very real threat to the planet that transcends the tragedy of mental illness in old age and other domestic problems. In a few years, the world's population is likely to reach

9 billion and the vast majority of scientific opinion tells us this figure is totally unsustainable."

"Many demographic experts claim that figure is hypothetical," Lennox countered. "They say it's pure fantasy based on computer predictions that ignore natural disasters such as earthquakes, epidemics, nuclear wars, asteroid strikes…"

"I recognise there are imponderables but it's certainly not fantasy. The scientific consensus is overwhelming…that drastic action is needed *urgently* to reduce population levels." She noticed the producer's wrap signal and switched on her 'animated and impassioned' manner. "The United Nations have set us a realistic target on pain of sanctions. It's our duty as citizens of the world to meet it. Future generations will never forgive us if we don't."

The punch line was perfectly timed. She had the whole interview cut and dried. Lennox couldn't even claim a draw.

"Prime Minister, thank you for talking to us. We must now wait for the decision of the British Medical Association on what is literally a life-and-death issue for our most vulnerable citizens. With that, it's back to the studio in London."

*   *   *

So *that* was where the cash-for-honours slush money was going! Why hadn't he thought of it before, Lennox wondered during the post-interview inquest with the production team back at their hotel. Dame Jessica's fact-finding in the Bahamas tax haven concerned the value of her property portfolio. After a couple of tequilas too many, Meg had let slip to one of the security guards that her illustrious partner needed to sell one of her luxury beachfront apartment blocks.

She owned several in different names, all yielding astronomical rentals free of tax. The income would provide for a comfortable retirement once her days of conning a gullible British public were over. But now one had to be sold to meet Meg's crack cocaine addiction. The only reason Jessica was in Nassau was to instruct a real-estate company via several discreet third parties.

Lennox had no doubts about the authenticity of this information. Camera crews and production staff often knew more about what was going on in the world than he did. The problem was, it was impossible to prove any of it. But even if he could, and Jessica's non-dom, tax-free earner were to be exposed, it would cause only minor problems for the hard-nosed politician.

There was nothing illegal about it, after all. Hundreds of MPs had climbed aboard the gravy train years ago, lining their pockets at the taxpayers' expense. There'd be a short burst of phoney outrage in the two-faced media but it wouldn't be a resigning issue. Nobody resigned any more. The term 'honourable' to describe an MP fell into disuse after the sleaze scandal of 2009.

Lennox realised he could never prove any wrongdoing by the sly old Sheila or exert any pressure on her to realise his burning ambition of a knighthood. But after much thought and several gins he figured there might be another way. It would cost an arm and a leg, but what if he were to make an offer on her beachfront property…?

EIGHTEEN

Sally was feeling depressed. It wasn't like her. She'd finished her t'ai chi meditation for the day, which usually left her feeling calm and positive but this time, strangely, it hadn't lifted her at all. The black mood was still with her. There was no way she could work when she felt like this, and anyway the weather had closed in again, with the wind getting up, rattling the shutters of the former olive press that served as her studio. She turned up the room heater, made herself a cup of herbal tea and nibbled a sugar-free biscuit.

She thought of calling Eduardo but decided against. Perhaps later. He'd be busy in his gallery and his phone would almost certainly be switched off. It seemed to be switched off most of the time. Three weeks had passed since his last call and that had been strictly business – a possible commission that had slipped away leaving her hard up. She had been reduced to doing freelance work for advertising agencies, which made her even more depressed.

Of course, there was no telling where men were concerned, especially Spanish men, but intuition suggested he was losing interest and her intuition was rarely wrong. She couldn't blame him really. He'd been patient with her but, like most Spaniards, patience was not his strong point. He'd offered to marry her if she agreed to live permanently in Spain, a condition she regarded as unacceptable and even chauvinistic.

And yet...time was passing and her hormones were becoming increasingly demanding. Her deep yearning for a child had started to challenge the strength of her feminist convictions. Eduardo, after all, would make an admirable father. Perhaps she needed to compromise. She could live permanently in Spain and still make flying visits to see her family – as she did now. Eduardo would surely agree to that.

It was the finality of the arrangement that disturbed her, the cutting of the umbilical cord with her homeland. Deep down she knew she was being unrealistic. In a few short years, Britain had become financially and morally bankrupt. People were desperate to get out. Why did she want to get back in?

She resolved to call Eduardo later in the evening and accept his terms, if he was still interested. But when the time came to make the call, she found her smart phone battery was flat. Maybe it was a sign that she should keep her boyfriend on the back burner, where he evidently preferred to be. At least she'd be flying back to Britain for the Christmas holiday. Then she could consider the problem from a new perspective. That usually helped.

She turned over on her studio couch and sank into a deep sleep. She didn't dream of Eduardo. She dreamt of home.

*   *   *

Despite the combined efforts of the atheist/ liberal/humanist coalition to replace Christmas with a secular 'Winterval' festival, the Mitchell household's celebration of the birth of Jesus Christ followed the formula observed for 40 years without the slightest deviation. William still helped his father install the Norwegian spruce in the lounge, hung with streamers and multi-coloured balloons. Sally still decorated the tree with fairy lights, tinsel garlands, the ornaments and miniature angels she remembered from earliest childhood, and its crowning silver star. On Christmas Eve, Howard's mother – 'Great Gran' to them all – joined the family gathered round the Bluthner for carols, with Barbara at the keyboard, as the tantalising aroma of roast turkey wafted from the kitchen.

Howard might not have been the greatest believer in traditional values but when it came to Christmas he was prepared to defend them with his life against claims that the festival caused offence to minorities. It amazed him that, even when the minority groups in question denied any offence was caused – and actually welcomed the Christian message of peace and goodwill – the secular bigots kept repeating their mantra, like a needle stuck in an old gramophone record.

As Barbara said, causing offence to Christians seemed to have been overlooked. Because of this double standard, few intelligent people took the PC censors seriously. But they were not without friends on national television, where all traces of Christianity had long been purged – the sole exception being *Songs of Praise*, relegated to BBC4. Religious services and carols had gradually given way to recordings of rock concerts and, to rub salt into the wound, *Life of Brian* repeats.

Even the five minutes allowed annually to the Archbishop of Canterbury had been scrapped.

The sovereign's Christmas speech (renamed his Winterval speech by the BBC) was spared on condition that it contained no references to God. Despite this and Howard's gentle efforts to dissuade her, Great Gran refused to change the habit of a lifetime and insisted on tuning in. It turned out to be an unintentionally entertaining performance. The head of the world's most dysfunctional high-profile family waxed lyrical on the importance of family life while keeping a perfectly straight face. There was no shortage of public laughing stocks these days, Howard thought. With this exalted addition to their ranks, competition for the coveted John Prescott Memorial Prize was sure to intensify.

Even Great Gran had to laugh at the ludicrous charade but when it came to the sign-off line, "May the force be with you," (replacing the traditional "May God bless you all") her lifelong royalist sympathies began to wear thin. "Turn it off," she ordered Howard. "I've had enough of the hypocrite." And that was how the TV set remained – firmly switched off to prevent further poisoning of the festive season.

For Christmas dinner, Howard, Barbara and Sally were joined by William and Louise, who had now combed her hair and wore a red dress with a plunge neckline. She helped to cut up Great Gran's turkey so she could eat with one hand, and regularly topped up her wine glass. It was not long before the frail guest of honour looked remarkably less haggard under her paper hat.

They'd all been disappointed when Bernard, now one of the family, had cried off from the party. He was forgiven since Christmas was the only time he saw his brother and sister in Liverpool. Just make sure you're back in one piece in the New Year, they told him. Fred and Lilian were also excused. They were spending the holiday period in Brittany while checking out local properties. But try as they would, there was no way the close-knit family could overlook the most painful absentee: their eldest son.

Christopher had taken Amanda and their baby to spend Christmas with his wife's parents. Amanda had insisted, apparently. Howard and Barbara had not seen the couple or their grandson since the bust-up over Howard's OBE and it was clear the wounds had not healed. Their son did send them a card, 'from Chris, Amanda and Sebastian', which told its own story.

So as they pulled their illicit Christmas crackers (still widely available on the internet) without mishap and toasted 'absent friends' in champagne, the moment held a special sadness for the Mitchell family. In this season of glad tidings and great joy, tears were not far from Barbara's eyes. Or from Great Gran's.

*　　　*　　　*

Not unexpectedly, in view of the Met Office's forecast that global warming indicated a mild winter, 2019 began under several inches of ice and snow. A lull in activity at Keep Breathing's command centre in Howard's study prompted a rare night off so he and Bernard booked a taxi to their club for a frame or two and a jar or three.

Bernard had just potted the black to complete a break of 16 and was feeling pretty pleased with himself when Howard held up a hand and gestured to one of the TVs. The late night news bulletin had switched to the BMA's headquarters in a frosty Tavistock Square, where a male reporter was relaying the doctors' verdict on the government's desperate plan for population control:

"The BMA have just announced the result of their ballot on whether to participate in the Health of the Nation Bill, with its controversial Maturity Contract. The association's 160,000 doctors have voted by a large majority *not* to co-operate with the Bill in the event of it becoming law."

The statement brought cheers from Howard, Bernard and the predominantly grey heads grouped round the screen. Heedless of the Arctic conditions, crowds in square were equally buoyant as they pressed in on the TV camera crew. Reading with difficulty from his notes, the reporter added:

"The official statement, issued a few minutes ago by the BMA's general council, said that more than three-quarters of their members responded to the ballot, 85 per cent of whom rejected any further involvement with the Bill. It adds: 'Since the measure legalises assisted suicide for patients not terminally ill – and even for those considered healthy – the BMA regards it as incompatible with the medical profession's integrity'."

The mood of the moment was one of relieved celebration as the reporter interviewed opponents of the Bill, among them a jubilant Dr Armstrong, the NPF leader. He described the result as a historic victory not only for common sense but for basic humanity. Every doctor in the country had been alerted to the Bill's fatal flaws and they had taken the message on board. It was a long time since he'd felt proud to be a member of the medical profession.

Sylvia Pullar, the Bill's long-time spokesperson, was interviewed by the reporter immediately afterwards. She

185

described the outcome as deeply disappointing and a missed opportunity. But the feisty feminist struck an ominously defiant note. The fight was by no means over. It was the duty of responsible, forward-looking political leaders to persevere with their campaign, despite the reactionary forces ranged against them. They were not prepared to write-off their Bill.

The doctors had forced the government's hand and it would be necessary to consider a "fall-back position" they had hoped would not be necessary. Third Reading would be postponed while amendments were made. It sounded like the usual politician's ploy of talking up a pretty hopeless situation. Nobody was really listening.

They should have been.

*   *   *

For Barbara Mitchell, the BMA's decision to wreck the Health of the Nation Bill was due to one cause and one cause only – the power of prayer. It represented the climax of weeks of persistent pleading on her part, and by other members of St Chad's congregation whom she had enlisted in her spiritual campaign. God had heard their prayers and answered them; there was not the slightest doubt in her mind about that.

The day after the announcement, she roused her husband at the unearthly hour of 10 am and informed him they were both going to morning Mass at St Chad's to give thanks for the act of divine intervention. Howard's protestations were long and eloquent. What about the mailing shot produced by George Armstrong and himself...hadn't that had anything to do with the doctors' decision? The ongoing media campaign, with people willingly going to prison to support Keep

Breathing's message…the internet petition that had already attracted half a million signatures…didn't they play some part?

"Of course they did. But they're merely instruments of a higher purpose," was the confident reply. "There's a special reason we need to go to Mass today."

He levered himself painfully out of bed. "Go on."

"Don't you know what day it is?"

"It's Wednesday, isn't it?"

She sighed patiently. "It's January 24th…the feast day of St Francis de Sales."

"Francis who?"

She sighed again, this time more loudly. "Howard, I despair of you at times. St Francis de Sales…the patron saint of journalists. Today is his feast day. That's why we both have to go to Mass and give thanks for his intercession."

He felt suitably humbled. Somewhere in the recesses of his mind he knew about St Francis de Sales, but the muscular pain in his back and chest was not conducive to deep thought at the moment. Barbara had made her case and there was no arguing with her. They were going to Mass and that was that. As it happened, he remembered he needed to take a repeat prescription to the chemist's, so they could call at the Co-op pharmacy while they were out.

They sat in a pew half way to the altar and Howard adjusted his hearing aid to the 'loop' position, which always worked perfectly in church. Not that the experience helped him much. He heard but he failed to understand. He had a mental block when it came to spirituality and it worried him sometimes. Barbara was a highly intelligent woman. She had unreservedly embraced the concept of a loving Christian God in a world overflowing with wickedness. Why couldn't he even scratch the surface?

The bell rang and the congregation stood. Howard counted about 40 of them which, for a weekday, was impressive. The youthful Father Fitzgibbon strode in energetically, vestments swinging, before stooping to kiss the cloth on the altar with its two lighted candles. Not for the first time, Howard reflected on the strangeness of calling someone almost young enough to be your grandson, Father. Then everyone except Howard crossed themselves and the Mass began with the words all except Howard knew off by heart:

Priest: "The Lord be with you."

Congregation: "And with your spirit."

Ever the observer, Howard proceeded to pick holes in the repetitious nature of the liturgy, its meaning, as he freely admitted, passing well above his head. All the ritual kneeling, sitting and standing irritated him and aggravated his painful joints. Why couldn't they just do one thing and stick to it? At least, as it was a weekday Mass, there was no hymn singing which he always found acutely embarrassing. That meant the ordeal would be shorter and they'd soon be off to the Co-op to collect his repeat medication.

When they came to the homily, the priest gave a potted biography of the saint of the day, St Francis. During the 56 years of his life, the 16th century doctor of law had achieved many conversions to the Church at a time when it faced fierce hostility – rather like today. As a means of reaching people's hearts and minds, he began writing leaflets setting out Christian teaching. These were copied many times by hand, as printing had not been invented, and had a profound effect on the community. The power of the written word, when widely distributed, was established and the saint's tracts were seen as forerunners of today's newspapers.

He was canonised in Rome in 1665 and declared a Doctor of the Church in 1887 but when Pope Pious XI appointed him patron saint of journalists he probably handed him his toughest assignment, if the state of the modern profession was anything to go by. Barbara gave Howard a gentle nudge at that, and he had to smile. The priest was right there. Hacks were not the holiest of people. But as Alistair had taught him all those years ago, they were servants of the truth. So they must be doing something right. After all, didn't Jesus say: "I am the way, *the truth* and the life"?

Finally, they reached the Lord's Prayer and, after all the unfathomable responses, Howard was able to recite the familiar words along with everyone else. He found the prayer that followed, 'Deliver us Lord, we pray, from every evil...safe from all distress....' held a special significance in the light of recent events.

On the way out through the church porch they passed stacks of hymn books, parish notices, magazines and newspapers including *The Catholic Herald* and the *Tablet*. Barbara bought a *Herald* by placing coins in the slot of a wooden box. Then she took a copy of the *Tablet*, grimaced at the kitsch front cover and turned it face downwards. "Liberal Catholics," she explained. "What I call a contradiction in terms."

That was something else, Howard reflected, as they drove to the Co-op supermarket: the different factions in the church. It appeared to have become a house divided against itself, with conservative and liberal wings. As he understood it, the conservatives wanted to play by the rules and the liberals didn't. Apparently, Father Fitz was one of the dissidents, which seemed bizarre. To a neutral observer for whom theology was not his strongest suit, it was all baffling.

They had the usual wait at the Co-op while the pharmacy assembled Howard's package of blood pressure, arthritis and cholesterol drugs. The assistants knew him well from his regular visits and they'd joke that he was keeping them in business. Other supermarket staff, particularly the elderly shelf-stackers, recognised him from his TV appearances and wanted to shake his hand. "Keep breathing, Howard," they joked, little realising he sometimes needed an oral spray to help him do so. Life was full of such ironies, he thought. You just learned not to take them too seriously.

Of course, younger employees failed to recognise the grey, stooping figure in the twill cap and shabby anorak. You couldn't blame them. He wasn't their idea of a celebrity, after all. He paid for a lager six-pack for Bernard and the checkout girl held the crisp new banknote up to the light to check it wasn't a forgery. When she handed him his change including a grubbier lower denomination note, he took it, held it up to the light and examined it carefully. It seemed to annoy the girl although it amused Howard no end. Like all newspapermen, he had a childish sense of humour.

Barbara pretended to be embarrassed. "Really, Howard, there was no need for that."

"But there *was*," he insisted. "Do I look like the sort of person who'd pass a counterfeit banknote?"

His wife looked him up and down critically. "Do you really want me to answer that?"

*   *   *

There's nothing quite like a bracing stroll along Brighton promenade in the middle of February to improve the circulation and sharpen the appetite. But after some 15 minutes battling against a stiff breeze blowing off the Channel, four intrepid figures in padded coats, mufflers, woolly hats and a cavalry twill cap staggered into a seafront shelter and collapsed on a wooden bench.

Barbara and Howard were staying with Fred and Lilian over the weekend. They had not visited the Craigs for several months and were anxious to sound out their emigration plans. To their surprise, they were well advanced.

"We've surfed the net and decided on a little farmhouse near Nantes, in Brittany," Lilian told them when they'd all got their breath back. "It's a beautiful place…all mod cons…three bedrooms…so you can come and stay any time. We've put a deposit on it and they're holding it for us."

Fred had been a PE instructor in the RAF during the 1960s but time and his later career as a forestry manager had taken its toll on his muscular physique. Now a hunched and wasted figure, he walked with the aid of a stick and frequently wiped his mouth with a handkerchief. "We're flying over next month to view it…sign up for our residential permit," he said, his words slurred and hesitant.

Barbara was surprised at the speed of their decision. "It's a big move to make, Dad…at your time of life. Are you sure you're up to it, the two of you?"

Lilian took her husband's wrinkled hand and replied for him. "We think we're doing the right thing, Barbara. This country's finished. It's very sad. We remember when it was a good place to live…a country you could be proud of."

Fred wiped his mouth again. "Now we're just ashamed of it."

"We'll have no regrets," Lilian added. "Except for leaving you both and the family, of course. But you'll all come and visit us, won't you?"

"Try keeping us away," was Howard's answer.

"They've even got a Women's Institute in Nantes and a lot of members are English, so it'll be just like home in a way. The health care there is far superior. We've checked and Fred'll be able to get the drugs he needs…that's what decided it really."

The sprightly great grandmother, her windswept white hair tucked tightly under a brown woolly hat, smiled gently. "We've just got to wait now until we sell our flat…"

"And they give us our residential permit," Fred reminded her.

"Then this couple of aged rosbifs will be off to the land of garlic and frog's legs. So we'd better start swotting up our French."

"I can't see Dad eating frog's legs, somehow," Barbara laughed.

"No way," Fred said with feeling and perfect clarity.

But when they called at a seafront café later for tea and doughnuts, he kept dabbing his lips with his handkerchief and it was noticeable that his speech had become increasingly slurred in the few months since their last meeting. He was still his cheerful old self and there was no sign of unsteadiness or mood swings, but Lilian's fears over the onset of Alzheimer's appeared well-founded.

There were tears all round as Howard and Barbara took their leave on the Monday morning. They could still keep in touch by telephone and pop over to see them any time, they were reminded. The grandchildren would always be welcome to visit and perhaps when their great-grandson was a bit older, Christopher could bring him as well. They hadn't seen the boy for ages. And anyway, they wouldn't be going just yet; not for a few months at least.

Two silvery-headed figures waved from their apartment window as their daughter and son-in-law drove away in their old Rover. Barbara waved back until they turned the corner and were out of sight. She settled back in her seat and adjusted her seatbelt. "It's very sad, Howard...being forced to emigrate at their time of life. Are they doing the right thing, do you think?"

Howard was full of admiration for his in-laws. "Absolutely. You've got to hand it to them. They need to get out while the option's still open."

"Do you think it'll soon be closed?"

"That's the consensus among our members. A lot of them are already fleeing the country. If the trickle grows into a flood our great leaders are sure to find a way of stopping them..."

"But there's no panic, is there?"

"Not yet."

"I mean, the BMA have killed the Bill, haven't they?"

"This time round, maybe. But you know how these things work. Jessica will soon be back with another. Older and wiser people have heard it all before. That's why they're getting out...while there's still time."

Barbara sighed and closed her eyes. "Surely things can't get much worse...can they?"

He negotiated a roundabout and headed for the A23. "I wouldn't bet on it."

NINETEEN

This time, the politicians needed an exceptionally good day to bury the bad news. It seemed a long time coming. A terrorist outrage, an earthquake or a major plane crash failed to materialise. So they had to settle for a disaster of almost equal magnitude: the failure of the English football team to qualify for the European championship – and the summary sacking of the team's manager as a result.

Of course, the newspapers fell for the ploy. All except one covered their front pages with 'Day of Shame'-type headlines (the team had lost their crucial match against Malta, 5-0), pictures of the disgraced team manager heading for the Caribbean with a handsome payoff cheque, and agonised speculation over his successor. But the real Day of Shame story was lurking just below the surface.

The odd paper out was *The Announcer*. Its editor, Hugo Michaelson, who had friends in places almost as high as Barbara Mitchell's, had received a tip that an announcement was about to be made signalling vast social change and even eclipsing football as the major news story. It came minutes before the nationals' first editions rolled off the presses. A low-key and cleverly disguised statement released to the Press Association declared that, after careful consideration, it had been decided to amend the Health of the Nation Bill at its Standing Committee Stage. Following the BMA's decision to withdraw support, an alternative strategy was proposed "as a measure of last resort".

The NHS would be extended to include a new profession of state-registered thanatologists. These specialists would need to pass a training programme and join a professional association. They would operate in regional clinics 'subject to stringent health and safety regulations' but would also provide a fully mobile, 24-hour service to hospitals, care homes and private houses. The amendment would be proposed at the forthcoming meeting of the Standing Committee, when the Bill was expected to be approved before proceeding directly to Third Reading. Voting in the Commons debate would be conducted along party lines subject to a three-line whip.

That was it. No mention of terminal sedation or the usual assertions of the Bill's crucial importance. By keeping the statement brief and couched in euphemistic technical terms, the government's spin merchants hoped the public would fail to see through it, at least until football fever had subsided. Few people would know what a thanatologist was. Even fewer would bother to find out.

Michaelson was a notable exception. He consulted his dictionary and read:

Thanatology: the scientific study of death;

Thanatography: a narrative of death;

Thanatologist: a scientific practitioner of death.

Devious to the last, New Phoenix had found a euphemism for a state-licensed suicide collaborator.

*   *   *

With hindsight, Hugo recognised it had been a mistake to play down Howard Mitchell's Keep Breathing campaign. He'd allowed personal animosity to blur his professional judgment. But this was no time for self-recrimination. He was facing yet another run-in with the culture of death. Battle lines needed to be hastily drawn up. With less than an hour to go before *The Announcer's* second edition, he decided to completely rejig Page One. All mention of football was removed apart from a small single-column picture of the disgraced England manager happily posing with two voluptuous young ladies at Heathrow Airport and a cross reference to 'Malta meltdown – see Sports section'.

Irene Thomas, the social affairs editor, was delegated to write the splash, leading with the 'thanatologists' announcement and picking up on extensive background material on the controversial Bill. The subs would tag on quotes from supporters and opponents, being hastily solicited by news desk reporters.

The splash sub's headlines almost wrote themselves:

New Phoenix's answer to the population crisis

WE'LL HELP YOU TO DIE

Picture desk supplied most recent shots of Sylvia Pullar, Dame Jessica Sykes and Dr George Armstrong, plus the

197

famous image of Howard Mitchell trashing his ONEBE. Despite regrets over playing down Keep Breathing there was no way Hugo could forgive its leader for depriving him of 'his' gong. He approved all the pictures except the one of Howard, which he swept impatiently into a waste paper basket.

Then he switched on his computer and reached into his desk drawer for the bottle. It was time for another landmark editorial:

The new Jews

They're called thanatologists. It's a word few of us are familiar with. It means 'practitioners of death'. Having failed to persuade the BMA of the legitimacy of obligatory euthanasia, our great social reformers now propose to bypass doctors altogether. The job is to be handed over to a new profession whose sole purpose will be to help pensioners broken by the Maturity Contract to kill themselves.

These so-called specialists, no doubt recruited from our rising class of politically correct control freaks with a morbid desire to help others die, will perform their duties in special clinics 'subject to stringent health and safety regulations' – a cynical oxymoron that would be laughable if it were not highly offensive.

But in cases where patients are unable to attend, an angel of death will arrive, not on a white chariot but in a white van to assist their 'life closure procedure' in the comfort of their own homes. We face a scenario which until recently would have been regarded as a nightmare of neo-Nazi malevolence.

The Health of the Nation Bill is a first step on the slippery slope of eugenics. The policy has been tried before, notably in 1930s Germany, with unspeakable consequences.

Of course, it would be more civilised this time, mental brutality in the form of subtle economic pressure replacing the physical kind. Nothing as crude as ghettoes or gas chambers. But the end result would be just as deadly. Those who ignore history are destined to repeat it. Only a free vote for MPs in the forthcoming debate will protect pensioners from becoming the new Jews.

TWENTY

The Mitchells held their council of war in their dining room, a haven of peace and calm in an ominously threatening world. Seated round the polished mahogany oval table were Howard, Barbara, Bernard, William and George Armstrong, who had driven over from Hay-on-Wye in his Land-Rover the day after the shock announcement.

Howard's opening words to the meeting were: "This means war," a phrase that sometimes held humorous connotations but this time nobody was smiling. "Just when we thought the doctors had seen them off, the euthanasia merchants have raised the stakes. We need to change our tactics...make them take us seriously. Passive protests haven't worked."

George nodded. "Our joint lobby for a select committee on their wretched Bill fell on deaf ears. Letters to MPs have ended up in their waste bins. They've ignored our emails and voicemail messages."

"And our members are going to jail in vain," Bernard lamented. "That's very hard on them and their families. Ditching their gongs was one thing but making that kind of personal sacrifice and seeing nothing come of it...well, it's demoralising."

"So what do we do?"

William had an idea. "Sabotage their death vans."

It was a moment of light relief. "We're all too old," George laughed. "And in any case there'll be hundreds of them – all unmarked."

Howard answered his own question. "I'll tell you what we do…we get mobilised. Plan B – Operation Scooter – a strategy for direct action that'll paralyse central London. On the day of the Third Reading, a rolling blockade of supporters' scooters will drive up to 10 Downing Street to present our online petition in documentary form. How many signatures have we got so far, Bernard?"

"Over a million, believe it or not. We'll need several sacks for the printouts."

"Then we'll all drive along Whitehall at a top speed of eight miles an hour and fan out into surrounding streets up to Trafalgar Square, bringing traffic to a standstill." He produced a map of central London and indicated streets where the rolling roadblock would be likely to cause the greatest chaos.

Bernard and George had sounded out members of Keep Breathing and the NPF on the plan and been impressed by the positive response. But it was the first Barbara and William had heard of it.

William was all in favour. "Great idea, Dad. Go for it…at least they can't nick you for speeding!"

Barbara was less enthusiastic. "I thought you could only drive those scooters on pavements. You'll be arrested, the lot of you."

George reassured her. "It's all perfectly legal. Some mobility scooters can only be driven on the pavement but what we're talking about here are models licensed for the road. I've brought one to show you."

She sighed resignedly. Her husband was embarking on another of his publicity stunts and nothing she could say would make any difference. But that didn't stop her from trying. "Aren't you all asking for trouble? I mean, men of your age…"

"There'll be women too," George assured her. "We've canvassed all our members, and all yours, and we've found lots of women with road-legal scooters."

"But they're all *old*, George. You know as well as I do that these demos can get out of hand. Things go wrong. Then the police start throwing their weight about…you know how violent they can be…"

"They're still careful when they see the TV cameras," Howard reminded her. "There'll be plenty of Press in attendance, I'll make sure of that. It'll be a peaceful protest but highly disruptive. We expect about 500 scooters to turn up, from all over the country."

"How will they all get there, they're only battery-powered aren't they?"

"Most of them fit in vans or car boots," George told her. "I've got one in my Land-Rover. Come on, let's have a look."

They adjourned the meeting to the driveway and watched as George unloaded a top-of-the-range electric scooter from his Land-Rover. With a few deft motions, it was assembled and the sprightly NPF chairman drove it sedately backwards and forwards to demonstrate the vehicle's remarkable manoeuvrability.

"It's a Cordoba Roadrider…quite nippy," he said, dismounting. "I borrowed it off a disabled friend. He won't be able to get to the demo so he kindly let me use it. It'll do 0 to 8mph in 4.5 seconds," he laughed. "Front suspension, indicators, beefed-up brakes, front and rear lights, adjustable seat…very comfortable. But, like all these machines, it's got a limited range between battery charges. So we'll have to concentrate our fire power on a narrow area. We'll also need plenty of back-up from our support teams on the day."

"That's been made clear to all our volunteers," Bernard said, as he took over for a test drive. "Everyone knows where to park their cars for a smooth getaway afterwards."

Howard turned to his sceptical wife. "I know I can rely on you as my support team, my dear," he said with the mischievous grin she remembered from way back.

Her eyebrow arched a trifle higher. "I had a feeling something like that might be coming."

His voice grew more persuasive. "Look, we do need to do this…to show Jessica we've got some muscle. If there's one thing politicians respect it's the power to stop the traffic. This is our secret weapon – scooter power!"

Barbara turned back to the house to hide her unease. "I'll make some tea."

She watched them through the kitchen window as she waited for the kettle to boil. They were taking it in turns to ride the scooter round the back garden, across the frost-covered lawn and in between the beds of frozen rose bushes, without a care in the world – just like schoolboys.

It would be a rather more challenging scenario when the time came to halt London's traffic. She feared heavy casualties among the gallant volunteers – not so much from police brutality as from natural causes. After all, the reason they drove round on mobility scooters in the first place was because they were immobilised. What would happen if they needed urgent medical treatment?

In Howard's case alone, she was worried about the demo bringing on his angina. Emergency first aid facilities would need to be on hand throughout the entire demonstration. She would supervise these herself with the help of nursing colleagues. Howard would need to agree as a condition of her support.

Yet, despite all her doubts, she realised drastic measures had now become unavoidable since the government was determined to push through its ruthless legislation. As Howard used to say about industrial disputes, you had to speak to people in the language they understood. You had to be as determined as they were. It was pointless appealing to people's better nature when they didn't have one.

That was always the sticking point for Barbara. She believed everyone, even MPs, had a better nature. If you persevered long enough, you'd find it and meet them on common ground. Her optimism was the by-product of prayer – prayer that had sustained her family through all Howard's hazardous assignments. She never had any doubt about that – until now.

Just when it seemed the power of prayer had again been vindicated by the BMA's decision, events had conspired against her. The sinister introduction of thanatologists was a bitter blow to her faith. So much for her friends in high places, Howard had teased. They'd kicked her in the teeth when she needed them most. It was just his colourful language but she had to admit it did feel a bit like that.

Her disappointment was the harder to bear because Father Fitzgibbon was not the sort of priest to provide much comfort. But at Mass the previous day she believed the Gospel reading carried a significant message. It had been about the man knocking on his neighbour's door asking for a loaf of bread to feed an unexpected guest. It was the middle of the night and his neighbour, tucked up in bed, didn't want to know. But the man kept knocking on his door and, in exasperation, he finally got up and gave him the bread so he would go away and leave him in peace. The message was obvious: you had to persist in your efforts if you expected God to give you a break.

TWENTY-ONE

They planned Operation Scooter with military precision, thanks to the retired colonels, captains and squadron leaders among members of the Keep Breathing and NPF Coalition. In an online conference, a master plan was devised for the rolling blockade on the day of the Health of the Nation Bill's Third Reading. For maximum impact, a pincer strategy was devised, targeting Trafalgar Square and Piccadilly Circus.

The first priority was to establish base headquarters within a mile or so radius of the operational area due to the scooters' limited range. Russell Square, with its surrounding long-stay car parks was selected as the ideal location. Two task forces would be deployed simultaneously with communication between them using the latest smart videophones.

Howard and Bernard would be in joint command of the main unit, heading south to deliver the groups' mammoth petition to 10, Downing Street, then returning to base through Trafalgar Square towards Aldwych, Kingsway and along Southampton Row. The second arm of the pincer movement would be led by George Armstrong and would make for Piccadilly

Circus along Shaftesbury Avenue, turning west into Regent Street and heading back to Russell Square via Euston Road and Woburn Place. In this way, an area of some five square miles of London's busiest streets would be effectively blockaded.

All volunteers were advised of the crucial importance of arriving in their cars at Russell Square well before the morning rush hour in order to secure their parking spaces. Once their scooters were unloaded and assembled, with their riders in position, they would await telephonic orders to take their places in the procession. Only then would they learn the operation's definitive route, since precise details were to remain secret until the final moment.

In keeping with military procedures laid down by the Geneva Convention and rigidly enforced by Barbara, full provision needed to be made for possible casualties. Middlesex Hospital lay within the target area and St Thomas's Hospital was less than two miles away. But bearing in mind the advanced age and frailty of many of the demonstrators, Barbara insisted on additional medical cover. Each column would be accompanied by a first aid vehicle with a red cross prominently displayed on a white background. George had offered his Land-Rover as one makeshift ambulance and Bernard had borrowed a large white van from a retired white van man to serve as the other.

Each vehicle would be staffed by qualified nurses and needed to be equipped with oxygen, insulin, asthma inhalers, nebulisers, glyceryl trinitrate sprays, the latest portable defibrillators, blood pressure machines and a comprehensive range of dressings and painkillers. By way of security, a team of young able bodied men recruited by William would walk the route acting as stewards.

To everyone's amazement, everything went smoothly. By dawn on the appointed Friday in early April, more than 450 Coalition Force volunteers, men and women from all over Britain, took up battle stations in their concrete car park bunkers. Some had travelled through the night from distant towns and villages in the Scottish Highlands. Some had driven from industrial cities in Northern and Central England, some from the Welsh valleys and others from comfortable retirement homes in the West Country and the Home Counties. All shared a single mission – to fight for justice for a marginalised generation and their basic human right to keep breathing.

Placards on the back of their scooters spelt out their message. They read: 'Not dead yet', 'Keep Breathing,' 'Grey Power rules', 'Life with dignity', 'Nurses Opposed to Euthanasia', 'Doctors Opposed to Euthanasia', 'Who says we've got no clout?' and other variations on a theme proving that they were alive and, if not exactly kicking, still strong enough to challenge their political persecutors.

Great care had been taken over preparation. The volunteers all carried a multi-function phone for smooth communications, bottled water and iron rations. They were dressed against the early morning chill in warm coats, mufflers, and an assortment of headgear ranging from cloth caps and woolly hats to crash helmets, deerstalkers and Commando berets. A bleary-eyed Howard, for whom dawn remained an indecent four-letter word, huddled into his sheepskin, his treasured cap at a rakish angle. Many of his troops sported war medals, awarded for military service and acts of gallantry – not to be confused with the outdated gong famously ditched by their leader.

With the patient discipline of their generation they waited, phones at the ready, for zero hour. Then, as the sun peered nervously over the East End skyline, Howard relayed the pre-arranged signal to move out with the laconic text message: '*Let the good times...ROLL!*' In serried ranks of three abreast and at a stately speed of 8mph, Granddad's (and Grandma's) Army swarmed onto the potholed streets of London.

Operation Scooter was up and running.

The main 250-strong unit carried boxes of the petition's printout pages in special panniers fitted to their scooters. On the slightest uphill gradient the paper's weight slowed their vehicles down still further. As they drove along Southampton Row and into High Holborn towards Shaftesbury Avenue, a cacophonous tailback of traffic built up within minutes.

Nelson turned a blind eye to the chaos as the procession trundled round Trafalgar Square and into Whitehall en route for the presentation of their mammoth petition. But heavily armed police officers manning security gates across the entrance to Downing Street took a more suspicious view. While they'd received advance notice of a group of people with a petition, they had not expected the group to stretch the length of Whitehall. After close inspection of the panniers and their contents, and a thorough body search, three war veterans wearing their campaign medals and black berets were allowed through. Progress was slow as the infirm trio struggled to unload the heavy boxes from the scooters. Several officers stood around watching but none offered to help.

Eventually, the petition was dumped on the famous doorstep and then an unscripted moment occurred. In recognition of the record total of signatories – the largest ever achieved by a public petition – Dame Jessica Sykes herself smilingly emerged to accept it as if it were a gift to be cherished. Which, in a way, it was. It allowed her to demonstrate for the benefit of the media penned on the opposite pavement, how much she really cared for the nation's senior citizens. Of course, once inside No 10, the voluminous petition would be immediately binned.

Meanwhile, the other half of the Coalition's pincer movement, a 200-strong detachment led by George Armstrong, dressed in combat fatigues (he'd served in the Medical Corps as a young man) on his top-of-the-range Cordoba Roadrider, was surging around Piccadilly Circus with a half-mile tailback of rush hour traffic in its wake. But they soon found themselves hemmed in along Regent Street. The police had arrived on motor-cycles.

Not that there was much they could do. While their training manuals included full instructions on detaining football hooligans, anarchists and animal rights fanatics, no mention was made of how to deal with your more mature agitators. You could hardly spray them with tear gas, drag them off their scooters and beat them over the head with your truncheon. You could try to arrest them on some dubious pretext – a charge to be conjured up afterwards in standard fashion – but that could take time. It would first be necessary to ask the rebel to dismount from his vehicle. This could involve shouting into his hearing aid which, in all probability, would be switched off.

Further time would elapse while the old codger fiddled around with the instrument, only to find that its battery had failed. A resourceful officer might then take out his notebook, tear off a page and write on it: PLEASE GET OFF YOUR VEHICLE, SIR, whereupon, after a lengthy search, its rider would discover he had not brought his reading glasses. All this, of course, might loosely be interpreted as obstructing a police officer in the performance of his duty, which would justify 'assisting' the suspect to alight from his scooter.

But here again there would be problems in view of the rider's inability to move any faster than a glacier in winter. Back-up would become necessary which would entail further delay while a colleague was summoned to help prise the recalcitrant from his vehicle as painlessly as possible. The only snag here was likely to be that the colleague in question was experiencing similar problems himself with another unco-operative cove and was just about to call upon you for assistance. It was hardly surprising, therefore, that the heavily outnumbered officers quickly recognised the limitations of the task confronting them and decided not to bother.

Even if they managed to arrest a few old-timers there was no way police vans and cars could reach them through the gridlock. And on suspicion of what charge? Obstructing the highway? That wouldn't stick because their scooters were all licensed to be driven on roads. They had as much right to be there as other vehicles. Driving without reasonable consideration on account of their slow speed? The scooters had a top speed of 8mph. Unlike vehicles used in previous rolling roadblocks by able bodied hauliers, fuel tax protesters and others, they couldn't go any faster. So in what way were the veterans breaking the law?

Faced with the prospect of claims for wrongful arrest and surveyed as they were by the media's cameras, the officers knew when to cut their losses. They remained seated astride their motor-cycles with their flashing blue lights and tried to look intimidating while speaking constantly into their two-way radios. Eventually, they received orders to allow the scooterists to disperse in small groups. But the volunteers did not remain scattered for long. Using their phones as walkie-talkies, they regrouped further up Regent Street and continued their disciplined scootercade.

Following the unexpected publicity coup of the Prime Minister herself accepting their petition, Howard's task force weaved their way back to Trafalgar Square through a forest of static cars, trucks, vans and buses, some of their frustrated drivers shaking their fists and shouting insults. On reaching the square, however, they received an altogether different reception.

It was now packed with foreign visitors photographing the statues, the fountains and the pigeons in the bright spring sunshine. As the long procession of OAPs rolled into view it attracted special attention from hundreds of Chinese tourists. Their guides told them about the Health of the Nation Bill and translated the slogans on the placards. In a gesture of spontaneous solidarity, they flocked round the scooters, excitedly photographing their riders and stopping traffic completely.

The tourists, belonging to a civilised culture of respect for elders, were shocked to discover the exact opposite in Britain. Waving miniature Union Jacks and Chinese flags, they pressed bottled water, soft drinks and exotic snacks on the startled pensioners. Some transferred garlands of flowers they'd been wearing round the scooterists' necks, while shaking their hands and embracing them. Although the tourists could speak only limited English, their body language said it all.

But the emotional scenes were short-lived. As traffic solidified in surrounding streets around the square, police rapidly moved in. Black-clad officers in riot gear roughly manhandled the Chinese into a penned area around the fountains. Some of the tourists were knocked over and injured in the melee, cameras were damaged, garlands and English/Chinese phrase books trampled on.

Through their zoom lenses, TV cameras perched high in surrounding buildings captured the horror on the tourists' faces. This was their first experience of state elderphobia. A measure as barbaric as the Health of the Nation Bill would be inconceivable in their homeland. It was completely alien to their culture, a culture centuries ahead of the decadent West.

Overwhelmed by the unexpected outpouring of goodwill by the tourists and disgusted by the treatment they had received, the demonstrators reluctantly turned and headed back towards their Russell Square base through a warren of side roads, jammed with abandoned vehicles. During the flurry of violence in the square, a grandmother had been knocked off her scooter and sustained minor concussion, another rider had his spectacles broken and a third suffered an angina attack. But otherwise the expedition's casualties had been confined to cases of insulin deficiency, lost medication and dehydration. All were dealt with by the mobile first aid centre staffed by Barbara and a nursing colleague, their water bottles topped up and iron rations replenished. The stewards and support teams of families and friends, following the procession on foot, were kept informed by phone and text message. Not a single case required hospital treatment – so far.

As their convoy reached Aldwych and turned into Kingsway, a police helicopter droned overhead, obviously checking on their progress, but then flew off. Shortly afterwards another helicopter appeared, this time larger and unmarked. It could only be the media. The scooters all stopped, their riders waving as it hovered overhead. Howard's multi-phone bleeped. When he answered, it sounded like a reporter in the chopper trying to talk to him but the noise of the aircraft made conversation impossible.

"How time flies when you're having fun," the garlanded Bernard called to Howard as he zig-zagged along a line of motionless, diesel-powered juggernauts like a teenager. The vehicles' drivers, standing in an impotent group, were not amused. They jeered and applauded sarcastically as the scooters went past.

Howard looked at his watch. It was half past eleven already. He signalled to his followers and they crossed over High Holborn into Red Lion Square. It had been a busy morning and it was time for a spot of lunch. Here, as both the retired hacks knew from their Fleet Street days, could be found a selection of eminently suitable hostelries. After making sure there were no police either on the ground or airborne, the cavalry chained their trusty steeds to railings outside several up-market watering holes and, with remarkable alacrity bearing in mind their various handicaps, disappeared inside. They were all texted to regroup in the square an hour later and reminded that the drink-drive laws applied to road scooters.

"What do you think of it so far?" Howard asked his perspiring lieutenant as the pair settled arthritically on a plush banquette with their favourite tipples and studied the bar snacks menu. The establishment had not yet filled up with its lunchtime clientele and the landlord was watching a rolling news channel on a TV behind the bar. It showed an aerial view of blocked streets, described by the reporter as "like a gigantic car park".

Before Bernard could answer, four heavily built men in jeans and leather jackets pushed their way through the door and strode aggressively up to their table. It quickly became clear that their objective was not to shake hands with either Howard or Bernard, both of whom still had Chinese garlands round their necks, which did not help to endear them to their visitors.

Eschewing the formalities of introducing himself and his colleagues, their leader, a head-shaved tough guy in his thirties wearing a thick gold neck chain and several chunky gold rings, asked what the effing pair of old masturbators thought they were doing by fouling up the effing highways. The old geezers were well-off retirees who could afford expensive road scooters, he maintained. What right did they have to stop honest working men from earning their effing living?

Howard recognised the men as the group of hostile HGV drivers they had passed earlier. He had to admit that, stripped of expletives, it was a good question. The men had a grievance. But he and his supporters had a much stronger one. He wondered if the lorry drivers had heard of the Health of the Nation Bill and was about to ask when the belligerent tirade continued.

Pointing to the scenes of traffic meltdown on the TV, the bling king wanted to know if Howard and his clapped-out masturbators were proud of themselves.

There was no effing way all the HGVs trapped in that chaos would complete their day's effing work schedules. Two of his mates were Geordies – he gestured towards them and they volubly indicated in their native tongue that they couldn't hope to make it back to Newcastle that night. At least that was what Howard thought they said.

"We're not doing this for the fun of it," he managed to squeeze in to the impassioned if colourful dialogue. "Have you heard of the Health of the Nation Bill?"

"The what?"

"The Health of the Nation Bill…the government wants to kill people off when their 15-year state pension expires. It's been on television."

The aggression began to drain out of the HGV heavy but he remained standing within punching distance of Howard, his tattooed arms folded. "We don't see much telly on the road."

"It's been in all the newspapers."

"Not seen anything about it in the *Sun*."

"You will if you look hard enough," Bernard said, joining the debate in his down-to-earth Scouse manner. "Look mate, you're bound to feel bad about the blockade but it's only for one day."

"That's bad enough. We'll all lose a day's pay."

"Tough, I know but it's not the end of the world. It *could* be for your grandparents. Are they still alive?"

"My granddad is."

"How old is he?"

"He's 85, I think. He's got cancer but it's in remission."

"Does he rely on his state pension?"

"I've never asked him."

"Maybe you should. Our caring government want to cut it by half...or preferably bump him off and hijack all of it."

The trucker sat down on an adjoining chair and twisted one of his gold rings uneasily. Somewhere at the back of his mind Bernard's words rang a bell...something to do with assisted suicide and helping people in agony to die with dignity. It had sounded like a good idea but the stresses of daily life had crowded out further thought on the subject. There was so much else to worry about...his estranged wife's maintenance demands, his delivery schedules, the tyranny of the tachograph in his cab, not to mention West Ham United's dodgy away form...

"Can they really do that?"

Bernard and Howard looked at each other and shook their heads in despair. Such was the level of public concern over the life-and-death legislation being debated in Parliament at that moment. You had to hand it to Phoenix's PR team. They'd done a brilliant professional job of mind conditioning.

Howard stood up and delivered a line that never failed to soothe the savage breast: "Let me buy you lads a drink."

*   *   *

While Howard and Bernard were pleading the case for OAPs' basic human rights to a saloon bar filling up with either hostile or apathetic lunchtime drinkers, George's detachment of the Coalition task force snaked its way from Piccadilly Circus along Regent Street, now dominated by Tesco fashion houses and McDonald's 'People's Restaurants'. They just happened to be

217

passing BBC Broadcasting House in Portland Place when they were ambushed by radio journalists and a TV camera crew.

The broadcasters waved down the procession and the camera crew took a great interest in George's combat fatigues. A young man dressed in denims with shoulder-length hair, a wispy beard and earrings, the archetypal hippy from Central Casting, approached him and shook his hand limply. His other hand held a microphone.

"Dr Armstrong, I presume," he said with a slightly effeminate accent. "I'm Dominic, BBC Radio. Can I ask you how your protest march is going?"

Over the years, George had developed an instinctive dislike of people with limp handshakes. He also had a deep suspicion of anyone who declined to give their full name. The age of chivalry might be long gone but it was only common courtesy to tell people your full name, especially when they knew yours. But he was well aware that radio was the poor relation in broadcasting, attracting people rejected by television on account of their uncouth manners and low IQs. Dominic appeared to qualify on both counts.

"Actually, it's a rolling roadblock. If you look carefully you'll see we're all on wheels."

Dominic ploughed on regardless. "You certainly seem to have stopped the traffic."

"That was the object of the exercise."

"And upset a lot of drivers."

"The government have upset *us*. Don't our lives mean more than a few blocked roads? We're talking about ageism carried to its lethal conclusion here. The BBC condemns sexism and racism. Now's your chance to condemn ageism."

In view of the BBC's obsession with youth – a policy that extended to sacking most presenters on reaching the age of 40 – Dominic was smart enough to realise it would be unwise to accept George's challenge. BBC staff who retired automatically disappeared from the radar. Life went on without you in the same way as if you were dead. To Broadcasting House mandarins, ethical issues involved in the Health of the Nation Bill were largely academic. The elderly, to all intents and purposes, were as good as dead already.

As he looked down the long line of silvery heads, some balding, some with eccentric headgear, drinking from their bottles of water and waving cheerily to the TV camera, the pathological elderphobe suppressed a shudder of distaste. God (if such existed) forbid that he should ever end up like one of these. Avoiding the thorny issue of ageism, he tried one last lame argument on George. "People are saying there are other ways of protesting without causing such large-scale disruption to the travelling public."

"We've tried them. They don't work. Unfortunately, the only thing politicians understand is direct action. We think we've made our point today."

"Thank you, Dr Armstrong." Dominic was about to approach other members of the procession to ask if they had any regrets over their anti-social behaviour when George gave the signal to move off. From a publicity point of view, the stop had proved disappointing. The next one – a lunch break at a drive-through McDonald's should prove considerably more entertaining.

*　　　*　　　*

A different kind of ambush greeted Howard and Bernard's troops as they finished their lunch break. On resuming the last lap of their trek back to base, mission accomplished, they found their way blocked by a temporary barrier erected across the exit to Red Lion Square. This time the police had arrived in large numbers and, judging by the squad of male and female officers wearing high visibility jackets and armed with intimidating electronic equipment, they meant business.

An officious chief inspector approached Howard and informed him that, acting on information received, they had reason to believe he and his associates had been drinking. They would all be breathalysed and, if over the limit, arrested and charged with driving a motor vehicle while under the influence of alcohol.

Howard and Bernard had to laugh. This was the best the authorities could contrive by way of a crackdown on a blockade that had caused them unprecedented disruption. The scooterists had seen it coming. They'd restricted their alcohol intake to a minimum, not least because their medication regimes demanded it. Most had also perfected a highly effective system for dealing with breathalysers. They were confident they would survive this belated counter attack, although Howard did notice one or two stragglers scooting off down side roads some distance away.

The remaining diehards were ordered to line up in a queue stretching all the way round the square while the breath-test squad swung into action. The young constables weren't heavy handed about it but they weren't exactly gentle either. Although accustomed to encouraging young and middle-aged motorists to blow into their high-tech gadgets, the training manuals said nothing about ageing scooterists incapable of blowing a kiss on a windy day. Problems ranged from angina and asthma to emphysema and chronic bronchitis, with the odd case of collapsed lung and severe tracheitis thrown in. Several riders explained that they could only blow properly on removing their full sets of dentures. Could the young officers kindly provide trays or small plastic bags for the purpose? The officers consulted the chief inspector, who in turn radioed for advice on the matter, when it was decided that these facilities could not be provided. The 'suspects' concerned were therefore eliminated from enquiries. The same decision was eventually reached on other veterans who claimed exemption on medical grounds and produced doctors' certificates confirming their afflictions.

The chief inspector did contemplate taking urine samples but was advised against in further radio contact with his superiors. Bearing in mind the suspects' average walking speed – estimated at 0.01mph – it was calculated that it could take several months to escort them all to the police station toilets and back to their vehicles. Even if wheelchairs were used, assuming that a couple of hundred could be found, the operation would probably still take weeks.

There was also the strong likelihood that, on reaching the test area, further problems would be encountered in the form of chronic prostate and bladder complications. In desperation, with almost three-quarters of his suspects eliminated from enquiries and not a single red light showing up on a breathalyser, the investigating officer's thoughts turned to blood tests. But these would involve an even longer timescale since they would have to be performed by qualified medical staff in a clinical environment. You couldn't just jab a hypodermic needle into a pensioner's arm out there in the street, however much you might feel like it.

With his carefully planned operation growing rapidly pear-shaped, the frustrated officer focused his baleful gaze on the demo's two leaders. The pair had been acting as stewards while their supporters were breath-tested and their own procedures were left until last. The chief inspector had a feeling he knew one of them, the taller one with the stoop. He searched his policeman's photographic memory and Howard's face clicked into place.

"You're the guy who threw his OBE in the river, aren't you?" the doughty servant of the Crown asked Howard, with barely disguised glee. All was not lost. It might still be possible to save face if he could discredit the man who'd shamelessly insulted king and country not long ago.

Howard did his best to smile. "Right first time, chief."

If there was one thing the officer detested, beside republicans, it was being called 'chief' – and by this old Leftie of all people. He couldn't wait to thrust the breathalyser into Howard's face. "Blow hard into the tube, *sir,*" he ordered.

Unfortunately, with the best will in the world, that was something Howard was unable to do. The day's exertions had started to affect him earlier and he'd had to use his angina spray twice to relieve his breathlessness. Now seriously groggy, he extracted it from his pocket again and took another puff. It didn't seem to help.

"I appear to be running out of grey power," he quipped.

The humourless officer was not amused. "Can you provide evidence of your condition?" he asked, as if the nitrolingual spray wasn't evidence enough.

Howard sat down abruptly on his scooter. The tightness in his chest was now accompanied by palpitations. He didn't hear the question because the crackle of the officer's two-way radio interfered with his hearing aid.

"I'm talking to you, sir. I asked you for evidence of your medical condition."

Again, the police radio jammed the sensitive high-tech aid. All he could hear was a loud buzzing.

Years earlier, at the Police Training College, the chief inspector had been taught there could be a simple explanation for people ignoring you: they might be deaf. But the instruction, like so many others, had long been forgotten. If people ignored you, what you did was nick them.

"I'm arresting you on suspicion of obstructing a police officer in the course of his duty..." As he recited the obligatory rubric, the officer signalled to a male constable and between them they hauled Howard off his scooter and frogmarched him across Theobalds Road to the police station 100 yards away.

Once inside the police station, Howard's hearing aid returned to normal, which was more than could be said for his breathing. Still struggling for breath, he was propped up against the duty sergeant's desk and relieved of his watch, wallet, phone, diary, pen, comb, nail file, reading glasses, tie, small change, keys and, crucially, his address book containing all the contact numbers of his volunteers.

He was allowed to keep a handkerchief, prescription drugs and his vital angina spray. His hearing aid was minutely scrutinised. They needed to test it for 'bugs', it was explained. If he hadn't felt so ill he would have found the idea laughable.

Then he was marched off to be strip searched, fingerprinted, photographed and finally DNA'd by a policewoman built like a shot putter, whose technique with an oral swab precipitated another attack of palpitations. The shot putter gave him a glass of water and he was led to the custody suite, where he was ushered into a cell with an unceremonious push between the shoulder blades. After that, his recollection of events grew hazy. He remembered a tightening knot of pain in his chest, of trying to sit on a hard trestle bed but collapsing on the floor, sweating and trembling.

Then nothing, until an unbearably loud pounding in his ears.

TWENTY-TWO

Nurse Mitchell had been attending an octogenarian campaigner, a frail great grandmother who'd suffered a fainting attack, when Bernard called on her videophone to tell her of Howard's arrest. He'd gone with him to the police station and had just been told he was unconscious in a holding cell. It seemed like a heart attack. Could she come at once?

Barbara realised the day's events were not over yet. The stresses and exertions of organising the demo had taken their toll on her husband as she had always feared. Right now she needed to get a grip. "Is there a doctor with him?"

"No. They've sent for one."

"Has he been given oxygen?"

"I don't know. They won't tell us anything."

"It's vital they put him on oxygen, Bernard. You'll need to blag your way in there and insist."

"I hear you, Barbara."

"If a doctor arrives, tell him to give him an intravenous thrombolytic drug – a clot-buster."

"You'll have to spell it, I've got a pen…"

After she'd spelt out her instructions and Bernard had speedily written them in his notebook, she added:

"Tell the police his wife's a nurse and I'm calling for an air ambulance. There's a helipad on the police station roof. There's no way a road ambulance would get through. Please hurry, Bernard. I'm on my way now."

She immediately phoned the Air Ambulance Service on its direct emergency line, then grabbed a hypodermic syringe and a heavy portable oxygen cylinder from her makeshift ambulance. With these, she staggered through crowds of pedestrians and snarled up traffic to the police station. On arriving at the reception counter gasping for breath, she demanded to know where her husband was being detained. She was his wife and she was a nurse.

There was a delay while the appropriate officer was traced and when she finally reached her husband's cell she found him lying on the floor, unconscious and blue in the face. A young, frightened looking policewoman was trying to remove his jacket but had not even turned him into the recovery position. There was no sign of any oxygen.

"Here, help me with this," Barbara barked, handing the officer the hefty oxygen cylinder. After feeling his pulse, checking that he had not swallowed his tongue and turning him on his side, she hastily applied the mask to Howard's nose and mouth and switched on the vital air supply.

Eleven minutes later, the air ambulance touched down on the police station's helipad and paramedics connected him to their own oxygen supply before stretchering him aboard. When everyone was strapped in, the aircraft rose swiftly into the darkening sky and headed for St Thomas's Hospital, a few minutes away. As they sped across the river and the twinkling street lights of a city still gripped by gridlock, Howard stirred and opened his eyes. The pounding of the helicopter's rotors, amplified as they were in his hearing aid, had roused him from what the paramedics and even Barbara had feared might be a coma.

Barbara, who was bathing his hot forehead with a handkerchief wrapped round ice from the aircraft's refrigerator unit, bent to kiss him and hold his hand. He coughed thickly and with the aid of a crew member, she helped him to sit up.

They half expected him to say: Where am I? But instead he spluttered into his oxygen mask: "They'll have to change their contact numbers..."

She had no idea what he was talking about. He seemed delirious. "Relax, darling. We're taking you to hospital. We'll be there in a couple of minutes. They'll have you right in no time." She really meant it although she knew the chances of recovering from a heart attack were 50/50. His BP was dangerously high at 210:100 on the paramedic's electronic machine, his pulse was racing and his temperature way off limits. But his respiration had improved and he was struggling to speak.

He released his hand from hers and lifted the oxygen mask. "The phone numbers..."

Barbara bent forward to calm him. "Don't try to talk, Howard. You can tell me later."

His wheezing returned and she replaced the mask firmly. "Deep breaths, darling. Nice and slow...just keep breathing..."

As soon as she said the words, she knew they would connect with his resilient sense of humour. It was difficult to smile under the oxygen mask but his hand found hers again and squeezed it tightly. As he used to say whenever the job's pressures were enough to drive normal people up the wall, you had to take the rough with the intolerable.

The moment the helicopter landed at St Thomas's, the crew whisked their patient into the Accident and Emergency Department. Specialist nurses unhooked his oxygen and replaced it with their own. As Barbara described his symptoms and medical history, they took his pulse, did a blood test and then connected him to an ECG machine to monitor his heart.

Barbara had to admire their smooth professionalism – in contrast to the slapdash care she'd seen the elderly receive in her own hospital – although the perceived 'celebrity' of their patient might have had something to do with it. They had defibrillators and intubation equipment on standby in case of respiratory or cardiac arrest. But Howard's condition seemed to be stabilising by the minute. She offered up a silent prayer of thanks.

He was breathing evenly and a healthier colour had returned to his cheeks. A specialist in cardiac medicine entered the cubicle and listened to Howard's wired-up chest with his stethoscope. After several minutes he smiled in his best bedside manner. "You'll live, Mr Mitchell," the tall and distinguished looking Afro-American doctor told him.

"That's made my day," Howard replied into his oxygen mask. "I was beginning to wonder."

"But you've had rather a narrow squeak so I'm going to keep you in for observation."

"That's fine by me. I don't feel like going anywhere."

Outside the cubicle, the doctor's prognosis was encouraging. He told Barbara her husband hadn't suffered a heart attack but acute angina aggravated by oesophagitis. He'd keep him in for a day or two and increase his blood pressure tablets and statins. He'd also prescribe oesophageal medication. On returning home, Howard would be given a portable oxygen cylinder in case of further attacks and would need to rest for a week on a fat-free diet with plenty of fluids. The doctor elaborated on the narrowness of Howard's 'squeak'. "It could have developed into a myocardial infarction. He was lucky you got to him in time."

That was no thanks to the police, Barbara thought. She switched on her videophone and called Bernard, who had now led his exhausted blockaders back to base without further problems. It was then that she learned the full story. The alarm had only been raised due to a fellow occupant in Howard's cell. The ongoing 'overflowing prisons' crisis meant that holding cells at major police stations had been pressed into service to house remand prisoners. But for his cellmate, Howard could have died. She offered another silent prayer: for the man, whoever he was, regardless of his alleged crimes.

Bernard also told her that, as Howard had not been charged with anything and the police no longer wished to proceed with his case, he could consider himself released unconditionally without police bail.

"That's kind of them." It wasn't the first time her husband had been wrongfully arrested. She knew it was an occupational hazard for journalists. But he was retired now. Surely at his age and in his condition...? Her anxiety was rapidly giving way to barely suppressed anger. There needed to be a full enquiry into the outrage but, for the present, someone would have to collect Howard's belongings from the police station and complete the formalities. Bernard, who looked completely exhausted himself, told her William had offered to make the journey by Tube later that evening.

When she returned to her husband's bedside, she found him sitting up and drinking a cup of tea, the oxygen mask temporarily discarded. She told him about the return of his belongings and he remembered what he had been muttering about in the helicopter. "All the members' contact numbers in my notebook...they'll need to be changed. You can bet they're listed on the police computer by now. We don't want any more old sods hassled...one's enough for today." He took a gulp of his tea and grinned at her. "I mean, do I look like the sort of person who would obstruct a police officer in the course of his duty?"

He was more philosophical about his arrest than she was. She replaced his mask gently while making no reply.

"All right...don't answer that."

*   *   *

They gave him his own room when he was wheeled up to the ward. Not because he'd asked for it but because the ward sister immediately recognised the name on his notes as that of the man who'd thrown his gong in the Thames and whose face was appearing in all the TV news bulletins.

"We don't often have a celebrity on our ward," she told him as she briskly tucked him up in bed and fitted his oxygen mask.

"Please don't call me that. I'd much rather be out there with the other patients."

"I'll be the judge of where to put you if you don't mind, Mr Mitchell."

Howard thought she sounded exactly like his wife. Barbara had left minutes earlier to take the Tube home.

A taxi was out of the question as many roads were still blocked. Their Rover would have to stay in its Russell Square car park collecting penalty charges. She'd return later with his pyjamas, toiletries, change of clothes and hearing aid batteries. Poor Barbara, he thought. Wisely, she'd taken the week off work but she must already be feeling as shattered as he was.

Perhaps she was right after all and they were getting too old for this kind of thing. But as he watched the news coverage of the rolling roadblock on his room's wall-mounted TV, the scale of its success told him she was wrong. All the planning and organisation, the day's enervating schedule and his own incapacitation had been worthwhile. Reporters along the demo's route declared that London had experienced nothing like it since the riots over Thatcher's poll tax last century.

As luck would have it, a major power cut had blacked out all traffic lights, leaving the central area's one-way system – baffling at the best of times – inoperable. Plug-in battery-charging points in car parks also failed, leaving thousands of vehicles stranded. In the absence of a workable contingency plan and with police unable to implement diversions, the havoc was unprecedented. Commercial offices reported widespread staff absence and shops an unprecedented drop in takings. An exclusion zone of several square miles between Bloomsbury and Clerkenwell had been enforced with dire penalties for drivers who ignored it.

The earlier scenes in Trafalgar Square received extensive coverage, with the brutal treatment handed out to the Chinese tourists described as a 'clash of cultures'. Viewers were told that, during the last hour, the Chinese High Commissioner to the United

231

Kingdom had lodged an official protest over the incident.

There was plenty more footage of the day's unique act of civil disobedience, including mug shots of its leaders, Howard, George and Bernard, with updates on the drama of Howard's arrest, his dramatic collapse and latest hospital bulletins. One programme producer allowed his impartiality to slip when the blockade's organisers were described as 'ringleaders'. When the camera teams ran out of different visual angles on the disruption they fell back on eye-witness accounts, along with the usual street interviews.

Frustrated bus, truck and taxi drivers – especially younger ones – maintained in forthright terms that such demonstrations alienated the older generation from the rest of society, who were trying to go about their lawful business. But most interviewees were supportive. If these were the lengths infirm people had to go to in order to stay alive then good luck to them, seemed to be the consensus.

The usual studio guests from both sides weighed in with their six penn'orth. The Bill's ardent advocate, Sylvia Pullar, appearing on *Newsline*, condemned the blockade for preventing ambulances and fire service vehicles from attending emergencies. Lives had been needlessly put at risk by a selfish and irresponsible minority.

A weary but still on-the-ball Dr Armstrong reminded her that, in the last decade, the roofs of most office blocks had been adapted as helipads precisely because of traffic congestion problems. Air ambulances and fire service units now dealt with emergencies more quickly and efficiently than ground vehicles. His colleague, Howard Mitchell, had himself been taken to hospital by air ambulance after his arrest and life-threatening collapse. It was Ms Pullar's horrendous Bill that was needlessly putting lives at risk, with a potential death toll running into millions.

As for the Bill itself, the media's political staff reported that the Third Reading debate had been adjourned for a week, when the guillotine procedure was expected and a vote taken immediately. Approval by a narrow majority was widely predicted. The measure would then proceed immediately to the Lords for dutiful endorsement. This was something of an embarrassing formality since five peers were serving prison sentences, two more on bail awaiting trial and a further 12 under investigation by the Serious Fraud Office.

It would be a straightforward rubber-stamping exercise without any meaningful debate. A matter of days later, after formal Fourth Reading and Royal Assent, the Bill would become law. Its backers were right about one thing. Once the sound and fury from public protests had subsided, the controversy would soon be forgotten. They quoted a felicitous Bedouin proverb, translated from Arabic:

"The small dogs bark…
And the big dogs bark…
But the caravan passes."

*　　　*　　　*

Propped up comfortably on several pillows, Howard was dozing off when a nurse entered his room and told him the Press had arrived and wanted to interview him.

"Please tell them I'm not well enough. I'm critical but stable." The term was usually effective in getting rid of intrusive reporters.

"We've told them you're comfortable."

"I'm still not well enough to be interviewed."

"Your son's also arrived. Are you well enough to see him?"

He looked at the clock on the wall. It was 8.30pm. William had certainly moved fast to collect his belongings from the police station.

"Of course. Show him in."

Moments later the door opened and Christopher, not William, strode in carrying a large bunch of flowers and a plastic carrier bag. His eldest son wore a smart grey pinstripe suit and an expression of anxiety mingled with embarrassment. He placed the flowers and the bag on the bedside tray.

"I brought you these. Heard you were in a bad way...came straight from the office...traffic's impossible. "

It had been a rollercoaster of a day but this was Howard's biggest surprise of all. He had not seen Chris since he'd disappeared out of camera range along the Embankment on the day of the investiture. He had even boycotted the family Christmas, which had been unforgivable. There was an awkward moment as his middle-aged son stood at the foot of the bed, drained of his customary self-confidence.

Howard eased his oxygen mask aside and grinned. "Well, hi stranger..." He held out his hand which Chris shook with his usual iron grip. "Good to see you. Have a seat." He restored the mask to its former position. "Got to wear this thing. Otherwise I'm okay."

His son sat in a bedside armchair. "They told me you were dangerously ill…that you'd collapsed at the police station. So I came to say sorry…you know, for the bust-up and everything. Amanda and I were out of order."

Howard waved away the apology. "Forget it, Chris. I understand how you felt. You were under a lot of pressure. How's Amanda…and Sebastian?"

"She's fine…and we're still calling our son Howard. I didn't mean what I said about changing his name."

Howard was relieved. "Glad to hear it. Best not to confuse the lad…"

Christopher's smart phone trilled and he answered it. It was Amanda. He told her where he was and that he'd be home in about an hour – hopefully. "She sends her love," he said, replacing the phone in his jacket pocket. "She was very worried about you. So was I, Dad. I don't care what you say, you'll have to slow down now. Mother's right…you can't carry on like this at your age and in your condition."

"Have you spoken to her?"

"Yes, I phoned her about an hour ago. She was on her way home. She says your angina attack was a warning – that you can't keep fighting the system."

Howard reached for a glass of water on his locker. "It's a corrupt system, Chris. Someone has to fight it."

"Maybe, but not you. You need a break, Dad Let someone else have a go. Leave it to Bernard and George Armstrong."

"They're already working their socks off…can't ask any more of them." He paused. "I could ask *you*." He wasn't really serious.

Chris rocked back in the armchair and laughed loudly. "You know that's a non-starter. I don't share your negative view of the world. This Bill that you're fighting...I know it's not perfect but most people support it. Surveys have shown that..."

"Surveys give a distorted picture. They ask loaded questions...that way you can get any answer you want. You're an advertising man, Chris, you must know that. And anyway doctors don't support the Bill. They want nothing to do with assisted suicide."

"But it's not compulsory. Nobody's forced into it. There's an opt-out clause."

Howard pulled a face. "You've got to be joking! Sure, you can opt-out...but then they slash your benefit by half. What kind of a choice is that? People can't live on their pension *already*!"

The Maturity Contract was still a long way off for Christopher Mitchell, the dynamic high-flying executive. But he could see his father had a point. "The state will look after them in some way or other. It'll have to."

"Don't kid yourself, Chris. The state's got it in for us this time. It won't be taking any prisoners." He made a throat-cutting gesture.

His son sighed theatrically. The old animosities were starting to resurface, which he was determined to avoid. He changed the subject. "Did the Old Bill give you a hard time?"

"Not really. I'd felt the attack coming on before they arrested me. They just went through the motions...dabs, mug shot, DNA, strip searched. They let me keep my angina spray, medication and hearing aid."

"Is that all?"

"Yes, they took everything else – even my tie in case I might try to hang myself!"

"Do you want me to collect them?"

"No thanks, William's doing that already."

"You should sue them for wrongful arrest…make them destroy all your personal records."

Howard had to laugh and it made him cough. "Waste of time, dear boy. They'd never do that. It's a police state. Your kind of system, remember."

Chris hadn't changed his allegiance to capitalism despite its ongoing frailties. But this was no time to defend it. He got up and began extracting his purchases from the carrier bag. "I got you a ham and tomato sandwich…a couple of bananas…some chocolate…" He placed the items on the locker. "They should keep you going for a while."

"That's very kind of you." They'd finished serving supper when they brought Howard in and he suddenly felt hungry.

"You're welcome. I know they don't feed you properly in these places – unlike private hospitals." He couldn't resist one plug for the system. "I'd better be off now. I'll give these flowers to the nurse."

Howard smiled and waved in appreciation. "Thanks for coming, Chris. You've made my day."

"I'm just glad you're still with us, Dad."

He turned and waved cheerily from the door. "Just stay where you are, okay? Don't *go* anywhere!"

His father turned wearily on his side, switched off his hearing aid and closed his eyes. "No danger. Give my love to Amanda – and Howard junior."

TWENTY-THREE

He was in a helicopter flying to a distant land where he could spend one day without pain. That was what he'd asked for in a prayer at St Chad's. He didn't want to push his luck, as he wasn't a Catholic. So he settled for just one day without all his physical burdens. His prayer was answered and he'd been granted a special permit – a one-day opt-out from pain in the independent republic of Shangri-la, where no-one grew old or became ill.

But as the helicopter soared above the clouds, he noticed that the pilot was Father Fitzgibbon. Suddenly the noise of the rotor blades grew louder and the priest lost control. The aircraft started to drop and he gave the order to bale out but there were no parachutes. As it fell, the helicopter rocked from side to side...

"Wake up, Mr Mitchell," the nurse said, shaking him gently. "Your other son's brought your belongings."

Howard raised himself stiffly on one elbow. The movement triggered the usual arthritic spasm in his back. So much for a day without pain, he thought. The clock on the wall showed 9.55pm. He'd managed little more than an hour. All the same, he was glad to see William. He needed to make urgent calls on his mobile, most importantly to warn members to change their contact numbers.

His younger son brought in two bags, a grip containing his pyjamas, change of underwear, razor, toiletries, hearing aid batteries and medication; the other a plastic bag holding the phone and other possessions taken from him at the police station. He sat on the edge of the bed and held his father's hand solicitously.

"Hi, Dad...how're you feeling?"

Howard eased his mask aside and coughed into a paper tissue. "I'm coughing better. The doctor says I'll live..."

William smiled at his old man's unfailing cheerfulness. "We were all very worried. We've been phoning the ward and they said you were over the worst. So Mum said to tell you she's too tired to come tonight. She's got another migraine..."

"Poor dear, she must be worn out."

"She'll visit you tomorrow with Sally. I've brought all your things. If there's anything else you need, let me know. Have you had anything to eat?"

Howard pointed to the bananas and half-eaten sandwich on his locker. "Chris brought me these. They'll be fine."

His son was surprised to hear of his brother's visit. He sat on the armchair and pushed back his shoulder-length hair. His honest young eyes watched as his father carefully checked his returned possessions. They were all there but Howard knew everything in his wallet had been scrutinised. The duty sergeant or one of his sidekicks had been careless how they'd replaced his driving licence and insurance card. The two had previously been inserted the other way round.

From experience, he realised that his diary would also have been minutely examined. He'd been arrested once before during a particularly sensitive *Announcer* investigation into people regarded as untouchable. The police had read his diary which contained his mother's address, among others. Not long afterwards, she became the victim of harassment, including a late night police raid on her sheltered flat on a spurious pretext. Coincidence? But of course. Since then, however, he'd made sure his diaries contained no names and addresses and that any remotely significant entries were encoded.

No doubt impressions of his keys had also been taken. They would all need changing. There was no limit to the hassle that could result from an innocent person being taken into custody. Howard knew only too well how police minds worked. The disruption the rolling blockade had caused would incense them. They would be sure to retaliate. William was just a naive young man with little or no knowledge of such things. Sooner or later he would discover the murky nature of the world. But when he tried to explain his concerns he was surprised to find his son knew more than he thought.

"They'll come after us now, won't they, Dad," he said, as if reading his father's thoughts. "Don't worry, Bernard'll know what to do. I suggest we encrypt all our computerised records and make back-up copies…"

"Good idea…in case they come for the laptop. Smart lad. We'll make a journalist out of you yet."

William shook his locks dismissively. "No way. Football's much more exciting."

After his son had left to take the Tube to Wimbledon, Howard made his all-important phone calls. Then he replaced the batteries in his hearing aid.

While he was at it, he painstakingly checked the device – for bugs. The police had taken a great interest in it. Nothing could surprise him any more. It was exactly the kind of stroke they were likely to pull.

Paranoid or what?

* * *

It was either porridge or corn flakes for breakfast. Howard chose porridge and found himself almost agreeing with Chris on the comparative merits of NHS and private hospital food. He quite enjoyed porridge when made the right way and served with hot milk and maple syrup. But the concoction he was offered was solid, the milk was cold and there was no syrup or even sugar. The toast was like cardboard but the tea was good and strong and he polished off a couple of bananas Chris had brought. He must be getting better, he thought, to be fussing over his food in a hospital struggling to feed hundreds of patients on an ever-shrinking budget.

His diagnosis was confirmed when doctors made their morning round. They took turns at listening to his chest, striking his knee with little hammers and shining powerful lights down his throat. They seemed pleased with his progress. He could dispense with the oxygen but they'd keep him under observation for 48 hours, when he should be well enough to go home.

When Barbara and Sally visited him an hour later, he was sitting up in bed reading the morning papers, their front pages devoted to the previous day's paralysis of central London. They carried huge pictures of immobilised traffic and venerable scooterists with headlines including: **Not dead yet** (*Sun*); **Victory for**

Granddads' Army (*Mirror*); **Golden oldies shock for Sykes** (*Express*); **Scooter power comes to town** (*The Announcer*); **Pensioner power on a roll** (*Mail-Telegraph*); **Blockade will not block humane Bill** (*Guardian-Independent*).

"There can't be much wrong with you, Howard," Barbara teased as she bent to kiss him. "We're all frazzled with worry and here you are wallowing in newspapers as if nothing's happened." The jocular manner was slightly strained. Her face was pale and drawn, and there were dark rings under her eyes. "They seem to be looking after you very well."

"Home from home. No complaints, apart from the breakfast."

She flopped into the bedside armchair. "Porridge?"

"Not as we know it."

Sally, in artist's regulation gear of baggy brown jumper and tattered jeans, her wild sandy coloured hair tamed by a red ribbon, kissed him warmly and held his hands in hers. "Dad, it's great to see you. How are you feeling?"

"Still breathing, Sal. Thanks to your Mum and someone up there." He gestured heavenwards. "The air ambulance pilot!" As soon as he laughed he started to cough and Sally handed him a tissue.

"It's nothing," he spluttered, waving her away.

She had to admire her father's indomitable spirit although it had its downside. It was not only taking its toll on him but also on her mother. You had only to look at her lined face and pain-filled eyes to see that. "You don't think you might be pushing yourself a teeny bit too hard?" she asked as tactfully as possible. "I mean, you *are* supposed to be retired – and Mum soon will be."

"It can't come a moment too soon," Barbara said with feeling.

Howard remained defiant. "Never underestimate the power of a pensioner. Sykes made that mistake and look what happened."

But his daughter's concerns were not lost on him. He'd noticed Barbara's drained face and the weariness behind the flippant manner. For over 40 years she'd shared the barely-tolerable burden of his profession while struggling with the demands of her own, not to mention raising a family. Sally was right. Enough was enough.

"I'm serious, Dad. You need to slow down…the pair of you."

"All right, I can take a hint."

"You've said that before and nothing has happened. This time, I insist you both come and stay with me in Canillas for a while. It's a great place to chill out. The air doesn't come any purer than on the Sierra. .just what you need to recuperate, Dad, and for Mum to get over all these migraine attacks."

Howard turned to Barbara in mock protest. "You've put her up to this haven't you."

She managed a weak smile. "No, darling. But I think she's right. We both need a break."

"I can't leave it all to Bernard. He could do with a break as well."

It was a valid objection but Sally was ready for it. "I've talked to William. He says he'll be happy to take over now his course has finished."

Not for the first time, Howard realised he'd been stitched up. On the other hand, his younger son's vigilance and streetwise qualities had impressed him the previous evening. He was bound to know the ropes, having helped to run Keep Breathing since its inception. Yes, William would make an admirable deputy. "It all seems to have been decided. When do you have in mind?"

Sally beamed and stroked his hand. "Soon. I'll fix it up... flights and everything. Just relax, Dad, everything's under control."

"Famous last words!"

*　　　*　　　*

Dame Jessica Sykes switched off the 60-inch. 3-D plasma TV in the cosy love nest she shared with Meg Meredith above the shop at No 10. She was in a foul mood. The unrelenting scenes of chaos she'd been watching represented an affront to her personal authority as Prime Minister but she was uncertain how to respond. So she did what any self-respecting politician would do in her position: she called her image consultant on her secure direct line.

Would it be appropriate to make a statement on television, demonising the ageing troublemakers as 'the enemy within' and assuring the nation that everything was under control? Or would it enhance her public profile if she remained aloof from the whole squalid business and let it blow over?

These were questions requiring much thought and, at several thousand an hour (cash only – no cheques or credit cards), Rex Clifton, 'adviser to the stars', was happy to take his time. "Wonderful to hear from you, Jessica. Keeping well, I trust. And the lovely Meg?" he said in the genial East End accent he'd used since his early days as a bingo caller at the former Hackney Hippodrome.

Dame Jessica wasn't in the mood for his usual flannel. "We're both fine, Rex," she said impatiently. She repeated the questions, reminding him that she was a very busy woman and would appreciate a prompt response.

"What's your Press secretary telling you, Jessica?"

"She's advising a general Press release saying the situation is under control and everything's likely to be back to normal in 24 hours. But I need to know if it would enhance my image to say that on TV."

Rex spun out his reaction for as long as decently possible. "I'm not going to hedge my bets with you, Jessie. We've known each other a long time and you're too valued a client for me to do that. At the end of the day, I'd have to say you should stick to the handout. If you went on TV, we'd need to give you gravitas, make you appear statesmanlike – sorry, I mean stateswoman-like. But, as you know, you don't do 'gravitas'. You come across more positive when you smile. Remember Blair...always grinning, even while cluster bombs were falling on Iraqi markets. He had the same problem with 'gravitas'. It made him look indecisive."

"You're going back a long way, Rex. What about Brown?"

"Son of the manse...know what I mean? He was *expected* to look solemn all the time. It suited him. It doesn't suit you, Jessie...take my word. You need to project a more human side to soften your hard-line policies."

"*Hard-line policies?*" she was genuinely offended.

"Well, you do seem to have got it in for folk with one foot in the grave. It's not exactly improving your image."

"It's strictly in the national interest, Rex. The country needs them to put the other foot in as well."

Rex laughed. "That's what I mean, Jess...insensitive. You're coming across as insensitive. You need to be more sympathetic to the golden oldies, show your human side."

"I tried to do that by accepting their wretched petition in person. It was a big mistake...made it seem I might support their campaign, which of course I don't."

"You took it at face value. You didn't know it came with a quarter-mile attachment of mobility scooters. Someone should have told you."

"They made me look a fool, didn't they."

"Nobody does that, Dame Jessie."

"So maybe we need to think in terms of damage limitation."

"I don't think you'd limit the damage by going on TV. You might increase it by reminding the public of a nasty experience. Better to turn the situation to your own advantage...show the old folk you have a kind, understanding side to your nature. I'd suggest a token concession, something to soften the blow of your euthanasia Bill."

"Such as?"

"Well, why not give them the commissioner they keep demanding?"

She thought for a moment. "Hmm...maybe you're right. But not a Cabinet appointment...just a figurehead with no clout. We've had them in the past. Nobody takes them seriously."

"But it would be seen as a goodwill gesture. You could say you'd listened to their demands and you'd picked a famous figure – I'd suggest some clapped out TV luvvie – to champion their interests. Of course, whoever it was would have no actual power."

As an example of gesture politics, it seemed like a good idea. And right now Dame Jessica was desperate for good ideas. "I'll think about it, Rex."

"Just a gimmick, you understand...to distract them from the real issue."

"I take your point." She believed she knew just the right man for the job.

"Don't lose any sleep over the demo, Jess. Wait till it all blows over. It won't take long...these things never do."

"Thanks for your help, Rex. I'll do as you advise."

She replaced the phone and buzzed for her private secretary. Her old pal, Sir Wally Alcock, the ageing rock singer, would be summoned to No 10 and offered the strictly nominal post of Pensioners' Commissioner. He had all the right credentials: dim as a 40 watt light bulb and ready himself for his Maturity Contract. But he was still sprightly and garrulous, with the sort of genial manner that appealed to the elderly. More to the point, Dame Jessica remembered him from way back as a fellow member of the British Euthanasia Society – before it changed its name to 'Die With Dignity' and then again to the cheery, pop-style 'Way To Go'. Yes, dear old Wally would make the perfect pensioners' tsar.

But, having shown her more human face, the Prime Minister was still fuming at an inexcusable breakdown in communications over the petition. Someone should have told her about the massed ranks of scooters in Whitehall. Her intended photo opportunity had seriously misfired, boomeranged in fact. She'd been humbled by Keep Breathing's organisers and she wanted revenge. She called Sir Justin Beryan, her State Security Minister. From now on, retired people's groups would be added to the list of subversive organisations requiring intelligence surveillance – along with Muslim jihadists, animal rights activists, Catholics and trade unions. It was time for a thorough review of national security.

*   *   *

Great Gran, of all people, was first with the news. "They've just announced it on the telly," she told Howard breathlessly from the payphone in her care home's communal lounge. "It's what you've been campaigning for – a special tsar for pensioners. Isn't that amazing – after all this time! You'll never believe who they've chosen."

He had to admit she was ahead of him. "You've scooped me on this one, Mother. Who is it…Lord Lucan?"

"It's Sir Wally Alcock…the pop star as was. You know who I mean…he's always on the telly."

At first, he thought she was pulling his leg. "You're having a laugh, aren't you, Mum!"

"No, I've just seen it on the news. It showed him on the step outside No 10 with Jessica Sykes. She said he was the new OAP icon, whatever that means. He's only 75…a bit young for the job but he's better than nothing. We've finally got someone to stand up for us…and not before time."

You had to marvel at Dame Jessica's deviousness, Howard conceded. Alcock was an ex-punk rocker who now hosted TV talent contests, game shows, reality romps – anything that would keep the fat cheques rolling in. He was a serial adulterer and divorcee who'd had more wives than Henry VIII and, as such, a public figure of fun. Such was the ridicule he inspired that, when he'd been awarded his knighthood, hundreds of people sent back their own gongs to the Palace in protest. But he still had plenty of admirers among the older generation.

Howard seemed to recall that Alcock had also been a leading light in the euthanasia movement, which made his appointment even more controversial, but he hadn't the heart to disabuse his mother of her new-found optimism. Before hanging up, she told him that Alcock was billed to appear on *Pandora* the same evening. She'd be disillusioned soon enough.

When the celebrated old humbug duly presented his credentials as Pensioners' Commissioner to Adrian Lennox for his all-important TV seal of approval, millions of viewers were also left in no doubt as to his manifest unsuitability for the role. After much back-slapping, with extravagant congratulations modestly accepted by Wally (as far as was possible for a man who didn't do 'modest') the great TV inquisitor dropped the old pals' act in favour of his familiar intimidating manner.

His guest, with dyed shoulder-length hair and regulation grubby T-shirt of the elderly hippie, settled in his chair, his rubbery, stubbled features fixed in a permanent expression of undiluted happiness. It diluted slightly at Lennox's first serious question.

Would he, in his new capacity, advise the government to raise the state pension above the poverty level instead of cutting it? Wally's manic grin hardened into a frown as he tried to concentrate on the soundbites he'd rehearsed. Then it came to him…he was not a member of the government or an ombudsman. He had no powers to increase benefits. All he could do was sympathise.

Lennox pressed on. "What about the oil, gas and electricity sharks raking in obscene profits while pensioners freeze to death?"

"There are generous home insulation grants. You just need to claim them!" He gave viewers his trade-mark wink and thumbs-up sign.

The non-committal soundbites were going nowhere. *Pandora's* researchers had filled the presenter in on Alcock's antecedents so he adopted a sterner tone. "I understand you support plans for obligatory euthanasia. Shouldn't an old people's tsar be trying to protect them not kill them off?"

Good ol' Wally did manage a grin for the cameras now he was on slightly firmer ground. "I've always believed the old and vulnerable should be given help to end their lives if that's what they wish. The elderly do worry about dying, y'know. They want some control over it."

"They also worry about *living*," Lennox cut in. "They'd like some control over that as well but you don't seem able to help them."

The geniality now returned, undimmed. "But I *can* help them at the end of their lives," he insisted. "When life becomes unbearable and they find themselves a burden on the state – through no fault of their own, mind you – I can advise them how to apply for assisted suicide. No fuss, no bother and absolutely free! That's how I see my role…doing pensioners a big favour when they really *need* one. I mean…why end your life in pain when you can end it in pain-free comfort?"

The grin widened into a clown's frightening mask of love for all humanity. "My message to all patriotic pensioners is simple: if you love your country as much as you love yourself, you can save the nation with terminal sedation!" He winked broadly at the cameras in recognition of his rhyming prowess and repeated his thumbs-up gesture. "Take it from me…it's the modern Way To Go!"

Watching the bizarre performance in their lounge, Howard and Barbara could only wince at the crude, slapstick approach to the euthanasia Bill. But they grudgingly admired Dame Jessica's double-edged publicity coup. Wally clearly had no interest in making pensioners' lives easier, only in how he could help them kill themselves. With a tsar like him ruling his silver serfs, who needed thanatologists?

TWENTY-FOUR

State terrorism varies in style and intensity throughout the world. In Russia, for long specialists in the field, secret police would drag you out of bed in the middle of the night without warning or explanation and ship you off to Siberia, where you would perish amid the permafrost. Those seen as threats to national security in African countries tended to meet a swifter and hotter end as their homes were burned down with them inside.

Some Pacific island rulers preferred to make a meal of their opponents and in Afghanistan you'd simply be staked down naked among the poppies under a hot sun while ants did the same. The sort of nepotism American subversives used to expect from Uncle Sam took the form of a long holiday in Cuba with the term 'room service' given a whole new meaning.

In Jessica Sykes' Britain you got an altogether better class of state terrorist. Recruited from public school/Oxbridge/Home Counties backgrounds (none of your ghastly oiks from 'oop north'), they were suitably unscrupulous, ruthless and amoral but in a very polite way. These well-bred secret agents enjoyed the euphemistic description of 'spooks' since, although they did not officially exist, they gave every appearance of doing so. They were in every sense the direct opposite of angels, who do exist but are not thought capable of assuming physical form.

In common with their international counterparts, Sykes' spooks excelled in leaning on and occasionally eliminating dangerous anti-Establishment figures without leaving the slightest attribution to the Powers that be. But unlike their crude contemporaries, they practised their art with finesse and unfailing courtesy. Once a victim had been deemed a threat to national security, he or she was invariably favoured with a friendly word of warning before being harassed or meeting an untimely end. The warning was usually delivered in a brief telephone call from a gentleman with a cultured voice, using an untraceable number.

In Howard's case the subtle intimidation lasted rather longer. He had left hospital a week earlier and was sitting in his lounge toying with *The Announcer* crossword when the phone next to his armchair rang.

It was the cultured voice. "Is that Mr Howard Mitchell?"

"It is. Who's calling?"

"Let's just say I'm an admirer, Mr Mitchell. I must congratulate you on your rolling blockade."

"Thank you but I need to know your name."

"I don't have one."

"That must be very inconvenient for you."

"I'm a senior civil servant in the State Security Department and can't identify myself for obvious reasons. Perhaps you'll allow me to give you a word of advice."

Howard was all ears. "Go on."

"I don't know whether you experienced any hostility to your demonstration yourself but there does seem to be a growing element of alienation towards the elderly as a result. Does it occur to you that your demo might have been counter-productive?"

"If you read the newspapers you'll find that most people support us."

The supercilious voice continued smoothly. "That may be so, Mr Mitchell, but there are those in positions of authority who find your activities unacceptable."

"That's too bad."

"What they find particularly offensive is that not content with insulting the Crown by defiling your Order of the British Empire, you now plan a rival award for those who break the law. They regard that as intolerable."

So they knew about the alternative OBE. Was there anything they didn't know? "I find it intolerable to mug old people for their pensions."

"I'm only trying to help you, sir. You're approaching 70 and in poor health...it's in your own interests to consider a range of consequences that could result if you persist..."

"You bet I'll persist."

"Think about it, Mr Mitchell. In your position, the pressure of adverse events..."

"What kind of 'adverse events' are we talking about?"

"Who can say? It's a dangerous world as you are well aware. Accidents can happen..."

Howard knew the polite code for a death threat. He'd heard it before. He felt the same mixture of apprehension and anger rising as he did on that occasion. This time he also felt palpitations. His breath was short and shallow but you never showed the enemy the slightest sign of weakness.

"Do me a favour, buster. Get lost."

He slammed the phone down. His hand shook and he was sweating freely. After a few puffs on his spray had calmed him down he tried to trace the call. It was 'number withheld', of course.

The crossword forgotten, he poured himself a stiff whisky to calm his nerves. Here we go again, he thought. At least they hadn't threatened his poor mother this time. You couldn't help but marvel at their malice. As a journalist he'd dealt with all levels of human nature, from teenage yobs who stabbed their victims to death for their smart phones, to low life who swung their babies round by the legs and battered their heads against the wall. Yet even at that level – the dregs of society – nothing compared with the premeditated cruelty of the ruling class if they deemed it expedient.

*   *   *

At the first opportunity, he told Bernard about the call. They agreed not to inform Barbara at that stage since the histrionics of the rolling roadblock were still affecting her health. Her GP had signed her off sick and advised her not to return to work until the migraine attacks had disappeared.

There was also a chance that the spooks would back off. It was part of the crash course they'd all taken in applied psychology. The fear of violence was often as effective as violence itself. It could be a bluff in a lethal game of poker. On the other hand, Howard could have pushed his luck too far. He'd already been labelled an enemy of the state by trashing an Establishment honour and had reinforced the image by helping to bring the capital to its knees. Now he was rubbing salt in the wounds by launching an alternative OBE that rendered the old version redundant. The Powers that be were notoriously bad losers...

The veteran partnership agreed to tighten security and to be careful what they said on the phone. William had already encrypted the group's computer records and hidden back-up copies of everything in places that even Howard didn't know about. It would also be necessary to keep checking his old Rover. Although kept in its locked garage most of the time, that presented no problem for spooks. Tutored by the cream of the nation's burglars, they could unlock any door in the country.

As far as Bernard was concerned, his old *Announcer* colleague would remain fireproof whatever the security goons threw at him. He'd proved several times that he was one of life's great survivors. On a holiday to the Isle of Man years ago, Bernard had been fascinated by the three-legged symbol displayed all over the island. He asked a bartender what it meant and was told it represented the indestructibility of the Manx people. Their motto was: 'Whichever way you throw me, I'll stand.' It could have been coined with Howard in mind – and he had only two legs.

Even so, indestructible though he regarded his fellow scribe, he had mixed feelings about the small package that was burning a hole in his jacket pocket. For a moment – just a moment – he thought about telling Howard there'd be no problem if he wanted to back out of the deal. Then he dismissed the unworthy thought. His old comrade in arms would be deeply offended.

As they sat with mugs of coffee in the study, long since converted into an untidy general office, he opened the small presentation case and unwrapped a round, gleaming gold medal from its tissue paper packing. "Our alternative OBE...the Owen Bryn Evans medal...for services to humanity." For some reason, Bernard's deep voice and Scouse accent added a gravitas to the words that no refined tones would be likely to capture.

Howard took the medal and admired it almost reverently.

"It's the prototype," Bernard said. "If you're not happy with the design it can be melted down and changed."

"It's perfect...exactly what we'd agreed."

One side carried Owen's embossed profile complete with full beard and the name Owen Bryn Evans, the initials tastefully but not ostentatiously enlarged. The reverse bore the inscription: 'For services to humanity', with laurel leaves at either side.

"It's an amazing medal, Bernard. But it's pure gold. Can we afford it?"

Bernard's rugged features creased into a wide beam behind his goggle-like spectacles. "No problem."

He unwrapped another small package and produced a selection of different coloured silk ribbons. "I thought you and Barbara might like to choose the ribbon." He took one, a lustrous crimson, and held it aloft. "I prefer this one myself – for obvious reasons."

Again Howard was amazed at the superb quality of the ribbons and clasps as he turned them over in his hand. "You're right there. But we must ask Barbara – and William. He's become a full partner in this operation now." He handed the ribbons back to

Bernard. "You've still not told me how we're going to pay for this."

Bernard extracted a small notebook from his inside jacket pocket and turned several pages. "I hadn't been able to check the balance until this morning. Since our little expedition round Bloomsbury and back, we've moved into six figures. Like to guess how much?"

Strictly by way of a joke, Howard said: "Quarter of a million?"

"Half."

"Half a million?"

Bernard grinned. "Correct."

"That's amazing!"

"It'll buy a lot of gold medals."

"You're not kidding. How many are we going to need, do you reckon?"

Bernard did a quick calculation. "Not all that many, really. Roughly 100 members have served prison sentences for non-payment of fines. Most have asked us not to pay their fines as a matter of principle. All of them deserve our special OBE don't you think?"

"Of course. And certain others I can think of. So how much will a hundred cost?"

Bernard gave the gleaming gong a little polish with his handkerchief. "I'll need to ask the goldsmiths. I only ordered this one as a prototype…before all the donations came rolling in…thought we'd need to cast the rest in copper or something like that."

"But now, hey…the sky's the limit. They won't call our members golden oldies for nothing!"

High fives and tens were in order.

Bernard's enthusiasm was infectious. "We'll need to have an investiture, of course…a proper ceremony like they have at the Palace…invite all the medal winners and their families."

"Now you're talking…with full Press and TV coverage. We'd make the front pages all over again! Where do you have in mind…for a venue?"

"Well, we can expect hundreds of people. I was thinking about somewhere like the Royal Albert Hall but we don't really want anywhere with 'royal' in the title do we?"

Howard laughed. "They wouldn't want republicans like us either. Far too expensive, anyway."

"I wondered about the Press Club but it's not big enough for all those people. We need a spacious, high profile venue…so I thought: what about the Millennium Stadium in Cardiff? Owen was Welsh after all."

"Spot on, think big…the bigger the better."

"The rates for their conference centre are quite reasonable and they've a date free in July so I suggest we book it while we can, assuming we're all in agreement."

"Sounds good to me, Bernard. I'll run it past Barbara and William, and get back to you as soon as possible. Once we've cleared the date, I'll organise a Press release. There's just one slight problem."

"What's that?"

"Who'll present the medals?"

"You, of course. You're quite a celebrity now in case you haven't noticed."

"And I won't charge a fee so it won't cost us anything?"

Keep Breathing's treasurer returned the medal to his jacket pocket and grinned. "That as well!"

It was always going to be close, bearing in mind New Phoenix's slim overall majority over their combined opponents. But in the days leading up to the fateful vote on the Health of the Nation Bill, intensive lobbying by members of Keep Breathing, the National Pensioners' Forum and disabled groups suggested there might yet be a back-bench rebellion.

All calls for a free vote had fallen on deaf ears but there were reports that several government MPs were tempted to defy the three-line whip. Along with millions of TV viewers, some older back-benchers had been moved by the scenes in Trafalgar Square during the scooter demo. The Chinese tourists' spontaneous outpouring of affection for the demonstrators had proved that humanity recognised no frontiers.

The MPs prided themselves on their support for endangered animal species yet here was a highly vulnerable human group threatened with extinction by their own leaders – and it had taken people from another culture to highlight their plight. Sometimes you needed an outsider to help put your own house in order. And, in this case, that house was the House of Commons. The rebels knew that to defy the Prime Minister on crucial legislation would inevitably wreck their careers but there were times when conscience transcended politics. This was one of them.

When the day of the vote arrived, thousands of demonstrators, young and old, able bodied and disabled, gathered outside the Palace of Westminster in a bitter easterly wind. Watched from his plinth by Oliver Cromwell, who'd had his own methods of population control, they overflowed out of Old Palace

Yard into Millbank and Parliament Square, blocked off to all vehicles, including scooters, to avoid a repeat of the previous week's debacle. They tirelessly waved their banners and chanted:

"Not dead yet…Not dead yet…Not dead yet…Not dead yet…Not dead yet…"

Inside the packed Chamber the atmosphere was charged with drama, plus a whiff of treachery on government benches. Rumour and speculation abounded, not least in the overflowing Press gallery where wordsmiths of differing political hues struggled to make guesswork appear plausible, and dilettante 'political analysts' contrived superficial soundbites for radio and TV. Such was the public interest in the occasion that the television audience – normally no more than a few thousand for everyday Commons debates – outstripped that for *EastEnders*, a phenomenon unequalled before or since.

As soon as the Speaker called for order the excited buzz of conversation in the Chamber subsided. With the ponderous solemnity of his office, he announced the resumption of the debate on the Health of the Nation Bill, and the ineluctable Sylvia Pullar rose to speak. Two crucial amendments needed to be made to the Bill, which she would propose as briefly as possible before applying for the Parliamentary guillotine procedure – known as an Allocation of Time Order – to curtail debate on them.

She came straight to the point. "Mr Speaker, before formally moving for an Allocation of Time Order, I wish to announce two further amendments. The House will be aware that, in response to misguided pressure from reactionary elements, the British Medical Association has withdrawn its support for the Bill.

"We regard the decision as deplorable and socially irresponsible but it cannot be allowed to stand in the way of our vital legislation. Accordingly, it has been decided to replace doctors with fully-trained, state-licensed thanatologists to ensure the Bill's objectives are met. Once again, I must stress that our Maturity Contract offers a guaranteed safeguard for those who withhold consent. If they prefer to prolong their suffering, all they need do is sign the legally binding opt-out clause enshrined in the Bill.

"Secondly, I understand certain citizens are proposing to emigrate rather than comply with legislation enacted by their democratically elected representatives." To calls of "Hear, hear" and murmurs of disapproval, she continued haughtily: "That, of course, is their prerogative. They're free to leave whenever they desire. However misconceived their decision, we recognise their absolute right to take it. But the rest of the nation has rights too. In the circumstances, it is only reasonable to declare that those who desert their country in its hour of need can no longer rely on their fellow citizens to support them."

(More loud cries of "Hear, hear" from government MPs and shouts of protest from Opposition benches).

"Mr Speaker, I move that, henceforward, retired people who emigrate from these shores to frustrate the will of Parliament shall be deemed to have automatically forfeited their United Kingdom state pension. Accordingly, their benefit will be withdrawn from the date they leave."

The diminutive orator sat down abruptly and the Chamber erupted in uproar. "Order...order," boomed the Speaker, to no avail. Only when he could make himself heard and threatened to suspend the sitting did the nation's democratically elected representatives stop behaving like naughty schoolchildren. Like a bull that had just been stung by a wasp, Reg Wilkins, Leader of the Opposition, sprang to his feet to oppose the amendment.

With thinning hair, a paunchy physique and intimidating manner, Wilkins was regarded by his supporters as something of a rough diamond. In less than two decades, the retired police officer had succeeded in making xenophobia almost respectable. He had transformed the BNP from a poorly-educated Right-wing rabble into the main Opposition party, albeit by a slim margin. His remarkable achievement had been due to a passionate if unsophisticated eloquence and that vital ingredient of success – sincerity. As someone once said, if you can fake that you've got it made.

The John Prescott lookalike waded into the debate in his usual combative style. He accepted the need for thanatologists as long as they were properly trained and as long as patients still had the right to opt out of the Maturity Contract. But robbing British citizens of their pensions – to which they'd contributed all their lives – while we continued to subsidise the tidal wave of immigrants swamping our country was totally unacceptable. Wouldn't it be more patriotic to stop handing out billions to foreigners who see us a soft touch instead of victimising the aged? Miz Pullar, Dame Jessica Sykes and the whole New Phoenix Party should be ashamed of themselves.

The Prime Minister, seated opposite at the Dispatch Box, remained impassive, refusing to rise to the bait but, as Wilkins sat down to loud cheers from his supporters, Ms Pullar rose to denounce his remarks as characteristically racist and obnoxious. Although older citizens had contributed to their pensions, these were largely subsidised by the state and that meant taxpayers. They had their rights as well as those who'd been panicked into deserting their country. There was no need for them to leave. All they had to do was sign the opt-out clause.

There was no lack of righteous indignation from other MPs, many demanding further time to debate the amendments before implementation of the guillotine and others renewing calls for a free vote according to individual conscience. But the Speaker, a pompous pedant, overruled their demands. The debate had already exceeded its allotted time. To prolong it would jeopardise the Commons schedule, which he regarded as sacrosanct, even bearing in mind the life-and-death-nature of the issue. It was time for the House to 'pronounce itself' on the matter. Three votes would be taken, the first two on the amendments and the third on the substantive Bill itself.

When the division bells were rung and Members meekly filed into the lobbies in response to their three-line whips, it was noticeable that several government MPs remained seated on the green benches by way of abstaining. A few brave souls actually crossed the floor, under the withering stare of Dame Jessica. It was going to be close. Uncomfortably close. The drama heightened as the tellers totalled the votes, then solemnly carried the results from the lobbies to the Clerk, who in turn presented them to the Speaker to complete the archaic ritual. Once all the politicians had returned to their places, the Speaker rose to announce:

"In the first vote on the amendment, the employment of thanatologists, the Ayes...314; the Noes...320. The Noes have it."

There were gasps from the government benches, a waving of order papers from the opposition and applause from the public gallery. Dame Jessica raised a hand to her forehead and compressed her eyebrows with a thumb and finger.

"In the vote on the second amendment, the withdrawal of state pension entitlement from those leaving the country, the Ayes...312; the Noes...322. The Noes have it.

"In the vote on the Health of the Nation (Death with Dignity) Bill itself, the Ayes...322; the Noes...324. The Noes have it."

In the ensuing pandemonium, the Prime Minister rose quickly and stalked out of the Chamber, brushing aside her all-female entourage of secretaries and junior ministers. The forlorn figure of Sylvia Pullar sat in stunned disbelief, surrounded by a knot of sympathisers, while obloquy and renewed chants of 'Not Dead Yet' rained down on her from the public gallery. The Speaker ordered it to be cleared and suspended the sitting.

The Press gallery, normally a haven of silent, shorthand-writing probity, seethed with activity as backs were slapped and wagers settled. Representatives of the *Guardian-Independent* and the BBC were thought to have been the main losers. They looked less than happy as they filed their reports for the early editions and evening news bulletins. The days had long gone when you could claim on your expenses for losing bets.

Outside, the wind had strengthened and it had started to rain but the weather could not dampen the demonstrators' euphoria. Squads of police in riot gear roughly pushed the jubilant crowds back to clear a passage for the Prime Minister's bullet-proof, bio fuel-powered limousine and its motor-cycle escort. As the convoy swept away towards Whitehall, Dame Jessica scowled at all the happy laughing faces. For an Australian, losing was never palatable. For an Australian feminist, it was unthinkable.

She leaned back in the enfolding comfort of her leather seat and plotted her revenge. Although the battle had been lost, the war continued. Her long-cherished Bill may have been defeated – but it was not dead yet.

TWENTY-FIVE

When the Prime Minister's motorcade completed the short drive from the Palace of Westminster to No 10 Downing Street, Dame Jessica stepped briskly out of the limo and hurried up the steps without bothering to wave to the cameras. Once inside the austere hall with its Masonic square-tiled floor, gloomy paintings and slightly moth-eaten rug, she politely but firmly detached herself from her entourage. A very heavy problem was weighing on her mind and she needed time on her own to think, free from all the secretaries, researchers, bodyguards and hangers-on.

As Britain's second woman prime minister slowly climbed the Grand Staircase en route to her private apartment, she glanced briefly at the photographs of her predecessors – some more illustrious than others – until she came to Margaret Thatcher, when she stopped. What would *you* do, old girl? she thought. You'd never lie down and let them beat you, would you?

Dame Jessica recognised it as the ultimate rhetorical question. She quickened her step as if a load had finally been removed from her shoulders. Once in her private study, she locked the door, sat at her desk and tapped a number on one of her three bug-proof telephones – the direct line to the head of state's personal private secretary. It was an emergency, she told the languid cut-glass voice that answered. No, it couldn't wait until tomorrow. She needed an immediate audience.

Of course, nobody, not even the Prime Minister, could just drop in at the Palace for a chat whenever they felt like it. So she laid it on as thickly as possible. She knew that heavy was the head that wore the crown and he was very busy working on affairs of state, a role to which he selflessly devoted his whole life in the interests of his subjects. (She suspected he was actually watching the snooker on TV.) No-one admired him more than she did. He was a remarkable inspiration to the entire nation.

There was a pause and a further question. No, it wasn't another war, she replied. But it was a real emergency just the same. Another pause. Then: he would see her at 8pm, during the interval in the snooker.

Dame Jessica replaced the receiver with a scornful sigh. Englishmen and their snooker! It was the only game they could win. She switched on her computer and started to write her notes in readiness for the audience. For all his faults, the king was an enthusiastic supporter of population control and had given the controversial Bill his full backing in their discussions. Even after the doctors had backed out, to be replaced by licensed thanatologists, his support hadn't wavered. He would be as displeased as she was over its defeat.

She rang for some tea and reviewed her notes. Yes, she'd summarised the position cogently. It fully justified the emergency meeting at the Palace. The plan she had in mind for rescuing the stalled Bill's main provisions was undoubtedly Draconic but he would have to go along with it whether he liked it or not. He had no choice. By then, her chief speechwriter would be polishing her address ready for transmission to the nation on television.

*   *   *

Probably for the first time in his life, Howard found politics more interesting than snooker. Although the World Professional Snooker Championship was being played out on BBC2, the vote on the Health of the Nation Bill on the Parliament Channel was infinitely more gripping. The lives of his mother, Barbara's parents and millions of others depended on it. Grandparents and great-grandparents everywhere clung to the desperate hope that a ray of humanity would penetrate the utilitarian, money-obsessed minds of the politicians.

Howard had been banned from attending the Westminster demo on doctor's orders. Bernard had not gone either. He was occasionally allowed a life of his own and had escaped for a dental appointment. Barbara was working an afternoon shift. But William and Louise brought a six-pack of Howard's favourite beer and the three of them watched the historic event unfold on the lounge TV. When the cameras panned across the sea of faces in Old Palace Yard and beyond, picking some out in close-up, Howard thought he caught a glimpse of George Armstrong. He knew George was in there somewhere to represent the Keep Breathing/NPF Coalition. You couldn't keep a good man down.

When the voting figures were finally announced, the crowd went crazy. And the motley trio in the Mitchells' lounge followed suit. They jumped to their feet in a spontaneous reggae gyration mixed with elements of jive, while toasting their triumph with raised beer cans. Howard, who couldn't play a note of music apart from half-remembered versions of *Chopsticks* and *Jingle Bells*, sat at the Bluthner and thumped the keys in a glorious cacophony of discord. It was like midnight on New Year's Eve all over again.

As relative sanity was restored, they switched channels to watch the snooker and the anti-climax could not have been more marked. It was like walking from a fairground into a library. In the darkened auditorium with its brightly lit rectangle of green baize and coloured balls, the players went about their highly-skilled business in an atmosphere of total calm, cocooned from the frenetic outside world. Even a maximum break here would have been overshadowed by the excitement of events in Parliament – and it was not often you could say that.

Howard sent William out for another six-pack and settled down to watch the beautiful game. When Barbara returned from work she found him asleep on the sofa, slumped 'tight against the cushion' (one of his favourite expressions), with several empty beer cans and others unopened on the walnut coffee table. She'd heard the result of the vote on the car radio and smiled indulgently at the sleeping form. The snooker's afternoon session had finished and she switched the TV off.

She shook him gently. "When the doctor said plenty of fluids, he didn't mean beer."

Howard stirred and opened his eyes. He wasn't drunk, just 'relaxed', as they used to say in the newsroom.

"Have you heard…we won the vote! We won! We won!"

She laughed at his boyish exuberance and they embraced as best they could with him still semi-recumbent. "Yes, I heard on the radio. I could hardly believe it. The campaign…all that work…actually paid off."

"We had a few drinks to celebrate…William, Louise and I…"

"So I see." She kissed him lightly on the forehead. "I'll let you off this time."

He stood up stiffly, shrugging off the pain in his back and ribs. "How about you, Barbara…can I get you a drink?"

"I need something a bit stronger," she said slumping into an armchair, unbuttoning her dark blue uniform tunic and kicking off her shoes. "It's been one of those days."

He knew what she meant. He poured her a gin and T at the drinks trolley and handed it to her. "How about going out for dinner…celebrate properly?"

"Not tonight, Howard, thanks all the same. I'm too knackered. I'll let you take care of dinner instead. Just the two of us…William and Louise are going out."

In the end they settled for a Chinese takeaway washed down with champagne and accompanied by his evening medication – in defiance of doctor's orders not to mix the two. Then they curled up on the sofa to watch the resumed snooker championship. Barbara was soon flat out and he was nodding himself when, as one of the players was about to complete a long and painstaking century break, coverage was rudely terminated by a newsflash.

An announcer informed viewers: "We interrupt this programme to go over to our news studio for an item of breaking news."

It must be big for them to interrupt the World Championship, Howard thought. And it was. The picture cut to a regular newsreader seated at his desk in front of a screen showing a middle distance view of Buckingham Palace. Reading gravely from his autocue, the presenter said: "In the last few minutes, the Prime Minister, Dame Jessica Sykes, left Downing Street for an unscheduled audience with the sovereign at Buckingham Palace. The reason for the visit is not yet known but an announcement is expected to be made within the hour. Further details will be brought to you in our extended news bulletin at 10pm. Now back to the snooker."

Howard roused his slumbering wife with a gentle prod in the ribs. She woke with a start.

"Was I snoring?"

"No, there's just been a newsflash. Jessica's gone to the Palace to see the Special One...mysterious unscheduled visit."

"Did they give us any clues?"

"No, but you can bet it wasn't to take him fish and chips."

"Maybe she's going to offer her resignation...after the humiliation of losing her nasty Bill."

"Could be. I doubt it somehow but we live in hope."

Howard brought coffee from the kitchen and they watched the snooker without much interest until the next news bulletin. When it came, there were no headlines flashed across the screen in the usual brisk and breathless style; simply the same newsreader as before seated at his desk and looking even more solemn. Behind him were twin views of Buckingham Palace and No 10, Downing Street, both ablaze with lights against a darkening sky.

"Good evening," the newsreader intoned gravely. "Following today's Commons defeat of the Health of the Nation Bill, the Prime Minister made an unscheduled visit to Buckingham Palace for an urgent audience with the head of state. Dame Jessica has now returned to Downing Street and has agreed to address the nation on the outcome of their dialogue. We're going over now to No 10 for her live broadcast."

The scene cut immediately to a medium close-up of Dame Jessica seated in a winged armchair in her White Drawing Room. Shaded lamps glowed softly in the background and a vase of multi-coloured flowers stood on a small side table. The Premier's hair had been freshly dyed in a lighter brown and blow-waved to look less severe. She wore a businesslike but elegant burgundy two-piece with a white silk neck scarf and small gold earrings. Bearing in mind her image consultant's advice that she couldn't do 'grave', she did her best to look cheerful while mindful of the fact that what she was about to say was no laughing matter.

Across the foot of the screen a caption read:

'Dame Jessica Sykes speaking live from No 10, Downing Street.'

"Good evening to you all," she said in a firm voice, still with the slight Queensland accent that intensive elocution lessons had failed to eradicate. Reading from an autocue slowly scrolling at the side of the camera, she continued: "You're probably aware that the Health of the Nation Bill was defeated by two votes in the House of Commons today. As a result, government policy for tackling the global population crisis has been seriously compromised. I do not exaggerate when I tell you that survival of the entire human race is at grave risk if the world's governments fail to tackle the scourge of uncontrolled population growth. Our plans to comply with the United Nations emergency resolution simply cannot be allowed to fail. The alternative is too serious to contemplate. It would involve contingency measures to ration food, oil, gas, electricity and further cuts in welfare benefits including the state pension itself.

"As your democratically elected leader, it is my duty to take whatever steps are necessary to avoid such a disaster. Accordingly, after full consultation with the monarch, I have decided to invoke the Emergency Powers Act which became law in the early part of this century to protect the public from terrorism. Under the Act, I am empowered to order the reinstatement of the Health of the Nation Bill's provisions in the form of emergency regulations, to remain in force until further notice. I now solemnly make that order.

"In addition, I direct that the amendment to the Bill – demanding state pension entitlement be withdrawn from those who emigrate – shall be approved and incorporated in the regulations. No-one appreciates the severity of these measures more than I do. It is with a heavy heart that I am compelled to take them. My hand has been forced by today's events in Parliament, which elevated misguided moral issues above national and global interests. Our great nation has survived many difficult challenges in the past. With your help and understanding, we will survive this one."

The Prime Minister's well-fed features creased into a confident smile – the sort Rex Clifton would have approved. "Good night."

*   *   *

In the Mitchells' own white drawing room, better known as the lounge, the mood was as flat as what remained of the champagne. Barbara was the first to break the stunned silence. "I had a feeling it was all too good to be true. We're back to square one, aren't we?"

"Even worse. Grandparents are now branded the new terrorists. They're free to leave but without their pension. They'll be deporting them next."

Barbara's hand flew to her mouth. "Mum and Dad...what'll happen to them?" She reached for the telephone and called their number. No reply. "They've probably gone to bed. They go early. I'll leave a message."

Howard thought of his own mother in her comfortable nursing home. In five more years her widow's pension would be cut by half and inflation would have undermined her paltry private income – assuming she lived that long. If not, then at least she'd have died a natural death, spared from obligatory euthanasia. It was a macabre thought. What he needed, he suddenly realised, was another drink. He hobbled stiffly to the drinks trolley. "Scotch?"

"No thanks. And you've had enough for today...all the medication you're on."

He poured himself a large whisky and ginger ale. "Stuff the medication!"

They sat in silence, watching the obligatory collection of experts, commentators, analysts and Uncle Tom Cobleys offer their totally irrelevant take on the shock development. They were the usual suspects, the shrivelled Pullar, her head now completely shaved,

275

trying not to look smug behind her little round anarchist's glasses; a hirsute young man from the *Guardian-Independent* with a ring in each ear, an elderly balding Catholic priest and a glamorous Anglican priestess. No sign of George Armstrong or anyone from the pensioners' movement (presumably the priest doubled in that capacity). And nobody from a serious newspaper. Once again, the broadcasters' idea of balance could only be described as laughable.

Not that it mattered much since nothing the motley gathering said could in any way mitigate Dame Jessica's act of dictatorship under cover of emergency powers. The skinhead MP reiterated the urgent need to save the planet from disaster. Practical measures must take precedence over outdated moral values. This was no time to yield to deluded reactionaries. Surprise, surprise, the trainee journalist agreed, saying the international community had made that mistake over global warming and look what had happened. (Not a lot, actually.)

When it came to the priestess's turn, she vacillated, equivocated, flapped her arms and tied herself in knots in a performance of erudite-sounding, diluted Christianity. One had to balance the needs of the nation with those of the individual. While having mixed feelings about assisted suicide, it could be seen as "a final act of generosity by our senior citizens". In the context of the economic crisis, the Bill might be regrettable but necessary. On the other hand, could it be right for utilitarian considerations to transcend humanitarian ones? By a roundabout and tortuous route, she ended up asking the question she was supposed to be answering.

Finally, the priest was allowed to get a word in. He came straight to the point. The Health of the Nation

Bill was nothing short of state-sanctioned elder abuse. It signalled the ultimate collapse of the British way of life. For the Prime Minister to reinstate it after its defeat in Parliament was a further abuse of the democratic process. He and his Church would support any move to refer her indefensible action to the European Court of Justice. He tried to add that the government could solve most of its financial problems by abandoning futile foreign wars, starting with the one in Sri Lanka – but the programme had run out of time.

*   *   *

Fred telephoned early next morning. Barbara answered in the bedroom. Her father and mother had watched the previous day's events on TV and couldn't wait to flee the country.

"Who'd have thought it would come to this?" His speech was heavily slurred but his mental alertness was undimmed. "Great Britain...the wars we've fought...all those RAF heroes who died in the Battle of Britain...young lads in their prime...gave their lives for their country...tragic waste. Look at us now...a dictatorship."

Barbara had never known him so bitter. "Will you be able to go to France, Dad...I mean, if they take your pension off you?"

"No problem...they're welcome to it. Won't be much of it left anyway."

"But how will you manage?"

"My company pension...and we've got a bit put away. Plus what we get for the apartment."

"Have you sold it yet?

"Not yet…but as soon as we do we're off. Lucky we still can. Lots of people will have to stay now…and face the music."

"We'll miss you, Dad…you and Mum. The family's going to miss you."

"We'll miss you, too, dear. But we'll see you before we go. We'll keep in touch by phone. And you can always come over and visit us. Promise you'll do that."

Barbara was close to tears. "Of course, Dad. You know we will. I promise."

"That's my girl."

"Wish we were coming with you."

"You've every reason to stay, Barbara. You're still young…you've got all your family round you…"

"Dad, I'm 62."

He laughed heartily. "Wish I was 62 again!"

"Bye, darling Dad. Love to Mum."

"Bye, Barbara. God bless."

She hung up and sank back on the bed next to her slumbering husband. Even in his sleep he offered a shoulder to cry on.

TWENTY-SIX

Hugo Michaelson paced up and down his office's well-worn blue and grey diamond-patterned carpet, occasionally pausing to gaze out of the window at the dark city streets and run a hand through his famous mop of rumpled hair. It had come to this. Britain, the home of parliamentary democracy, was now a dictatorship. It had been a completely bloodless coup. With the aid of a gang of population control freaks loosely described as the New Phoenix Party, Sykes had used anti-terrorism laws to inflict state terrorism on a blameless public. It was an act of bizarre irony.

The Announcer's lawyers had confirmed there could be no challenge by way of judicial review since the terms of the Emergency Powers Act were absolute. Any appeal to the Supreme Court would be sure to fail. Its judges, the former Law Lords, were all solidly pro-Establishment. The TUC were threatening a general strike. If it went ahead the Emergency Powers Act would ensure troops manned power stations and other essential services. Experts in constitutional law planned to petition the European Court of Justice but the ponderous process would drag on for months, if not years. By then, the Maturity Contract would have taken a heavy toll.

Even the power of the Press was likely to be circumscribed under the new emergency powers. Hugo's executives had rushed out the early editions with front pages devoted entirely to the political bombshell and its widening fallout. How much longer they would be able to do that without the threat of imprisonment remained anyone's guess. There was already talk at his club about 'persuading' editors to sign the Official Secrets Act in the interests of national security, which would effectively hand over control of the Press to the government.

After that, as evidence from the International Federation of Journalists proved every day, it would be downhill all the way. UK editors would be on a par with those in Asia and South America. Hugo seated himself at his desk and scanned an early draft proof of the headlines:

SYKES SEIZES POWER TO REVIVE EUTHANASIA BILL

Disabled in national outcry; Vatican denounces 'crime against humanity'

He switched on his computer. What was clearly needed for the Leader Page was an act of leadership, a call for people power and a last stand against tyranny – before he felt the heavy hand of the censor on his shoulder:

Time for a British Spring

Just when we thought sanity had prevailed, an act of tyranny has returned us to the brink of despair. By reinstating the barbaric Health of the Nation Bill in defiance of the will of Parliament and the medical profession, Jessica Sykes has assumed the role of dictator at a time when dictatorships around the world are going out of fashion.

She has taken this retrograde step ostensibly to comply with an alarmist and misconceived United Nations directive on global population but her real motives stem from economic constraints and anti-life ideology rather than concerns for humanity. When it comes to human rights she has more in common with Wally Alcock than the director-general of the United Nations.

There is no denying Dictator Sykes has dealt a desperate blow to those of us who treasure the most basic human right of all – the right to life. It is vital that we rally in its defence. All is not lost. Any nation that can survive Thatcher and Blair can surely survive Sykes. It is time for a British Spring – for our long-suffering people to lead us on the road back from the brink. It will be a long road but in common with other nations who have confronted tyrants, we will get there in the end.

*   *   *

"You realise what this means, don't you?"

It was George Armstrong on the landline the day after Dame Jessica's shock proclamation. Howard had answered the phone as he and Barbara sat in their kitchen drinking coffee and discussing what to take with them on their trip to Andalusia.

"It means we're stuffed, at least for now," he replied.

"No way, Howard. What it means is another rolling blockade…only this time a bigger one."

"I'm sure you're right, George but Barbara and I need a break. We're escaping to Spain for a couple of weeks…doctor's orders."

"You've had a hard time, I know. Demonstrating is tough at our time of life…but it's all we've got left. They keep turning the screw…we have to respond…fight fire with fire."

Howard knew all about the need for persistence but George was a younger man, without his own catalogue of ailments. "We just need a breather, George. Give us two weeks and we'll be back in business."

"What about Bernard?"

"He needs a break, too. He's been working his socks off for months. He's going to the Isle of Man for a week. Don't worry, as soon as we get back, we'll be in touch. You're absolutely right. We need to keep up the pressure."

"Fair enough, Howard. I'll start laying the groundwork again. There's a lot to organise, as you know. I'll phone again in a fortnight. Have a good hol, you've certainly earned it."

"Thanks, George, we'll do our best."

"Whereabouts will you be staying?"

282

"Little place called Canillas…high up in the mountains. Our daughter Sally has a studio near there. It'll be good for my angina, I'm told."

"Inspired choice…you'll be a different man when you get back. Cheers."

*   *   *

They were due to take a midweek flight to Spain in late May and on the day of their departure Barbara insisted on her husband accompanying her to Mass at St Chad's. They'd bought their tickets, dug out their passports and arranged the necessary insurance. All they needed, to complete their preparation, was to say a special prayer for a safe journey.

Howard felt that, having paid a hefty surcharge on account of his various health problems, he already had sufficient insurance against all eventualities but reluctantly agreed to the additional protection since it didn't involve any extra premium. But, as always, he felt uncomfortable as they entered the church porch and Barbara crossed herself with holy water.

"Why do you do that?"

"All Catholics do it."

"But it's just water."

"It's *holy* water…for dehydrated souls…that's what the Church teaches."

"And you go along with that?"

"Of course."

"I didn't know your soul was dehydrated."

"Sshh…and for God's sake take your cap off."

They took their places in the half full church. Once again Howard was struck by the hushed silence. There was definitely an atmosphere, something you couldn't quite put your finger on. A phrase came to mind from somewhere in the dim and distant past...'the odour of sanctity'.

Everyone stood as Father Fitzgibbon swished in and they were off again:

"The Lord be with you."

"And with your spirit."

Howard smiled patiently. At least there would be no hymn-singing. As the liturgy progressed through the Lord's Prayer and the Sign of Peace, he even found himself recognising a few passages. When it came to: 'Deliver us Lord, we pray, from every evil...' he thought of the cultured voice on the telephone:

"Accidents can happen."

He hadn't mentioned the call to Barbara and there'd been no more since. But he was careful to check the car every day and bolt the garage door on the inside every night, entering the kitchen via an internal door. In Howard's book, prayer was fine. Trust in God by all means – but make sure you cut the cards yourself.

The Mass ended with the congregation being enjoined to "go in peace" but as they made their way out, Father Fitz was standing in the porch guarding a small pile of *Tablet* magazines in case certain people tampered with them. He didn't look all that peaceful so Howard bought a copy.

"Something to read on the plane," he grinned.

The young priest's manner relaxed. "Well, thank you, Mr Mitchell."

Barbara was not amused but her husband took her arm and steered her gently through the door before she could say anything about liberal Catholics.

"Blessed are the peacemakers," Howard quoted, as they emerged into the weak sunshine. "How does the rest go?"

"For they shall be called children of God," she sniffed.

"There's hope for me yet then?"

She managed a brave smile and squeezed his arm. "Just a glimmer."

*   *   *

News that an alternative OBE was to be awarded at a rival investiture organised by the Pensioners' Coalition ignited the public's imagination. Many felt it was high time to scrap the anachronistic honours system. Military decorations for bravery were admirable but medals glorifying a long-defunct empire had no relevance today. Ever since Howard had ditched his gong, the public mood had swung behind calls to sweep away a system rooted in the Victorian era, when Britain really was a land of hope and glory. Nowadays, in the words of the *Sun*, it was more 'a land of dope – and gory'.

The red-top tabloid launched a national campaign demanding a referendum on a republican constitution. Thousands of people across Britain – not just *Sun* readers – were interviewed and the result was startling. More than three-quarters of respondents were in favour. While most believed exemplary community service deserved official recognition, an obsolete medal was just a back-handed compliment. Confidence in the worthiness of recipients was undermined by ongoing 'cash for honours' scandals which kept getting brushed under the carpet.

The system had clearly become discredited – 'rotten from top to bottom' was a phrase widely used – yet nothing was done by the ruling class to change it. Normally the BBC could be relied on to squeeze the last drop of controversy out of the issue, mainly through the *Pandora* current affairs slot, but they remained strangely silent. It was probably a coincidence that the programme's celebrity presenter had recently been awarded a knighthood for services to broadcasting. Sir Adrian and Lady Rose Lennox were honeymooning in the Bahamas (they had been required to marry before the title could be officially conferred). They'd travelled by scheduled flight rather than private jet. Nobody quite knew why, though there were rumours of "certain cash flow problems". Perhaps, on their return, Sir Adrian would challenge the corrupt honours system in characteristically robust style. Then again, of course, he might not.

TWENTY-SEVEN

Deep in a wood at the foot of a steep hill somewhere in Buckinghamshire stands a small, quaint cottage with roses round the door. Though unoccupied it will never be put up for sale because it hides a very large secret. Behind it, tunnelling into the hillside to a depth of 200ft, a passage leads to a bunker complex designed to house over 1,000 members of the ruling class in the event of a nuclear war. The complex, powered by its own electricity generator, provides air-conditioned accommodation for the VIPs, their families, technical support staff and selected servants.

Behind 4ft thick reinforced concrete walls and heavy, blast-proof steel doors lie carpeted conference rooms, rest rooms, a computer room and, at the heart of the complex, an operations centre. The Cold War might be a thing of the past but the great and the good are not the sort of people to take chances, bearing in mind their provocative foreign policy and the world-wide proliferation of nuclear weapons.

Deserted now but still maintained by a skeleton staff and security guards, the bunker has few visitors. But once a month it hosts a most unusual event – a meeting between seven people who don't exist.

Whether composed of protoplasm or ectoplasm remains a matter for conjecture but the seven members of the State Security Service (SSS) who arrived for their May meeting looked solid enough. One by one, at the appointed hour, they stood outside the door of the operations centre for their iris recognition checks and tapped their secret codes into the electronic key pads. Then, having discarded wristwatches, rings, mobile phones, pens and anything capable of concealing miniaturised recording or filming equipment, they passed through an arched metal detector into the inner chamber.

The Secret Seven, as they called themselves (they were not without a black sense of humour), trusted nobody, not even each other. In Britain's police state highly sensitive microphones and cameras were everywhere, most of them installed by the spooks themselves, but there were also mavericks out there, anxious to spy on the spies. So the SSS had the chamber 'swept' for listening devices before each meeting.

No pleasantries were exchanged as the dark-suited, middle-aged men took their places round an oval table covered in a green cloth, with a single jug of water and seven glasses. There were no name cards but each place bore a number – from one to seven, denoting the heads of the seven departments. No 1, the chairman, was Cabinet State Security Minister Sir Justin Beryan, 'Beria' himself; No 2, the head of Muslim counter-terrorism; No 3, leader of animal rights counter-terrorism; No 4, head of the Catholic Church subversion unit; No 5, responsible for trade unions surveillance; No 6, head of republican infiltration, and No 7, leader of the newly-formed department monitoring retired people's pressure groups.

Not all the delegates looked villainous. Some, while embodying the ponderous alertness of secret policemen the world over, even appeared human. But under the harsh fluorescent lighting, the face of Chairman Beria called to mind a memorable phrase from Solzhenitsyn's classic, *The First Circle*: "The blackness of his heart stood out on his face." He was the only one with a beard, a triangular grey goatee, and with his little rat-trap mouth, hooded malevolent eyes and heavy eyebrows, could have stepped straight out of a medieval torture chamber as Robert Cecil, Earl of Shrewsbury.

In those days people labelled traitors (often erroneously) were hung, drawn and quartered – a process of cutting them down from the gallows while still alive, disembowelling them and hacking their remains into four pieces, which sometimes featured as trophies in the homes of Cecil's henchmen. But the SSS had come a long way since the days of its founder. Now you had to arrange for your victims to have tragic accidents instead.

The chairman opened proceedings with the obligatory rubric, delivered in short, clipped and cultured tones. "Gentlemen, a reminder that we do not exist. No minutes, notes or records of any kind will be taken. Understood?" The hooded eyes darted round the table and they all nodded. It was just a formality.

He took a sheet of paper from the inside pocket of his Savile Row jacket, and laid it on the table with his small, immaculately manicured hands: "Gentlemen, as we are all aware, the republican movement is gaining strength. Drastic action is needed if a constitutional crisis is to be averted. Sections of the media are openly rallying public opinion against the institution of the monarchy, while challenging our ancient system of royal honours.

"They have adopted as their figurehead one Howard Mitchell, a former *Announcer* journalist and trade unionist who, it will be recalled, insulted the Crown by defiling his award of the Most Excellent Order of the British Empire. He has since compounded his insolence by producing a so-called alternative OBE for those who break the law of the land – and by organising a mock investiture at which the bogus medals will be awarded.

"Moreover, he is the high profile leader of a national protest movement that was instrumental in sabotaging the Health of the Nation Bill, a measure on which our country relies for its very survival. His high profile stems from his ability to manipulate the media more effectively than we do, despite all our expenditure on public relations.

"Since this person's activities clearly undermine the established social order, exposing it to revolutionary pressures, they can no longer be tolerated. While every allowance is made for freedom of speech, there comes a point where persistent subversion amounts to treachery. That point has now been reached. The target has been given due warning but has failed to respond. Therefore, since no other remedy is available, he is hereby deemed a 'real and present threat to Crown and Constitution' who must be dealt with accordingly, as a salutary example to others."

The chairman folded the paper, replaced it in his pocket and turned to the newly-appointed departmental leader. "No 7, the target falls within your jurisdiction. Kindly outline your proposals."

No 7 was a bright young former section head who took his recent promotion very seriously. "Certainly, sir." He produced a voice recorder the size of a matchbox that had been given security clearance. "The target M has been kept under regular surveillance. He plans to visit Spain on holiday in the near future. This is a recording of a recent telephone conversation." He switched on the device which played an extract from George Armstrong's call to Howard a few days earlier.

"Have a good hol, you've certainly earned it."

"Thanks, George, we'll do our best."

"Whereabouts will you be staying?"

"Little place called Canillas…high up in the mountains. Our daughter Sally has a studio near there. It'll be good for my angina, I'm told."

"Inspired choice…you'll be a different man when you get back…"

No 7 switched off the recorder. "*If* he gets back. With the meeting's approval, two of our most diligent agents will ensure he doesn't. I propose that they follow our standard procedure. As we all know, accidents can happen."

There were smirks on the spooks' faces. Some suppressed slight coughs.

"Any questions?" asked the chairman.

No-one said a word. The man had been deemed a traitor. That was enough. They didn't need to know who had done the deeming, although they had a shrewd idea. And the less they knew about what form the 'accident' would take, the better.

"Then, all those in favour."

The vote was a formality. It needed to be taken for procedural purposes. Spooks were sticklers for procedure; it helped to give a kind of structure to their non-existence. It was unanimous, of course.

The chairman then closed the meeting in the obligatory manner with the ancient imprecation: "So mote it be!"

*   *   *

Sally met her mother and father at Malaga Airport late on the Wednesday afternoon. They looked tired and older than when she last saw them a couple of weeks before. The flight had taken its toll. It had lasted two hours but had been delayed by a further two hours at Gatwick. In addition to a gung-ho style take-off by a trainee first officer and excessive turbulence, there had been the usual hooligan on board, 30,000ft high on something other than adrenalin.

The flabby, pony-tailed lager lout let everyone know he was in holiday mood from take-off. Seat belt signs were not for him, nor were repeated requests to sit down by the flight attendants. He had smuggled his own alcohol on board and when refused more from the trolley, became aggressive. Only when the flight captain arrived to threaten him with restraint did he subside in his seat and fall asleep. If a parachute had been available there would have been no lack of volunteers to apply a gentle push.

It seemed an unwritten rule of air travel that these comedians were always to be found in seats immediately in front of the Mitchells, thus adding to the stress of the journey for Barbara for whom flying was itself an ordeal. So by the time they reached Malaga and spent another half an hour wondering if their luggage would ever appear on the carousel, she described herself as frazzled. They were both feeling their age and the unaccustomed heat of the Costa when they finally reached the exit and saw Sally waving. She hugged the pair of them and her dazzling smile helped lift their sagging spirits.

Their taxi had been specially reserved. It appeared in seconds, driven by Sally's regular driver, Felipe, who spoke no English except for "Manchester United" and "Ronaldo", which rather gave his age away although he didn't look that old. They all collapsed inside and Sally gave him his instructions in fluent Spanish. The journey to their hotel in the mountains would take less than an hour, she said, but the worst was now over.

At least, that was what they thought. But as the taxi sped away through the traffic from Malaga towards the Sierra Almijara towering in the distance, the thought may have been a little premature. Barbara sat in the back with Sally, chatting about the family and the fluctuating relationship with Eduardo, while the cab's radio played faintly and Felipe tapped one hand on his window sill in time to the music.

Everything seemed relaxed and cosy but after a while the road narrowed and became more tortuous. Howard, seated in front in an unfamiliar position with the driver on his left, noticed prayer beads and a small crucifix dangling from the rear-view mirror. Nothing special about that, this was a Catholic country. But after a while it became clear they were there for a reason.

In the course of a few minutes, dusk had darkened into night and the vehicle's headlights illuminated a continuum of hairpin bends, cliff faces rising sheer from the road on one side and falling steeply away on the other. There was little traffic now but when their taxi met an oncoming vehicle, both slowed down and passed each other at a respectful crawl, their wheels inches away from the unfenced edge of a seemingly bottomless ravine.

As the gradient grew steeper and the hairpins more hair-raising, only Felipe seemed unconcerned, although he'd switched off the radio and was now keeping both hands on the steering wheel. Howard noticed that the chatter from the back seat had stopped. He half turned to see his wife and daughter holding hands and gazing wide-eyed at the road ahead – or perhaps it was at the crucifix, swaying on the windscreen. It was too dark to be sure but both their faces seemed to have grown pale, probably matching his own. He had been a car driver for nearly 50 years but there was no way he would attempt to drive along this road.

At last, after negotiating a short, loose stone gradient of about one-in-four, the cab crunched into a small courtyard. They had reached the Hotel Murillo in one piece. Felipe turned to him and smiled nonchalantly. "Buenas noches, Senor."

Howard felt like hugging the man but realised such a gesture might be misconstrued. As his Spanish was strictly limited, all he could say was: "Gracias, muchas gracias…mucho gusto" while recognising the total inadequacy of the words.

When their luggage had been unloaded and carried into the hotel foyer, Pedro, the hotelier, asked in broken English if they'd had a good flight.

"It wasn't the flight," Howard told him. "It was the road that terrified us."

*   *   *

Sally had been right. The air on the Sierra Almijara was something else. If you could compress it and bottle it, you'd make a fortune in London, Howard thought idly. You could offer two varieties: sparkling or still. The sparkling version would be cool, crisp morning air while that in still form would capture the balmy ambience of a warm afternoon by the pool. Come to think of it, you could also offer a third variety, that of a sultry evening spent in the shade of a century-old olive tree.

He was sitting on the hotel terrace watching his swim-suited wife and daughter splashing in the pool when the chink of tea cups broke his reverie. A waiter, instilled with the importance of afternoon tea to the English, placed the ritual tray on a small table. Howard called to Barbara and Sally and they joined him in their towelling robes. It was early season and the only other guests at the hotel were a group of walkers from Germany. They spent their days roaming the rugged scenery and the quaint Moorish villages, leaving the Mitchells the run of the hotel. It was like having their own private villa.

Sally had some good news. "I was telling Mum…Eduardo phoned earlier. He's sold two of my paintings. Isn't that great…months without a sale and then he sells two!"

Howard and Barbara both smiled. It was good to see their daughter happy. They knew the on-off courtship was back on the agenda, though there were still no plans for a wedding. They'd met Eduardo soon after their arrival – over a week ago now – and both agreed he was admirable son-in-law material. There was no substitute for age and experience in assessing these matters.

Sally poured tea into china cups. "So, anyway...we're going to celebrate. I'm taking you both out to dinner tomorrow night. I'll phone my friend, Manuel, and make the reservation. He owns El Ghonero in Canillas, the best restaurant for miles."

Her parents were encouraged to hear of the sales. They knew little about art but both felt her prices were on the high side. Sally, on the other hand, felt they were too low. Her art celebrated the rhythms of nature, something which she maintained was far beyond price. She left the grubby commercial side of the operation to Eduardo. The day after the couple's arrival, she showed them round the studio she rented from the hotel. It was full of her canvasses, mostly figurative but some abstract. Howard found the latter impenetrable although Barbara was intrigued by them.

"I'll buy one myself when you get married," she told Sally.

"True artists are above bribery, Mum," her daughter laughed. But Barbara could sense that a sale might not be far off.

*   *   *

Hugo Michaelson faced the most agonising dilemma of his life. During a night's hard drinking at his club with Justin Beryan, his Cabinet 'insider', the SSS chief let slip something deeply disturbing. They were discussing the phenomenon of pensioner power and the conversation got round to "a certain thorn in our side".

"Who do you mean, Justin?" Hugo asked disingenuously.

"You know perfectly well who I mean, dear boy." Leaning closer and swaying slightly, the goatee-bearded grandee added: "He might not be around much longer."

"Are we talking about Howard Mitchell and his health problems?"

"A masterly euphemism, Hugo…very serious health problems." Beria leaned back in his hand-tooled, buttoned leather armchair and took another swig of his claret.

"He's off to Andalusia to recuperate but there's reason to believe the treatment might turn out to be terminal."

Hugo was several drinks behind his friend. "I'm afraid you've lost me."

"Strictly between ourselves…and strictly off the record…accidents can happen." He tapped the side of his nose with a bony forefinger. "Know what I mean?"

Hugo thought he knew what his friend meant, although he didn't want to. "Surely you're not talking about…"

"I can say no more, dear boy." His informant suddenly remembered he was talking to a journalist. "I've probably said too much already…"

The memory of the conversation aroused deep misgivings and an even deeper sense of conflicting loyalties when Hugo woke from a bad hangover next lunchtime. The club's claret had loosened the tongues of contacts in the past but none so indiscreetly as that of his high-level government contact.

His position as *Announcer* editor gave him a unique entrée to the ruling class hierarchy…a privilege he had achieved at the cost of many close friendships. It had been a long time since he'd exchanged his newsroom colleagues for boardroom toffs. There could be no going back. The thought of jeopardising his hard-won status as a toff himself with a lingering hope of a knighthood to compensate for the debacle over his OBE was not one he could entertain for long.

And yet...and yet...he was still basically a journalist. That was something that never left you. Howard Mitchell may have usurped his OBE before slinging it in the river – an unforgivable action – but for all his loony socialist ideas, he was still an old and respected colleague. They'd worked together for years before going their separate ways. Of course, he'd made enemies. All reporters did. It went with the job. But his Quixotic attack on the Establishment had made him one powerful enemy too many. He was a marked man.

Howard was a journalist of the old school, a throwback to a different world in which truth and honour still counted for something and human life was sacrosanct. Now, in Sykes' Britain, kids were killing each other on the streets every night while the state planned to exterminate their grandparents. Life was cheap and disposable – including Howard's. They'd take him out in a cynical 'accident'. His old colleague's big mistake had been coming out of retirement. He was about to pay for it.

Hugo lurched into his kitchen and made some strong black coffee. The paper's personnel department kept records of all present and retired employees. They would have Howard's contact details. He'd ask around at the Press Club for his videophone number. Then he'd find an unvandalised payphone and make a brief call.

A word in the old hack's ear, for old time's sake. It was the least he could do.

TWENTY-EIGHT

As it was early season and as a favour to Sally, their resident artist, the hotel offered her parents their de luxe suite at a standard rate. Over the years, the couple had stayed at numerous hotels, up to and including five-star rating, but had never seen accommodation like it. There were three rooms: a sitting room, bedroom and en suite bathroom. The sitting room was conventional, with comfortable armchairs, coffee table and wide screen TV, but both the bedroom and bathroom had been hewn out of the mountainside, leaving one rugged rock wall in each. The rock was painted white and the remainder of the rooms were elegantly appointed with marble tiled floors and contrasting colourful furnishings to create the effect of luxurious caves.

In the bathroom, a sunken bath with gold fittings lay in a kind of grotto with stone overhanging on three sides. The suite was certainly unconventional but it gave Barbara the creeps. There was something about it that filled her with a sense of foreboding. It was warm in the bedroom as she changed into a slinky green figured silk outfit for dinner but she still shivered. She'd experienced these premonitions before and they'd seldom been wrong.

299

The hotel's landline had been behaving oddly since the Mitchells' arrival and was now out of order, awaiting repair. So Sally used her mobile to phone for a taxi to take them to the restaurant. Howard showered, shaved and donned his uncomfortable 'investiture' suit. Then he waited outside on a flower-decked veranda and watched the sun slide behind the Sierra at the end of another perfect day. The chiming of a distant church bell carried faintly on the warm breeze but the relaxed moment was suddenly shattered by a louder ring from his jacket pocket. He took out his videophone and adjusted his hearing aid to its telephone setting. Its battery was running low and he'd forgotten to pack spares.

He switched the phone on. "Hello."

The instrument identified the call as coming from a public payphone in the UK, without a visual image. Reception was crackly and intermittent but he thought he recognised the voice. Then he realised it was Hugo Michaelson...of all people. How did he know he was here and what on earth could he want to talk about?

"Hugo, how are you?"

Hugo wasted no time in small talk. His voice was anxious and he sounded in a hurry. "Howard, there's something important you need to know...the SSS are watching you, they know where you're staying and they're planning..."

For a moment, Howard's hearing aid cut out. Then the faltering power returned in time to hear Hugo signing off...

"...so watch your back, old chap. Best of luck. Cheers,"

Howard switched off the instrument and returned it to his pocket. He cursed quietly as he snatched the malfunctioning hearing aid out of his ear. For all its advanced technology the device was useless without its tiny batteries. They were not the sort of thing the hotel would stock and the chances of acquiring them out here in the wilds of Andalusia were minimal. Even if he were to find another hearing aid user, you could bet the Spanish aids would be of a different design. He sighed and restored the wretched gadget to its case. There was nothing else for it: people would have to speak up.

He had a good idea what Hugo had been trying to tell him. The memory of the 'accidents can happen' phone call he'd received a few weeks earlier was still fresh in his mind. He'd stepped up security at home and took extra precautions when travelling. On arriving at the hotel, he'd covertly scrutinised the other guests, but they were just German walkers who disappeared into the mountains every day. As far as it was possible to tell, the staff were above suspicion. They were all known to Sally, who had a special affection for them as spiritual country people – a different species from city dwellers.

Surely he and his family would be safe enough out here in the middle of nowhere. He shivered and buttoned up his jacket all the same. Dusk fell quickly on the mountain, along with the temperature. By the time their taxi arrived for the short drive to Canillas it was dark and growing colder by the minute. Both Barbara and Sally wore shawls over their dresses and Howard was persuaded to wear a scarf that Barbara had packed for him.

It was the hotel's regular taxi, Felipe's comfortable Seat Toledo. He greeted them with his broad smile and ceremoniously opened the doors for them. "Buenas noches, Senora, Senorita, Senor." They settled in their familiar places, Barbara and Sally in the back and Howard next to the driver. It would only be a short ride to Canillas, about 15 minutes, Sally said. Although it was pitch black, with the cab's headlamps once more highlighting the stomach-churning mountain switchback, there was nothing to worry about; Felipe knew every inch of the road.

They did their best to relax, reassured by the crucifix and rosary beads swinging gently on the windscreen. The darkness was all-encompassing. There wasn't another vehicle on the road within miles – until a single light appeared in Felipe's mirror. He slowed down as the light grew brighter. Every taxi driver knew the drill on this road.

As they approached the most difficult hairpin, skirting an unprotected near-vertical drop of 750ft, the light was upon them. It was a motor-cycle, now alongside. There was a pillion rider. He was pointing something at their driver's window. A split second before the flash blinded him – a massive sheet of brilliant light that lit up the mountainside – Felipe braked sharply, pulled on the handbrake and switched off the engine. With a tremendous roar, the motor-cycle hurtled past, wobbled out of control and shot straight over the edge of the precipice into the aching void.

It was all over in seconds. But the taxi's occupants seemed to sit there for ever, too horror-struck to move. "Dear God...dear merciful God," Barbara breathed as the reality of what had happened sank in. Sally clung to her mother, shaking and sobbing quietly. Felipe was rocking in his seat, clutching both eyes and moaning. Howard could hardly breathe. For the first time since arriving in Spain, he needed his angina spray – urgently.

After several deep breaths he gasped: "Are we... are we all...okay?"

"Not Felipe," Barbara cried. She bent forward anxiously to comfort the driver whose quick thinking had spared them all from the abyss. He'd stopped rocking but was bent over the steering wheel, his head in his hands and trembling violently. The intense flash of light – laser, strobe, whatever – had exploded within a few inches of his face and had obviously blinded him. But there was nothing she could do in the way of first aid. She couldn't even communicate with him.

Sally's translation services were urgently required. Still trembling herself, she dabbed her eyes with a handkerchief and asked Felipe in Spanish if he was okay, an unfortunate question in the circumstances, but everyone was still trying to emerge from shock and a disorientating sense of unreality. He shook his head violently. No, he could see nothing...he could feel nothing.

Obviously, there was no way he could drive. One of them would have to take over. If the cab stayed in its precarious position it would be a hazard to other vehicles. There could be another terrible accident. They needed to move it immediately. Howard was quick to appreciate the urgency. No other vehicles had appeared yet, but when one did the consequences didn't bear thinking about.

"Tell him I'll drive. We'll have to change places."

"He can't get out of the car," Barbara told him. "He's completely blind...numb with shock. He needs time to recover."

"We don't *have* time. I'll get out and come round. Can you try to pull him across?"

303

"Howard," Barbara cried in alarm. "We're inches from the edge. You can't get out."

He looked out of his window and in the dimly reflected light of the car's headlamps could just see a grass verge about 18 inches wide bordered by some six inches of rock, then nothing. Nothing but blackness.

"It's all right. We're a good two feet from the edge." He opened the front passenger door and was immediately hit by a gust of wind that snatched his breath away. Pulling his scarf tightly round his neck, he opened the door again. Barbara could not bear to look. She crossed herself and offered a silent prayer.

"Dad, be careful," Sally shrieked. But the howl of the wind muffled her cry. With the door half-open, he eased his feet onto the grass verge. Then, still gripping the door with one hand, he grasped its frame with the other. Turning to face the car, he edged gingerly towards the rear, closing the front door inch by inch. A stone, dislodged under his feet, slid over the edge into the blackness. "Please, God," he whispered, for the first time since childhood, as a monstrous gust snatched his cherished cap from his head, hurling it into history, urging him to follow.

He clung on desperately. For a bizarre moment, fear gave way to indignation. He'd had that cap for 25 years...it was irreplaceable! Then the wind abruptly changed direction, gusting into his back and pinning him to the taxi. He found a handhold round the tailgate window and clutched at its wiper blade. Breathing heavily, he hauled his way round the car and opened the driver's door. Barbara and Sally had half pulled Felipe across to the passenger seat and he completed the process with a series of pushes. He sank into the driver's seat, gasping and weak at the knees, his heart palpitating. Phew…but so far so good. Still no sign of any other vehicle. He took a hurried puff from his trusty spray and noticed it was dangerously low. Then he scanned the Seat's unfamiliar controls. Felipe was holding his eyes with one hand while clasping the crucifix from the windscreen with the other. He was still completely blind and in intense pain, his limbs still numb. There was no way he could drive.

Howard had never driven a left-hand drive before. But with Sally's translation of Felipe's hoarse guidance he soon worked out what was what. He seemed to remember saying there was no way he would ever drive along this road. Never say never. There was a first time for everything. Nervously, he started the engine, released the handbrake and engaged first gear. He slowly steered the car round the hairpin until the headlamps showed the road straightening out. Everyone breathed more easily. Like a learner driver, he tentatively changed into second, then third, keeping well away from the beckoning brink on the right. He was getting the hang of it. Only one question remained: where were they going?

"Just carry on for about five kilometres if you can, Dad," Sally said. "Felipe knows a Dr Garcia in the next village. He needs urgent treatment." Then, for the first time, she noticed something different about her father. "You've lost your cap, Dad."

"Tell me about it. It's like losing an old friend."

"Don't worry…we'll buy you another."

"Thanks but it won't be the same!"

By the time they reached the doctor's house, Howard's control of the Seat had grown more assured, though he kept the speed below 30kph. Only once did they meet an oncoming vehicle, a small van, but they'd reached a stretch of straight, sheltered road. Both vehicles slowed to walking pace and passed each other without difficulty.

Howard and Sally led Felipe, limping heavily, into Dr Garcia's well-equipped surgery and, with Barbara's aid, helped him lie on the couch. The medic, middle-aged dapper and briskly efficient, applied drops to both the driver's eyes and produced dark glasses. After a thorough examination, the prognosis, translated by Sally, was that Felipe would be fine. His eyes were inflamed but retinal damage was minimal. He had split vision that would soon wear off. Feeling was returning to his limbs and he should be fit to drive in 24 hours. He could stay with the doctor and his family overnight.

When told the events of the last half hour, Dr Garcia insisted on treating them all for shock. They sat in his comfortable waiting room, draped in blankets, and the doctor's wife brought them strong tea. She offered biscuits and home-made cake but nobody felt hungry. As the doctor checked their pulse rate and blood pressure Howard asked him, via Sally, if he would phone the police. He had already called them.

They arrived in two cars half an hour later which, considering the nature of their route, was a commendable response time. There were two young constables and two older plain clothes detectives, all with the ubiquitous bearing of stolid alertness though more hirsute than their British counterparts. Laboriously, they took statements from Felipe, whose voice at least had returned, Howard, Barbara, Sally and Dr Garcia.

It lasted over an hour, by which time the officers possessed eye-witness accounts of a case of attempted murder that had, with supreme irony, turned into a tragic accident. They would investigate the scene immediately and at first light a helicopter would search the lower slopes for bodies. Meanwhile, as it was now growing late, they would be happy to drive the Mitchells back to their hotel.

Wearily, the effects of delayed shock kicking in, they trooped out to the police vehicles. But before leaving the surgery, a thought occurred to Howard. Dr Garcia had been so efficient he might be able to replace his angina spray. He also needed hearing aid batteries – if the medic had any – so that when he phoned *The Announcer* with his latest scoop he could hear people at the other end.

Amazingly, the doctor went straight to a cupboard and produced both spray and a small packet of the precious batteries. When Howard tested one on his aid, it worked loud and clear. "Ole!" He took out his wallet but Dr Garcia waved it away. "El Dios de mayo va con usted." ("May God go with you," Sally translated.)

Felipe hobbled out with them to the cars. Normal vision was slowly returning but he still wore dark glasses. He shook Howard's hand warmly. "Buenas noches, Senor. Gracias por todo usted hizo." ("Thank you for everything you did.")

Howard asked him how he thought he might make out if he were to take up taxi driving. Sally passed on the question and Felipe's reply. "He said you'd be sure to earn many fat tips."

TWENTY-NINE

It was the morning after two talented young spooks, with first class honours degrees from Oxford and middle class parents in the judiciary and civil service, embarked on their date with the devil. No 7, their newly-appointed departmental head, waited with growing impatience for the all-important phone call from Andalusia and the code words – 'the party's over'. He had waited all night but the message with its subtle double-meaning never came.

Now, as the grey sky lightened over Tower Bridge, he watched the early morning bustle return to the river in an effort to keep his eyes open. Despite the air conditioning in his expensively fitted new office, he felt the sweat moistening his palms and temples. He loosened his collar and Winchester College tie, mindful of the need to tighten them before his secretary arrived.

Something had gone wrong. He'd tried repeatedly to contact his agents but there was no signal from their state-of-the-art phones with their back-up global positioning. More ominously, the main location transmitters concealed in their crash helmets were also silent. The familiar bleeps had disappeared from the map on his computer screen at 8pm the previous evening. He had no idea where his spooks were.

The transmitters operated via satellite as did their multi-function phones. Although reception in the mountains was notoriously difficult, the transmitters were so sophisticated their signal could have reached him from the Moon. Granted, they were sensitive and easily damaged. One could have malfunctioned, but two? It was either that or…

He pulled himself together. No, it was unthinkable. They were his brightest operatives…mid-twenties, unattached, fluent in several languages, including Spanish. Their IQs were the highest in the section. And their training had been meticulous. They'd rehearsed the operation using sophisticated 3-D computer simulation. After several dummy runs their timing was perfect. There could be no possibility of failure.

True, one of them had expressed misgivings about wasting three innocent lives as well as the target but his lapse into old-fashioned morality was soon corrected. This was 2019, his section leader reminded him. Human life was cheaper than it had ever been. It wouldn't be the first time innocent people were taken out as well as the target. It happened regularly in similar 'accidents' throughout the world. All governments assumed a divine right to murder in the interests of expediency. Innocent victims were regarded as collateral damage. The Powers that be didn't think of them as human beings and neither should their secret agents. You were expected to carry out your professional training and put your country before your conscience.

In practical terms, the multi-victim wet operation offered a big advantage over single hits. It made the 'tragic accident' scenario more plausible. Certain strict rules needed to be followed: that the mission took place in a foreign country (to ensure maximum diplomatic obfuscation) and that it happened under cover of darkness, either in a remote area, at sea or in a tunnel where there could be no witnesses.

The Andalusia operation fulfilled every requirement but as the morning wore on without any word from the duo, No 7's anxiety turned to desperation. Was he about to blow his first wet operation after he'd only been in the job five minutes? He phoned Severiano Rodrigues, commercial attaché at the British Embassy in Madrid, on the secure direct line. His secret service colleague had heard nothing about any fatal accident on the Sierra Almijara but would make enquiries.

His secretary brought him coffee and the morning papers. They were full of the war in Sri Lanka and a new geological survey casting doubt on the size of the island's oilfield. No mention of Howard Mitchell, the traitor and pensioners' celebrity champion. If anything had happened to him it would have been front page news.

It was early afternoon before the call came, confirming No 7's worst fears. He had just finished a cheese and pickle sandwich with more coffee, and what his Madrid contact told him almost brought it all up in the waste paper bin. The police had found the bodies of two young men and a wrecked motor-cycle on the mountainside near the village of Canillas.

The pair had clearly come off the road on a hairpin bend 750ft above. The unidentified bodies were dressed all in black, with black crash helmets and night goggles. They'd been flown by helicopter to a mortuary in Nerja. Two crushed satellite phones and a smashed strobe light had also been found near by. The Press were asking questions. They seemed to think the men were British. Could London offer any input on that?

With an effort, No 7 suppressed his nausea and instinct took over. Deny everything. Disclaim all knowledge of the men. Disown them. That was standard SSS procedure. Everyone knew the score. Mendacity was their creed, their 'noble cause' that transcended everything. It had been drilled into them as part of their training.

Madrid would need to 'refute' the theory in the strongest terms. It should be emphasised that there was no evidence of the agents' nationality. It was a golden rule that agents never carried any ID while on missions. Their Japanese phones would have been unused and their ownership could not be traced. They'd served only to relay the coded message on completion of their mission.

No 7 knew the pair had rented a remote cottage a few kilometres from the Hotel Murillo after landing near Nerja by speedboat from Gibraltar. They'd been instructed to converse in Spanish at all times. The motor-cycle was Spanish with false number plates, Sevvy Rodrigues' team had seen to that. Where had the rumour come from that the men were British? Their helmet location transmitters were obviously damaged and may now be visible. If so, he was confident they carried no British markings. The strobe? That was Chinese but what about its high intensity bulb...?

He felt sick again. Beads of sweat stood out on his forehead. "Check the strobe bulb for markings," he almost screamed into the telephone.

"We can't. What's left of it is in police custody," Sevvy said.

"Then demand access under diplomatic immunity."

He slammed the phone down and mopped his forehead with a handkerchief. Had one tiny mistake proved fatal – literally? Or was he panicking unnecessarily? Even if the strobe carried a British mark it wouldn't prove the agents were British. They could be any nationality who just preferred a British model – like they preferred a Chinese-made strobe and Japanese phones. He needed to calm down. There was still a chance he could hang on to his job. With luck, his son's name could remain on the waiting list for Winchester.

To soothe his shattered nerves, he glanced at the photograph of his wife and their baby son on his desk and recalled the axiom: Eton College was where you sent boys not thought bright enough for Winchester. A weak shaft of afternoon sunshine slanted across his desk which, combined with lack of sleep and the ongoing stress, almost caused him to nod off in his executive leather armchair. The sudden buzz of his internal phone made him jump. It was the Minister, Beria himself. The jitters returned, worse than before.

"Update me on events in Spain, please."

"There's been an unexpected setback…"

"So I gather. Tell me."

"The target has survived and our agents are dead, sir."

"Have we covered our tracks?"

"Yes, sir, I'm confident we have."

"You'd better be right. If this gets out we're all stuffed. Keep me informed."

He wondered how Beria already knew about the cock-up but was too fatigued to dwell on the question. Before he could leave for home and some desperately needed sleep, there were other tasks to perform. Although it was obvious the bodies were those of his agents, he would need positive confirmation before informing their next of kin. He organised the electronic transmission of the necessary face recognition modules and thumbprints to the Madrid embassy with instructions for an agent to travel to Nerja and complete the process under diplomatic immunity. Arrangements would need to be made for the bodies to be flown home, once the Spanish police had closed their files on the case.

His newly purchased super electro-turbo Jaguar saloon waited in the underground car park but he realised it would be foolish to drive in his present state. He was about to call a taxi to take him home when his secure phone rang. It was Madrid and the news was not good. In fact, it was catastrophic. The strobe had been closely examined and a British imprint found on the base of the bulb. But worse by far was the revelation that one of the agents was still alive when rescuers reached him. He had managed to say a few words in English to a paramedic just before he died.

The paramedic, who spoke fluent English, clearly remembered the words as they seemed particularly poignant in the circumstances. They were:

"The party's over."

*   *   *

Howard sipped his freshly squeezed fruit juice and nibbled the bread and cheese that passed for breakfast at the Hotel Murillo. It seemed a poor way to celebrate surviving an assassination attempt. A bottle of champagne and a full English would have been more appropriate but if there was one fault to be found in an Andalusian holiday it was the absence of a proper breakfast. His first task on returning home, whatever time of day it might be, would be to cook a classic fry-up of bacon, eggs and sausages – laced with tomato ketchup, which did not seem to have been discovered in Spain.

Barbara and Sally sat opposite at the terrace table, looking pale, drinking coffee and marvelling at their narrow escape from death. They shuddered at the thought that the two motor-cyclists who'd tried to force them off the road had plunged to their deaths themselves. Who could have done such a thing? Howard had a good idea and recalled that Hugo had tried to warn him but he'd not heard the crucial details. Barbara also remembered her dark premonition the previous evening and attributed their survival to a miracle. Experience had taught her all about the spooks' deadly *modus operandi* but she hadn't expected it to reach them out here in Andalusia.

Sally, on the other hand, was too young to remember the full extent of the pressures her family had suffered as a result of her father's job. She knew all about his latest crusade to defeat elder abuse but had not understood its less obvious dangers. A sensitive and unworldly artist, she rarely read the newspapers or listened to the news. It was all too depressing and inhibited her creative instincts. She had suffered the worst of the three from the bizarre events on the mountain road, followed by the demands on her as an interpreter while under extreme stress.

But Sally had come out fighting next day, a true Mitchell, Howard told her, while describing as euphemistically as possible his troubled relationship with the 'authorities'. What horrified his daughter most – as it did Barbara and himself if the truth were known

– was the fact that the would-be assassins had targeted all four of them, including an unrelated Spanish taxi driver. Was there *nothing* they refused to stoop to?

How did you answer that? You couldn't, without dragging their naïve daughter into a murky real world beyond her comprehension. When ignorance is bliss...it's folly to be wise. Barbara's advice was to keep praying to be delivered from evil, and you had to admit that so far her method had proved effective.

The reassuring bit, her husband pointed out, was the fact that having scored such a spectacular own goal, it would be a long time before the spooks tried again...*if at all!* The thought cheered them up no end and after she'd finished her coffee, Sally hurried off to her nearby studio to practise her own form of religion – her mysterious t'ai chi.

As well as a full English breakfast, Howard also missed the morning newspapers. Unlike Sally, he needed to know what was going on in the world, in particular the fallout, to use an unfortunate expression, from the previous evening. There'd been no mention of it on Spanish radio or TV and it would be hours before the papers arrived. He wondered what *The Announcer* had made of the incident.

After the police had returned him and his wife and daughter to their hotel the previous evening, the trio had immediately fortified themselves with large brandies. Then, while Sally recounted the traumatic experience to Pedro, the hotelier, Howard found the right spot in the hotel's grounds to telephone an exclusive story to his former newspaper in London. There would be no-one there at this time of the morning so he phoned Bernard, now back from the IoM, to ask what they'd done with it.

The answer, Bernard said when told the full, unbelievable but true story, was nothing. There was no mention of it in any of the morning papers. Nothing on radio or TV either. It might be too early to suspect a cover-up as the story was only a few hours old. They'd see what developed during the day. As for Howard's remarkable escape, it merely confirmed Bernard's belief in his colleague's indestructibility.

"Can't wait to see tomorrow's headlines. We'll have to start calling you Houdini. How do you do it?"

"According to Barbara, it's all down to the power of prayer...and I'm starting to believe her."

Bernard laughed. "Come on, my old mate...I know you better than that."

Howard let it pass. "Anything else in the papers?"

"The *Mirror* and the *Express* have given us a good show on our investiture in July...good advance publicity. And, guess what, the Sri Lanka oilfield might be only a fraction of the size we were told. Scientists behind the hype are having second thoughts...blaming dodgy computers for over-the-top predictions."

"Computers...don't we just love them! How's George getting on with his latest rolling blockade?"

"It's been overtaken by events. The transport unions are planning their own large-scale version...trucks, vans, buses, taxis. Nothing decided yet ...but when they hear about your escape there'll be no stopping them."

"Am I glad to hear that, Bernard! Doubt if I could've managed a repeat performance on the old Roadrider."

"Jessica's spouting the usual stuff about 'standing firm' and not giving in to extremists. That's us golden oldies...extremists! But the public are turning against her. The opinion polls are swinging our way."

"Not before time…what about the thanatologists?"

"Shortage of recruits, apparently, despite mega bucks on offer. There's talk that the system could be unworkable…that Jessica might have to call in the army. Makes sense, I suppose…they're in the business of killing people after all."

"I can't believe even Jessica would stoop that low."

"Don't bet on it. She keeps telling us there's no alternative if we love our country…the usual stuff."

"Tell me about it. Who said 'Love your country but love it intelligently'?"

"Sounds like Orwell. Trouble is, there aren't that many intelligent people left these days. Anyway, my old mate, when are you coming home?"

"Next week…if we can face the road back to Malaga!"

*   *   *

As spooks do not exist, they obviously cannot die. But try telling that to their next-of-kin. Once the agents' formal ID confirmation came through from Nerja, No 7's last task as their controller was to inform the parents of their sons' deaths. For them it really *was* a tragic accident. Their sons had died in Spain, serving their country, so they were told, yet Britain was not at war with that nation.

There would never be an inquest and it would be months before their bodies were returned, since diplomatic relations with Spain had been strained for years over the Gibraltar issue. This latest incident would strain them further. When the funerals finally took place they would need to be conducted under a veil of secrecy. One family lived in Kingston-on-Thames and the other in Cheshire. When No 7 phoned, he identified himself by means of a secret code known only to the agent's father.

The first father, a senior Admiralty civil servant, took the news stoically. For a long time there was silence, then he said in a cracked voice: "Do you know...I'd half expected this. He was so clever, you see...too clever for his own good!" Another long silence, then: "I don't suppose you can tell me what happened."

"I'm afraid not, sir...except that it was a road accident...Official Secrets Act."

"When will you send us his body?"

"That may take some time...weeks, possibly months. There are certain formalities to be completed. One of our senior officers will visit you when convenient to discuss the funeral. He'll phone you first. Please accept my sincere condolences, sir. The thoughts of everyone in our department are with you at this difficult time."

The second bereaved father, a Crown Court judge, was less amenable. He didn't believe it when told his son had died on active service, despite being given the secret code. He demanded No 7's name and office landline number so that he could call him back but, of course, that wasn't possible. Instead, the spook gave his secretary's non-video mobile number and waited in her office for the call. The judge called back inside a minute and demanded the return of his son's body. When told that might take months, he threatened to order a writ of *habeas corpus* to be served on the State Security minister, followed by a personal complaint to the Lord Chancellor.

More aggravation, No 7 sighed as he wearily retired into his inner sanctum. But at least he'd be out of the firing line, ignominiously relieved of his short-lived promotion. Sadly, he wasn't wet operations material. The Jaguar would have to go and it would be back to the Volkswagen Polo.

And it looked as if the boy would end up at Eton after all.

THIRTY

It was one of those editorial conferences dominated by a single executive – in this case, Roger Ellis, *The Announcer's* foreign news editor. The mystery over the size of the Sri Lankan oilfield was developing into a major front page story but an even more intriguing one was emerging from southern Spain. Originally, agency sources reported that two motor-cyclists had fallen to their deaths from a mountain road in Andalusia, which hardly merited space in an English newspaper.

The same night, Howard Mitchell, leader of the Keep Breathing protest movement and the paper's former star journalist, had phoned an extraordinary account of the accident. Mitchell, who was on holiday in the area, said the motor-cyclists had attempted to force a taxi containing him and his family off the road and over a 750ft sheer drop, but had failed and had careered over the cliff themselves.

There were three other witnesses to the incident: Mitchell's wife, his daughter and the cab driver, who had been blinded by an intense flash of light on a hairpin bend. In addition, a local doctor who examined the driver's eyes confirmed that he had been temporarily blinded by a powerful strobe or laser light.

The local police had taken statements from all of them and would search for bodies below the cliff at first light.

Ellis had phoned the paper's Madrid correspondent, who contacted police in Nerja, the nearest town with a police station open 24 hours, but they could only confirm that an accident had been reported and they would search the area for bodies next morning. In the absence of any corroboration of Mitchell's dramatic version of events, the foreign editor had no option but to hold the story in his computer's pending file.

Confirmation that something very strange had happened had been arriving since and, as Michaelson and his other department heads listened attentively, Ellis brought them up to speed. The Madrid correspondent had flown by chartered helicopter to Nerja overnight and interviewed senior police officers. They confirmed there had been a large-scale search and the bodies of two young men found at the foot of a steep cliff, together with the remains of a strobe light and two badly damaged, unused satellite phones. The bodies carried no identification but the officers had reason to believe the men were British. One had spoken in English shortly before he died.

Inoperative location transmitters had been found in the men's helmets which, together with the other evidence, indicated they had been engaged in clandestine activities. The Spanish authorities ordered that the bodies be kept in the police mortuary until claimed. They also lodged a strong diplomatic protest against violation of their territorial integrity by a foreign government. The British Embassy in Madrid had denied that the two men belonged to the State Security Service. In London, the Foreign Office claimed the UK government had no intelligence agents at work anywhere in Spain at the material time.

That had been the story so far – but Ellis then added that in the last hour, a Madrid embassy official had inspected the bodies under diplomatic immunity and had refused to speak to the Press afterwards. However, 'sources close to the enquiry' indicated that the bodies would eventually be flown to the UK. The key word here, of course, was 'eventually', a word of some flexibility to the Spanish. With an international incident brewing over the affair, the translation could mean just about anything.

Bizarre though it had seemed at the time, Howard Mitchell's story now stood up and it was almost certainly an exclusive. Foreign desk staff were trying to contact him, his family, the taxi driver and the doctor for quotes. All the executives gathered in Hugo's office were convinced that, on the available evidence, they were looking at a familiar 'tragic accident' scenario reserved for so-called enemies of the state.

Hugo, of course, was certain of it. He had foreknowledge of the attempt from Beria himself and had tried to warn Howard of the danger. But he was a 'belt and braces' editor. In his position you had to be. *The Announcer* wasn't a red top tabloid but a quality paper of record. Although the spooks were obviously British – what else? – he needed independent corroboration.

It arrived two hours before the first edition deadline. A highly reliable source in the Lord Chancellor's Department called on his bug-free direct phone. There was a strong whisper in the department that one of the dead spies was the son of a Crown Court judge. His Honour was demanding immediate return of the body on pain of a writ of *habeas corpus*, the hearing to be held *in camera* .

It was the editor's clincher. He'd keep the ace up his sleeve by way of insurance – in case of flak from SSS lawyers. Stranger things had happened. There was no such thing as a hopeless legal action if there were fees to be had in the form of public money. He resolved to splash the story, relegating the war in Sri Lanka to the second lead. The paper's lawyers would tone down the assassination angle while leaving enough for the public to read between the lines. Any lingering doubts over class roots and divided loyalties had long since melted away for Hugo. His first priority was the truth.

The following morning, *The Announcer* had the story all to itself:

PENSIONERS' LEADER ESCAPES DEATH

Mountain drama as mystery motor-cyclists buzz taxi

By Roger Ellis, Foreign News Editor
THE founder of the Keep Breathing pressure group, Howard Mitchell, has narrowly escaped death after two motor-cyclists apparently tried to force his taxi off a mountain road in Spain. Both riders themselves died in the incident.

Mitchell, his wife Barbara and daughter Sally, were being driven along a narrow road on the Sierra

Almijara, Costa del Sol, on Tuesday night when a motor-cycle pillion rider reportedly blinded the taxi driver with a strobe-type light as they approached a hairpin bend at the top of a 750ft cliff.

The taxi driver managed to brake sharply but the motor-cycle careered out of control over the sheer drop, killing both riders. Their bodies, dressed completely in black with black crash helmets and night goggles, were recovered next morning when a police helicopter searched the remote area. The remains of a strobe lamp, mobile phones and satellite location transmitters were said to have been found at the scene. The men carried no identification but Spanish police believe they were British. One of them is believed to have spoken briefly to a paramedic in English shortly before he died.

Although badly shaken, neither Mitchell, a former *Announcer* journalist, nor his family were injured in the incident. Their driver was temporarily blinded and traumatised but recovered after emergency treatment.

The Spanish Ambassador in London has lodged an official protest over the incident, claiming the motor-cyclists were British agents but a spokesman for the State Security Service said in a statement that he 'utterly refuted' the charge. He insisted that no SSS agents were operating anywhere in Spain at the time. There was no evidence that the deceased men were British. What happened could only have been a 'tragic accident'.

The statement added: "Suggestions that the SSS could be involved in some kind of sinister assassination plot can only be described as the work of conspiracy theorists whose real aim is to undermine the nation's security. All necessary legal remedies will be rigorously enforced against those responsible at the appropriate time."

Ellis's story went on to include quotes from Howard, Barbara, Sally, Felipe and Dr Garcia, vividly describing their terrifying experience – plus pictures on an inside page of the vertiginous road in question, the heroic taxi driver and strobe lights similar to those found at the scene.

It reminded readers that Mitchell had publicly spurned an OBE the previous year in protest at age abuse and the life-threatening Health of the Nation Bill. With fellow activist and ex-*Announcer* sub-editor Bernard Baxter, he now headed Keep Breathing's high profile campaign against the controversial legislation.

The group were responsible for the scooter riders' rolling blockade that recently disrupted the capital. They had also produced an alternative OBE gold medal for members who had gone to prison for their beliefs. A special investiture ceremony was planned for July. It would still go ahead.

*   *   *

The British Spring, as might be expected, was rather different to the Arab and Prague versions. There were no tanks on the streets or demonstrators mowed down by small arms fire. No buildings were set alight and, as far as could be ascertained, nobody was injured. But a groundswell of public anger against the government, the Maturity Contract, Jessica Sykes and Wally Alcock had been smouldering for weeks. News of the assassination attempt on the man who'd spurned an OBE to protect the lives of his generation provided the final spark. The result was a rolling blockade several miles long that made Operation Scooter look like a picnic outing. This time it was monster articulated lorries, petrol tankers, fleets of buses, taxis, vans, trailers, cars and caravans that trundled at 8mph along London's grubby streets – past the fast food 'restaurants', licensed brothels and posters of a winking Wally, draped in a Union Jack, advising old-timers on The Way To Go. Once again, the capital seized up almost immediately but now the gridlock extended from Romford to Richmond, Barnet to Bromley. It took the best part of a week to clear the chaos. The cost to the economy was incalculable.

Sympathy for the pensioners' plight gathered strength as the public, at last shaken out of their apathy, recognised the grim prospect of thanatologists in their midst. Their own grandparents were in real danger. All too soon *they would be in danger themselves.* How could they have allowed such a thing to happen? The answer was simple: they'd all been too spaced out on their football, their porn, soaps and virtual reality games to notice.

They had finally woken up to real reality. Despite the soulless materialism of popular culture, it seemed there was still some humanity left in them. In the days following the blockade, overtaxed and over-exploited workers throughout the country adopted their own form of go-slow. Supported by their trade unions, they downed tools in a series of spontaneous 24-hour stoppages in a belated show of solidarity with their long-suffering elders. The message to the government was clear: drop the Health of the Nation Bill or face a general strike. The TUC met in emergency session. And so did the Cabinet.

The message was not lost on Dame Jessica. Amid the gathering storm, she realised strong action was

326

essential if a crippling general strike were to be averted. But she decided not to sack Beria immediately. That would only vindicate Hugo Michaelson's irresponsible coverage of the shambles in Andalusia. The name of the game had to be damage limitation.

She imposed a news blackout on the SSS scandal in the national interest but the public outcry it had aroused meant she could provide only limited protection to her State Security Minister. As part of a mini Cabinet reshuffle, the hapless Beria was shunted to the Department of Health, Safety and Political Correctness – the so-called 'graveyard department'. That would draw the sting of those calling for his head.

The announcement was made almost in passing when her 22-strong Cabinet assembled for their crucial meeting. There were more important matters to be discussed: urgent reports from Sri Lanka that the size of the prospective oilfield had been greatly exaggerated – plus equally grim news on the home front: only a trickle of recruits had volunteered as thanatologists under the Health of the Nation Bill.

Without these state-registered 'practitioners of death', the Bill was clearly unworkable. It had become terminally ill itself, ironically qualifying for the remedy it prescribed in such cases. The Prime Minister read the last rites in the form of an official declaration abandoning the measure and relinquishing her emergency powers to enforce it. A few moments of suitably solemn silence followed as the thoughts of Cabinet members turned to the little matter of meeting their UN-imposed quota of:

7 million IUCs

by the year 2040 without the aid of the Maturity Contract.

It was the Health Secretary who came to the rescue. He had taken soundings from eminent clinicians and it might still be possible to avoid UN sanctions and help save the planet if NICE introduced further economies on life-prolonging drugs. Previous decisions to deny cancer patients vital medications on the grounds that they were not cost-effective had been controversial but had resulted in a significantly increased mortality rate. If the institute could be 'persuaded' to make similar economies on drugs preventing heart attacks and strokes, the UN target might be met through 'natural wastage'.

There was one other possibility. His department had already withdrawn NHS-funded care for dementia patients in the later stages of their illness. Care could now be withdrawn progressively earlier, leaving patients' families to pick up the bill – which would concentrate their minds on assisted suicide procedures available under the Assisted Dying Act.

Ever the cynical opportunist, the Prime Minister brightened up at these suggestions. Perhaps she could still comply with the UN directive without the need for further social engineering, however visionary. But the unfolding events in Sri Lanka placed sterner demands on her talent for improvisation. Advisers were telling her there would be no oil bonanza after all. Estimates of the oilfield's potential had been drastically scaled down. Geotechnologists were blaming malfunctioning computers for flawed predictions. Sampling of the main sand had shown its hydrocarbons were residual and that the mobile fluid was water not oil. Unfortunately, computers were unable to tell the difference. Tests on what little oil there was showed it to be unsuitable for commercial use. Expert advice was that further exploration would not be viable.

After juggling with a complex economic equation and its likely political fallout, Dame Jessica came to a stateswoman-like conclusion. On mature reflection, military intervention in the Sri Lanka conflict might have been a trifle hasty, she suggested, fixing a beady eye on the Defence Minister. He readily agreed, claiming he'd only supported the island's invasion under American pressure. His latest intelligence from the war zone indicated that the army's task in training Sri Lankan defence forces was complete. They'd been transformed into a fine body of men able to resist the Tamil insurgents on their own.

"In that case," the Prime Minister declared, "British military presence in the area can serve no further purpose. Our moral duty to the islanders in their struggle for freedom is discharged. The time is now opportune to bring our boys home."

The sombre mood round the Cabinet table lightened as Dame Jessica continued: "Withdrawal of our armed forces would release substantial financial resources from our overseas defence budget. Accordingly, I now direct that these funds be diverted to our desperately overstretched Work and Pensions Department."

Both Chancellor of the Exchequer and Defence Minister did hurried sums on the backs of Treasury envelopes and came to the remarkable conclusion that the billions saved by withdrawing troops from Sri Lanka exactly matched the sum needed to clear the horrendous deficit in the pensions budget.

The entire Cabinet united in congratulating Dame Jessica on her inspired idea. Why, they asked themselves, had nobody thought of it before?

329

THIRTY-ONE

Every day since their return from Spain, Barbara had attended Mass at St Chad's to offer up thanks for their miraculous escape from death on the perilous road above Canillas. For the first week, Howard came with her but gradually the excuses started to kick in. The services were too early in the morning for him; his hearing aid had developed a fault and needed repairing; he was too busy organising the 'alternative' investiture in Cardiff with Bernard and George, and, most imaginative of all, the incense aggravated his angina.

Barbara pointed out that the only time there was incense was at requiem Masses. He maintained that there seemed to have been a lot of those recently, to which she replied he should be thankful that none of them had been for him. The fact that he was still alive, along with herself, Sally and Felipe, was clearly due to an act of divine intervention. In other words, a miracle.

Howard was no stranger to narrow squeaks. His life had comprised a whole series of them but he was more inclined to put them down to luck rather than divine intervention. As a journalist, he'd been trained to ride the punches and bounce back. You learnt to take the rough with the intolerable. Every so often, you got a lucky break. But that's all it was – luck. As far as he was concerned, prayer and journalism were mutually exclusive.

Yet, looking back at the hair-raising cliff-top ordeal when he'd almost been blown into oblivion along with his cap, he acknowledged there'd been a moment when, instinctively, he'd appealed to a higher power for strength. Immediately, the wind had changed direction and pressed him against the car until he'd struggled round it. Coincidence? Luck? Or a miracle? As a rationalist, he was determined to keep an open mind. But Barbara could very well be right. It had been known.

For the time being, he forced himself to concentrate on more worldly matters. There were interviews with the media on his reaction to the government's historic climbdown on obligatory euthanasia, which could only be regarded as the ultimate victory for grey power, although it had taken the threat of a general strike to secure it. Nothing changed, he reflected. It was still necessary to back politicians into a corner before money could be 'found' for humanitarian purposes. It was almost a miracle in itself when it happened.

But concentrating all his team's minds at the moment was the formidable task of arranging the investiture in the banqueting suite of Cardiff's Millennium Stadium. Almost 100 'martyrs' of the pensioners' movement and their families were expected to attend the reception to collect their Owen Bryn Evans awards. Overnight accommodation had to be found for them all, except for a few who lived locally.

Disabled access needed to be checked at various points while Barbara again organised medical facilities, including standby ambulances. Menus offering wide choices of dietary alternatives were selected and a 16-piece orchestra booked to supply music of the 1960s and 70s. In addition, Press and TV facilities needed to be laid on to cope with an unprecedented level of media interest. There was no problem in finding the money for it all, as contributions continued to pour in from those grateful to have escaped the clutches of the Maturity Contract.

But if anything can go wrong, it always does. Hours before the investiture was due to start, with flowers, balloons and streamers in place, tables laid and champagne on ice, the Powers that be stepped in. Poor losers to the end, they served a High Court injunction on the Welsh authorities, demanding the immediate cancellation of "this illegal and unconstitutional ceremony infringing Crown protocol".

Unfortunately, they had overlooked one vital detail. The injunction was in English. A declaration by the Welsh Assembly months earlier had decreed that all legal communications must in future be in Welsh. Dismissing the injunction out of hand, the Assembly's lawyers described the blunder as "an abuse of the diplomatic process, an intolerable interference in the affairs of the Welsh nation and a slur on our distinguished citizen, Owen Bryn Evans".

On a day of rolling power cuts and widespread computer failures, their emailed response in Welsh took several hours to reach London's High Court, arriving after 4 pm in broken-up and garbled text. The court's computer, operating on back-up power from its petrol-driven generator, normally translated anything from Greek to Swahili in seconds but mangled Welsh was something else. It crashed. Staff anxious to avoid the horror of the evening rush hour put the translation on hold until next day.

Meanwhile, Dame Jessica, having heard nothing from her judiciary, fired off her own top-level email to her Welsh opposite number. But as it was in English, the message ended up in a spam bin. In desperation, she tried her priority emergency phone link – only to hear a loop recording of *Land of my Fathers* sung by massed male voice choirs. With time rapidly running out, she did think about parachuting in an SAS squad to break up the illegal gathering in familiar style with smoke bombs and stun grenades. But the strong national Press and TV presence at the venue persuaded her it might not be one of her better ideas.

*   *   *

While Buck House investitures rewarded social climbers who had bribed their way in as well as the worthy, those honoured in the Alternative Investiture at the Millennium Stadium were all genuine VIPs who'd earned their gongs the hard way. Dubbed the People's Investiture by the Press, it paid homage to heroic senior citizens who had willingly suffered real hardship to defend their generation's human rights – martyrs to their cause who'd shared jail cells with criminals, disgraced MPs and other low life. Now it was time for a taste of the high life.

The sparkling lights in the opulent banqueting suite glittered and glinted on the crystal glass and silverware on the round dining tables with their red linen cloths. The champagne popped and fizzed, the orchestra played nostalgic music and, centre stage beneath powerful arc lights for the TV cameras, 100 so-called alternative OBEs gleamed pure gold in their purple velvet-lined presentation cases.

The guests dined in true VIP style on oysters and scallops, venison, caviar and vintage wines. Then, as the toastmaster announced each name in turn, they trooped up to the stage to receive their awards, some hobbling with the aid of sticks, others in wheelchairs. Many of the men proudly wore their military medals – meaningful decorations for acts of bravery in the service of their country – to which they could now add an OBE that also meant something.

Unusually immaculate in an expensive blue tuxedo, Howard presented the medals and citations, helped by George and Bernard, wearing lounge suits. Each recipient was given a hug – gingerly if they were very frail – and an affectionate handshake, while remembering not to squeeze too tightly. Taking the microphone, Howard told the exuberant audience these were the real stars of the show, true servants of humanity, in keeping with the inscription on their awards.

But the investiture had not quite finished. Sitting at the front table were Barbara, Christopher and Amanda, (Sally had failed to make it due to a Spanish air controllers' strike) and William, almost unrecognisable following a haircut. William waited for his father's signal, then handed him two further gongs in their cases.

"There are two more people who richly deserve the distinguished Owen Bryn Evans medal, ladies and gentlemen," Howard announced. He turned to Bernard and George, standing modestly in the background alongside the musicians in the band. "I refer to my colleagues, Bernard Baxter and George Armstrong, giants of our movement and an inspiration to us all. Without them, we certainly wouldn't be here tonight. They may not have served time in prison..."

"Not yet!" Bernard called out, and everyone laughed.

"...but I can assure you they're both worth their weight in gold."

The room erupted in sustained applause as Bernard and George came forward, bowing elaborately before Howard pinned their gleaming medals to their jackets. "And finally, two more special people," Howard continued. "Firstly, to our group's resident nurse and medical consultant, my guiding light, my long-suffering wife, Barbara..."

To more applause and cheering, a waiter and waitress brought in enormous bouquets of flowers for Barbara, elegance personified in a low-cut cream creation showing the pearls Howard had bought her for their 30th anniversary.

"...and secondly, my son William whose assistance has kept us all going throughout our long campaign." He took an envelope out of his pocket. "I've got a surprise for him." He opened the envelope, took out a letter and made a show of putting on his reading glasses. "You may not believe this, William, but it's a summons from the Palace."

William looked nonplussed and an anxious silence descended on the gathering. "It's okay," Howard grinned. "It's not from Buckingham Palace...it's from Crystal Palace. My son has been appointed first team physiotherapist at the club."

Laughter and relief followed as the sports science graduate went up to collect the letter, wagged it in mock admonition at his father for keeping it a secret, and raised it proudly above his head with both hands, as if it were the FA Cup. Short of actually playing for Crystal Palace, there could be no greater accolade.

Then George, his medal glinting in the spotlight, stepped forward, took the microphone and gestured for silence. "Ladies and gentlemen, all great protest movements have their iconic leaders and we are specially privileged to have ours…a man who threw his meaningless medal into the Thames and who, with his family, very nearly paid the ultimate price for his insolence. We cannot let this historic celebration end without expressing our sincere gratitude and admiration for the man who continues to make our movement headline news…the former distinguished *Announcer* journalist…the amazing, the indestructible…Howard Mitchell!"

For well over a minute, wild cheering, handclapping, discharge of party poppers, stamping, banging of wine bottles on tables and rattling of walking sticks reverberated round the banqueting hall and poured outside into the stadium, almost as if Wales had scored a try. Scores of hearing aids had to be hastily adjusted.

Howard motioned for Barbara to join him on stage. When she did she carried a small gold box, fastened with a purple ribbon. She gently relieved George of the microphone. "This is an entirely unscripted moment, ladies and gentlemen," she announced. "As you know, my husband cannot award himself our real OBE – although I'd say he richly deserves it…"

She waited until more cheering subsided. "…but I think you'll agree we can't let him leave empty-handed. So I'm delighted to make this special presentation which I sincerely hope will go to his head." She handed Howard the gold box and silence descended as he opened it, removing layers of tissue paper. Then, to his genuine surprise, he extracted a brand new, blue cavalry twill cap with a maroon silk lining and wide, rakish peak. He waved it aloft, grinning broadly.

When she could make herself heard, Barbara added: "It's an exact replica of the one blown away in Spain – when Howard was almost blown away with it – only a bit cleaner!"

He pulled the cap firmly on his head and embraced her. Tears were in both their eyes which, in the case of the hard-bitten hack who reckoned he'd seen it all, proved there was a first time for everything. He cleared his throat and took the microphone. "There was a moment back on that road in Andalusia when they tried to blow us *all* away – Barbara, Sally, our driver and myself – when I did wonder about carrying on with the campaign. But I have to say that tonight has made it all worthwhile." (More cheers and table-thumping.)

"I'd just like to add that the battle's not over yet – in case you thought it was! We still need to get rid of Wally and replace him with a *serious* commissioner to protect us from the pro-death brigade."

"Don't forget our opt-out fees?" somebody shouted.

"Too right," Howard replied. "The first thing our real tsar must do is refund the legal fees charged for opt-out certificates. The law is now defunct so we have a right to our money back."

Amid cries of support, he added: "We'll gladly award our OBE – the *real* one, remember – to any member of the government implementing these reforms. Now we've got our message across, we need to drive it home. The fight goes on. We've only just begun. Good night and remember…KEEP BREATHING!"

With a final wave to acknowledge the fervent loyalty of his followers, he stepped down from the stage hand in hand with Barbara and signalled to the band. They immediately struck up with the Carpenters' old hit song, *We've Only Just Begun*, familiar to almost every grey head in the room.

Exhausted, the hero of the hour collapsed into his seat, pushed his stylish new cap back on his head and mopped his forehead, glistening with sweat from the arc lights. Apart from the tightening in his throat and chest, his head ached and the pain in his back was killing him. It had been a long and gruelling day, with a highly stressful and emotional climax. He knew how a racehorse felt at the end of the Grand National... knackered.

Barbara reminded him his evening medication was well overdue but he reached for his champagne and drained the glass. "This beats isosorbide mononitrate any day," he grinned, and as it was a special occasion, she didn't argue. This *was* his night, after all. The medication regime would be firmly restored next morning.

He poured more sparkling medicinal alcohol for William, Chris, Amanda and himself. "Pity Sally couldn't make it." Their videophones had been switched off during the investiture. "I'll check my vidimail."

When he flipped up the phone screen he found Sally's smiling face telling him the long-awaited good news. "Eduardo and I are engaged. It's finally happened. Isn't it wonderful! We're both coming over to see you soon, so then you can have *another* party. Sorry about tonight. All flights to the UK were

338

cancelled, would you believe. Hope you have a great evening. Speak to you soon, darlings. Love you."

After they'd toasted Sally's good news, Howard pressed the menu button to find three other callers. The first was his mother, propped up in bed in her nursing home and looking remarkably sprightly. "Well done Howard and Barbara. You really deserve your success...you and William and Bernard, of course. I'm feeling a lot better now there's no more talk of a maturity contract. But I've told Matron not to throw my opt-out certificate away just yet." She laughed wheezily and tapped the side of her nose. "You never know with this lot! Night night, God bless."

Next came Fred and Lilian, Barbara's parents, seated at the kitchen table in their Brittany farmhouse. Fred's face was suntanned and he looked healthier, if slightly bewildered by the ultra-smart phone. Lilian did the talking. "Hello Barbara and Howard. Hope all goes well tonight and congratulations on sending Jessica packing! We're settling into our cosy cottage now...hope you can come over soon. No regrets about moving...give us a call when you've recovered from your party. Love to all." They both blew kisses and were gone.

Finally, familiar swarthy features appeared, with an even more familiar mountain road in the background. "Good evening, Senor Mitchell," Felipe said in hesitant broken English. "I hope you have good party this night...and come again and drive taxi, si? Dios te bendiga, mi amigo." With a wave and a laugh, their Spanish guardian angel faded from view.

At least, that was how Barbara described him as the tears welled up again. "Poor Felipe...how he suffered for us that night. Thank God he seems to be okay now."

339

The band struck up with *Thanks for the Memory* and the revellers could take a hint. It was getting late and past their bedtime. More than a little unsteadily in several cases, they filed out into the cold night air, hugging and shaking hands with Howard and his family. It had been a truly memorable occasion…a real investiture with real medals for real people. There was no substitute for the real thing.

A television executive handed Howard a full-length DVD of the evening's celebrations, extracts of which had been broadcast live nationwide. High on champagne and euphoria, he and Barbara resolved to watch it when they got home. In the taxi on the way back to the hotel, he put his arm round her and gazed down at the silk-ensconced cleavage. "The night is still young," he whispered in her ear. It was the alcohol and the adrenalin talking.

She raised her head and kissed him tenderly. "Yes, darling. But *we're* not."

He laughed and stroked her thigh. "We'll soon see about that!"

When they reached the door of their room, he lifted her in his arms and carried her over the threshold. Giggling like teenagers they collapsed fully clothed on the bed, Howard still wearing his smart new cap.

Within seconds they were both asleep.

EPILOGUE

"Well, what about it?" Barbara asked.

"What about what?"

"You know perfectly well what, Howard."

They'd just finished watching the DVD of the awards ceremony on the lounge TV, followed by replays of their videophone messages. Felipe's emotional greeting had triggered vivid memories of their miraculous escape from the clutches of the SSS.

"It does have to be a miracle that we're still here, Howard. Surely, looking back, you recognise that. All the prayers I've said for you and both of us...they were finally answered that night."

Now that the distraction of the investiture was over, Howard's thoughts kept returning to their ordeal on the mountain and the metaphysical implications would not go away. "I have to admit that you're very probably right, Barbara."

"Do you remember telling me it would take a miracle to make you join the Church?"

"Vaguely." The memory never left him.

"So, what are you waiting for?"

Howard was reliving the surreal scene of the motorcyclists disappearing into eternity...his brinkmanship around Felipe's taxi....his cap violently snatched off his head and flung into the appalling, beckoning blackness. At the same time, a small sceptical voice reminded him of the ritualistic nature of the Roman Catholic religion, the candles, the incense, the holy water...as well as the Church's strange divisions on ethics and morality. But the voice was growing weaker.

She took his hand. "Well?"

He felt the wind suddenly change direction, pressing into his back after his whispered prayer, the prayer of a doubting agnostic, and saw the crucifix swinging from the windscreen of Felipe's taxi. There had to be more to the scenario than pure luck. Rationality and good fortune had their limitations at such times. Having considered all other explanations and found them wanting, the claim of a miracle was not merely compelling, it was irresistible. But he still said nothing.

Barbara could sense that her husband, having fought conversion to the Church every inch of the way, had reached the moment of truth but couldn't bring himself to acknowledge it. The servant of truth hesitated to embrace his master.

"Let me help you, Howard. We have an initiates' course at St Chad's. It doesn't commit you to anything. There's no pressure to join. It just sets the record straight about the Catholic faith, corrects all the popular myths. I've got an enrolment form. All you need to do is sign it and I'll take care of everything...no problem."

Howard barely heard her. What he heard was the sound of the wind and what he saw was a swaying crucifix. She handed him the form and he slowly put on his reading glasses. Then he took out his pen.

"Where do I sign?"